Also by Edith Konecky

Allegra Maud Goldman
A Place at the Table

PAST SORROWS
AND
COMING
ATTRACTIONS

PAST
SORROWS
AND
COMING
ATTRACTIONS

Edith Konecky

HAMILTON STONE EDITIONS

The stories in this work were originally published in the following: The Kenyon Review, The Virginia Quarterly, The Massachusetts Review, Esquire, Cosmopolitan, The Saturday Evening Post, Mademoiselle, From Mt. San Angelo, Women on Women II, Martha Foley's Best Short Stories of 1964.

Library of Congress Cataloging-in-Publication Data

Konecky, Edith
    Past sorrows and coming attractions/by Edith Konecky
      p.cm
    ISBN 0-9654043-4-X
    1. New York (N.Y.)—Social Life and customs—Fiction.
      1. Title

    PS3561.0457 P37 2001
    813'.54—dc21

Manufactured in the United States of America

This book is dedicated to my
invaluable assistant and beloved son
Josh

CONTENTS

LOVE AND FRIENDSHIP

Rena Poswolsky was the smartest girl in the eighth grade, possibly in all of P.S. 193. Not only did she always know everything before anyone else, she knew considerably more than was required. Far from being ostentatious, her brilliance shone forth almost against her will, understated and sullen. She was just barely civil to her classmates and close to none of them.

The class, the cream of its age group, had stayed fairly solidly together from kindergarten on and, having skipped two half-terms, was to be graduated in June with some of its members still shy of their thirteenth birthday. Lois Robinson, who had managed to maintain a position in the middle of the class in spite of a tendency her mind had to wander, had not considered the possibility of friendship with Rena, though she had long admired and respected her, until two things happened. The first was when they were asked to tell what they wanted to "be" when they grew up. The boys all said doctors and lawyers and scientists and engineers, and the girls said teachers, movie stars, registered nurses, and ballet dancers (not one, Lois was to remember years later, said "housewife and mother"). Lois said she thought she might have to be a poet, and when Miss Roach asked her why she said because she only seemed able to have short, intense, vague ideas. Everyone laughed except Rena, who looked interested. When Rena's turn came she said, "I've no intention of making up my mind yet. There's still a lot I have to learn about myself."

Lois grinned at Rena with appreciation, but Rena just ducked her head.

The second thing that happened was the IQ's. Measuring intelligence was just coming into vogue and most teachers didn't yet know how to handle it. When the scores were in, Miss Roach did what she did in most situations: she called out their names and scores in descending order of excellence and had them line up in IQ places. It was no surprise that Rena was first, but it came as a shock to everyone, including Miss Roach, that Lois, just a point behind, was next. Lois was so dazed that Miss Roach had to call her name twice, and when she went to take her place at the front of the room she was trembling. She knew that her whole life had changed, that she would never again be the same.

"There must be some mistake," she mumbled.

Rena put her hand on Lois's arm. "I knew it," she said fiercely. "I always knew it. You don't have enough self-esteem."

That Rena should not only have noticed her, but taken the trouble to have an opinion about her, thrilled Lois. She had long suspected that no one understood her; now she realized that she had not even understood herself. She might after all be closer to her occasional fantasy of herself than to what she had reluctantly begun to accept as the reality: her parents' estimate of her, her older brother's, her teachers', that she was bright enough, articulate, often amusing, but certainly in no way outstanding. She would be passed on to high school without any special notice, possibly an honorable mention in English, but what had just been pinned on her was better than any medal. She had the equipment to be anyone she chose; she could now choose to be anyone she pleased.

The first thing she chose was to catch up with Rena after school.

"I'll walk you home," she said. "It's on my way."

Rena lived on East Twenty-ninth Street, three blocks from Lois, but in those three blocks there was a subtle status change. Rena lived upstairs in a stucco two-family house. Lois's house was private, much larger, all brick, on a corner plot, and had three bathrooms. Mr. Poswolsky was in butter-and-eggs and Rena wore skirts and middy blouses, but Lois, whose father was a dress manufacturer, often had to wear frocks, some of them from Paris, which she hated. Rena was always having to go to the store to get things for her mother. Lois's mother was seldom home and if the cook needed something, Arthur, the chauffeur, would drive over to Avenue J for it in the big Buick with the sliding-glass panel that separated him from the groceries in the back.

When they got to Rena's house, they sat on the stoop and talked.

"How did you know, if I didn't?" Lois asked.

"You have an original mind," Rena said. "But you haven't learned yet how to use it."

"I hardly every say anything much in school."

"That's one way I could tell. But when you do say something, it's usually unexpected. Getting good grades doesn't mean anything, you know."

Lois had been led to believe that it meant everything. It was the only yardstick there was for someone her age. When you grew up, the yardstick was how much money you made. Or if not you, since you were female, then your husband.

"But for example what did I ever say that you thought was original? I honestly don't know."

Rena laughed. Lois had seldom heard her laugh; she was usually so intense and serious and angry. It was a good laugh. "You're funny, Lois," she said. "I see there's a lot I'm going to have to teach you."

"Will you?"

"Yes, I like you. You're real."

"Isn't everyone?"

"God, no!"

"I don't know how you know so much," Lois said despairingly. "You must have terrific parents."

Rena gave a scornful, two-syllable snort. Across the street, a short, dark boy emerged and halloed. Languidly, Rena waved to him.

"That's Donny. He's the boy I'm in love with."

Lois peered at him, her heart inexplicably sinking. The boy had curly black hair, and his pants fitted snugly across his solid bottom as he trotted around the side of the house back toward the garage.

"My boyfriend's name is Leonard," she said. "I met him summer before last at Camp Sambering."

"Sambering? What's that supposed to be, Indian?"

"It was named for the owners. Sam, Berny, and Irving. It was a terrible camp. It was the third worst summer of my life."

All the intermediate girls were sending mash notes to boys one rainy week, so Lois had chosen a tall boy named Dicky, who seemed to her the best-looking boy in her age group, and sent him a note saying, "I think you might be my type. Do you want to be my boyfriend?" He had responded instantly with looks of such dark loathing that when, a few days later, Leonard Glassman, who was in her brother Philip's bunk, had written her a note telling her he would always love her, she had accepted his suit with gratitude.

"Leonard?" Rena said. "Is he fat?"

"Not really. Why?"

"It's a fat-sounding name."

"He's a little shorter than me."

"What's he like?"

"Actually, I don't see that much of him," Lois said. "He lives in Queens. He writes me letters every so often and last summer he sent me a ring he made out of a peach pit."

"But what's he like? How do you feel about him?"

The truth was that apart from the initial flattery, Lois felt nothing at all about Leonard.

"He has lots of personality," she said. This had been the general consensus at camp. "He's a pleasant person. Are you really in love with Donny?"

"How would I know!" Rena said impatiently. "I think he's attractive. I like his jawline."

Baffled, Lois now saw that Rena was as sophisticated as she was intelligent "What do you mean you like his jawline?" she asked. "What's there to like about a jawline?"

Rena traced the line between Lois's chin and ear with a finger. "You have it, too," she said. "That sharp, clean line."

Lois, her jaw tingling from the touch, looked at

Rena. She had known for years how Rena looked without thinking about it. In spite of the angularity of Rena's mind, her appearance was soft. Nearsighted, behind round gold-rimmed spectacles, her eyes were almost perfect brown-targeted circles; her snub nose was buttonlike, her mouth small and full. Though not plump, her b‹ dy, unlike Lois's, which was longer and leaner and not yet beginning to "develop," was all slopes and curves. Only her hair, seldom properly combed and often hanging over her face, was straight. She decided that Rena looked exactly the way Rena ought to look.

A window slid open overhead and a woman's voice called out. "Rena? Is that you down there?"

"Yes, Ma," Rena said, resigned.

"I want you to go to Nostrand and get me a Silvercup."

"She always wants something," Rena said, sighing. "She never makes a list, so it's one thing at a time. Well, I better go. And then I have to practice. I'll see you."

They parted. All the way home, rethinking the day, Lois's spirits rose and fell. Then, nearing her block, she began to run. She could scarcely wait for dinnertime, and she began to rehearse the nonchalance with which she would pass along the news of her IQ. Ignored, the youngest, a mere girl, unable to match her brother Philip's grades and the edge of his age, she could at last win their respect with this mysterious something that had been lodged, unsuspected, within the very fabric of her being all along. Now she had a vision of herself, grown and jaded, her cheeks sunken, wearing slacks and long earrings, chain-smoking, her heavy eyelids drooping. She was never going to push a baby carriage on Ocean Avenue.

It was two days, however, before Lois saw either of her parents. Her mother was asleep when Lois left for school in the morning, and Lois was asleep by the time her parents got home. On Friday afternoon when Lois came home from school, the game was in their living room and when her mother was dummy she got up from the bridge table and kissed Lois and asked her to empty the ashtrays. Her mother's Friday game, Jenny and Ruth and Ann, all said something friendly to her over their hands, and then it was as though she were dead. She emptied the ashtrays and went up to her room and wrote a poem about ladies with lacquered hair and fingernails, mannequins taking turns being dummies, and had to rhyme it with "certain kinds of mummies," and then tore it up and told herself that when she grew up she would have an operation and be a man. She had hardly seen Rena at all. On Thursday afternoon Rena had her piano lesson and on Friday she said she going to the library but that maybe she'd come to Lois's house on Saturday. Lois asked her to come for lunch, but Rena said she didn't know, she might have to mind Teddy, her baby brother. She never knew till the last minute, but she'd call and let Lois know.

By some miracle, her parents were home for dinner Friday night, though as usual her father was in a terrible mood. There was a depression on, and it made her father angry all the time. He made expensive dresses for large wealthy women and even they were economizing and in no mood for Belgian laces and Paris copies. He came home late, and you could see at once that he was waiting for the first chance he could get to holler. There was a standing rib roast for dinner.

"I suppose you paid your lover the butcher forty cents a pound for this piece of horsemeat?" he said. He made a big thing of slicing the roast, his face turning as red as the inside of the first cut. "Goddamn it!" he said, throwing the knife down. "This knife is no goddamn good. Haven't we got one sharp knife in this goddamn house?"

"Calm down, Sam, the knives were just sharpened in February. He should be back any day." She was talking about the Italian knife grinder who appeared on the block in a horse-drawn wagon, usually once a month.

"Then you carve it," her father said, sitting back in his chair, his eyes beady with hate. "Goddamn bunch of parasites, and I'm losing twenty thousand dollars this season."

Lois and Philip sat meekly eyeing each other in familiar despair across the table.

"A person doesn't see their parents all week and then when they finally show up for dinner this is the charming conversation," Lois murmured.

"What was that wiseguy remark?" her father bellowed.

She bolted from her chair, throwing her napkin down. "I don't know why you ever had children in the first place," she shouted. She slammed out of the dining room and ran up to her room, too furious even to weep, and sat on her bed clenching and unclenching her fists, wishing that her father, in one of his fits of temper, would be struck down by a just Old Testament God even angrier than he. Furthermore, she was hungry. She'd had four Fig Newtons and a glass of milk after school and not a bite since. In a little while, she heard her mother bounding up the stairs.

"Lois?" her mother said, opening the door.

8 · 8 ·

"Are you all right?"

"Oh, sure," Lois said, bursting into tears. "I'm just great." Her mother came and sat down on the bed beside her, which only made her cry harder.

"Sarah Bernhardt," her mother said, as she always did when Lois cried. Then, placating her with complicity, she sighed and said, "You should be used to him by now. That's just the way he is. He works very hard."

"If I have to hear how hard he works one more time, I'll vomit. Who asked him to work so hard?"

"You have to learn how to handle him."

"I haven't noticed that you've figured out how to do that yet, and you're his wife. I'm not even here by choice."

"Come on downstairs now. You must be starved."

Lois blew her nose. "Why don't you get a divorce?" she said. "All he does is yell all the time."

"Don't be silly," her mother said. "We don't get divorces in our family. Besides, he has his good moments. "

"Very few and far between," Lois said.

"Anyhow, how could I divorce him with two children?"

Her father didn't go to work the next day, Saturday. At breakfast, he was calm and in good spirits, sleep and the night having mollified him. Breakfast that morning was almost festive; the previous night, like so many others, almost forgotten. Sunlight streamed through the breakfast-room windows.

"It's a beautiful day," her father said. "How would you like to go to Coney Island for a walk on the boardwalk?"

"I have to practice," Philip said. Timid, unathletic, shunned by the boys on the block, he had turned to music for solace. He practiced the piano five hours a day, every day.

"My friend plays the piano, too," Lois said.

"What friend?"

"A new friend. Rena Poswolsky."

"Is she in your class?" Lois's mother asked.

"She's the smartest girl in the class. She may be coming to lunch today."

"If she's so smart," Philip said, "what does she want with a dope like you?"

Lois sat up straighter in her chair. "It just so happens we got the results of some special tests the other day," she said. "They're called IQ's."

"What's an IQ?" her mother asked.

"It stands for intelligence quotient," Philip said.

"Mine was the second highest," Lois said. "Just a point behind Rena."

"Is that so?" her mother said. "What does it mean?"

"It measures your basic intelligence," Lois said. "What you were born with, not your learning or what you know, but how smart you really are."

"So what does it mean?" her father persisted. "What good is it?"

"It means I have something called a potential, according to Miss Roach. Better than ninety-nine out of every hundred people. It means that some day I may be able to do something unusual, if I'm allowed to develop properly."

"I'd like to see it already," her father said.

"I think it's wonderful," her mother said. "I'm very proud of you, Lois. Sam, I think you should be proud of your daughter."

"When she brings home her first dollar I'll be proud."

Rena didn't come that day, nor did she call. Lois moped around all morning within earshot of the telephone, and spent the afternoon vacillating between anger and disappointment. On Monday she ignored Rena all day during classes and was surprised, after school, when Rena linked her arm through hers after they had filed outside.

"Let's go to your house today," she said, "and do our homework together."

Lois looked at her coldly. "What happened to you on Saturday?"

"Saturday? Oh my God, Lois, I'm sorry, I forgot all about it."

"Think nothing of it," Lois said grimly.

"Gee, Lois, I really am sorry. I'm just so absent-minded." She squeezed Lois's arm. "I haven't hurt your feelings, have I, Lois?"

"It's OK," Lois said, relenting. There was no doubting Rena's sincerity. "I guess that's just the way you are. I guess when you like someone, you just have to accept the way they are."

When they got to Lois's house, Rena's face darkened. Lois opened the door with her key and took Rena's coat to hang in the hall closet. When she emerged from the closet, Rena had vanished. Lois found her in the living room, scowling at the furniture. The room had been redecorated the previous year and, although Lois thought it gorgeous with its newly paneled fake-fireplace wall, the bookcases with their expensive leather-bound matching sets of books, the Lalique vase, and the rosewood tantalus from France, the thick, sculptured wall-to-wall carpeting, the needlepoint side chairs, and the damask draperies, she tried without success to see what it was in the room that was making Rena so cranky.

"You're rich, aren't you?" Rena said, going over to the grand piano. "A Steinway." She touched one of the keys, then played an arpeggio. "In tune, much to my surprise."

"My brother plays."

Rena leafed through his music books. "He's pretty advanced," she said. "How old is he?"

"Fifteen."

Rena went over to the bookcases and scanned the titles. "The Book of the Presidents. Sourcebook of the Great War," she read off the spines. "Who reads this crap?"

"Nobody," Lois said. "It's for show. Let's get something to eat."

"Is your father a boss?"

"Yes. He has a dress factory. He has 150 people working for him."

"Just as I thought!" Rena said. "A capitalist exploiter. Is he unionized?"

"I don't know. He's having trouble with the union."

Rena nodded sagely. "I'm a Communist," she said.

"No kidding?" Lois said, thrilled. "My father hates Communists."

"Naturally. What about you?"

"I guess I've never been too interested in politics. As a child I was mainly athletic."

"I'll lend you some books. It's important."

"Okay. Let's get something to eat."

They were in the kitchen having milk and leftover chocolate cake when Philip came home from school. He stood in the kitchen doorway, the light from the windows reflecting off his glasses, shielding his shyness.

"Rena, this is my brother Philip," Lois said. "Philip, this is my friend Rena."

"You don't have to do both ends of an introduction," Philip, who knew everything,, said. "It's both boring and redundant. I have to go practice now, if you ladies will excuse me."

"He was showing off," Rena said when Philip had gone. "He's probably afraid of girls."

"He's afraid of boys, too."

They could hear the piano in the living room. Rena listened thoughtfully for several minutes. "Technically, he's very good," she announced. "But he doesn't play with much feeling. You can't play Chopin the way you play Bach."

Lois drained her glass. She listened, trying to understand what Rena meant. Then, suddenly, she did.

"I never thought of that before," she said. "That there aren't only the notes that are there on the page. And the loud parts and the soft parts. But that there's the composer's meaning, the kind of soul, that the musician has to understand." She was enjoying herself, feeling the walls of her world stretch. Rena was nodding, her dark eyes warm and glowing.

"Like actors, musicians are kind of middlemen. Of course, boys of fifteen can't be expected to have all that much feeling yet. They're not like girls."

Carlotta, the houseworker, a gaunt black woman of indeterminate age, staggered up from the basement bearing a wicker basket filled with freshly laundered clothing.

"You makin' crumbs all over my clean floor?" she said.

"This is Carlotta, our maid," Lois said. Rena leaped to her feet, smiling as though at royalty, and with a forthright manly gesture extended her right hand. Carlotta eyed Rena with terror, then set down her basket, wiped her hand on her apron, and limply extended it. Rena pumped it with enthusiasm.

"I'm very pleased to meet you. Did you bake that cake we're eating?"

"Yes'm."

"It's marvelous, just about the best I ever ate."

Lois squirmed. "Let's go to my room," she said.

Upstairs, Rena turned on Lois. "What do you mean calling her 'our maid'?" she said. Lois stared at her.

"That's who she is," Lois said.

"First of all, she's not yours. She's not a slave, though she probably has no way of knowing that. Secondly, she's not a maid. A maid is a girl. She's a woman. Does she sleep in?"

"Yes."

"I suppose in a room about four feet square."

"It's not that small."

"How much does she make?"

"I don't know. Forty or fifty dollars a month. And room and board."

"How many days a week does she work?"

"She's off Thursdays and every other Sunday."

"Why Thursday?"

"That's the day they all go off."

"What do you mean, *they*?" God, Lois, doesn't it make you ashamed, having a poor oppressed woman doing all the dirty work?"

"I think she's glad to have a job. There's a lot of unemployment, don't forget."

"Who did those paintings?" Rena said, going to the wall opposite the bed.

"I did. Last summer at camp."

"This one isn't bad." It was a portrait of Barbara Bronffman, one of her bunkmates. "I didn't know you could paint."

"I can't, really"

"Yes you can. You put blue in her hair. Most people wouldn't do that unless she really had blue in her hair. You did it to make it look more black."

"That's what the painting counselor said. She's an artist. She told my parents to encourage me."

"Did they?"

"They sent me a box of oils, but I don't want to study painting. My father got all excited. He started talking about how I could be a dress designer and how dress designers make almost as much money as he makes."

"So?"

"I'd rather write poetry."

Rena flopped down on the bed and narrowed her eyes at Lois. "Good for you," she said. "Do you know why you reacted that way? Because you're in revolt against their lousy values. But that's no reason not to paint. You could do it and not be a dress designer."

"I know. But it made him so happy it killed all the pleasure for me."

"But don't you see, if you're acting only to rebel, then they're still making you behave in a way that's against your own feelings. They're still the focus. The important thing is to do what you want, to know what you want. Then you train your parents accordingly."

"My God, Rena, what do you mean, train my parents?"

"It's just as important to bring your parents up right as it is for them to bring you up right."

Lois looked at her as though she were insane. "You don't know my parents."

"I'm sure I'd hate them," Rena said. "And vice versa."

So it proved. Their homework done, Lois persuaded Rena to stay to dinner. It's broiled chicken," Lois said. "So thank God my father won't have to carve."

"Why? Doesn't he know how?"

"He has a very short temper and the knives are never sharp enough."

"I like my father better than my mother. He's not a happy man, but he's sweet. He collects stamps."

"Philip and I chip in and give them a new carving knife every year for their anniversary, but it doesn't seem to make any difference."

"My father couldn't care less about those things. He's very withdrawn."

"Well don't pay any attention if my father blows up about something. His bark is worse than his bite."

Rena put a hand over Lois's and squeezed it. "You're not afraid of him, are you, Lois?" she asked gently. Lois looked down at her feet.

"Boy, these sneakers are really getting ratty," she said.

"Look at me, Lois."

Blinking, she forced herself to look at Rena.

"It doesn't make any difference, Lois. I'm not going to hold your parents against you. You're you."

The meal was interminable. There was almost no conversation at first, just the sound of Lois's father inhaling his soup.

"I always say a meal without soup is no meal at all," he said, after a while. It was true; he always said it.

"We have soup every night," Lois said. Rena said nothing. Across the table, Philip, looking at no one, was letting it be known that although his corporeal self was unhappily present, his mind and spirit were profoundly engaged elsewhere.

"Where do you live, dear?" Lois's mother asked.

"Twenty-ninth," Rena mumbled, not looking up from her plate.

His spoon at last laid to rest, Lois's father turned his attention to Rena. "What does your father do?" he asked.

"Butter and eggs."

"A wholesaler?"

"He has a route."

Lois held her breath, waiting for her father to say that there wasn't much money in that, or something worse. By some miracle, he didn't. The soup plates cleared, Carlotta began to pass the big round silver platter, chicken mounded in the center, the vegetables flanking it. She started at the head of the table.

"The left!" Lois's mother said. She was perpetually training Carlotta. "Serve from the left, remove from the right."

When Carlotta got to Rena, Lois saw from Rena's awkwardness that she had never been served at dinner. From that point on, Lois watched Rena's manners deteriorate. She reached for a slice of bread and buttered all of it. She didn't pass her fork from her left hand to her right after using her knife. She kept her napkin crumpled at the side of her plate. She clattered her cutlery. When she spoke it was in monosyllables and her voice was sullen. For a brief, moment, Lois was embarrassed, and then, when it came to her that Rena's bad manners were deliberate, she was overwhelmed with admiration.

At last, released from the dining room, Rena gathered up her books.

"I'll walk you to the corner," Lois said, getting her coat. They walked in silence for a way and then, unable to restrain herself, Lois threw an arm across Rena's shoulders and hugged her. "I want you to know that I ... cherish you," she said.

"Your father's not so bad," Rena grunted. "He's just exactly what he is. But I'm not sure I can figure out your mother."

It was something else for Lois to think about. When she got back to the house, her mother looked at her with distaste and said, "You make the most peculiar friends, Lois. She didn't even say thank you when she left."

"No," Lois said, grinning. "She didn't."

In the months that followed, they were inseparable. They did their homework together almost every afternoon, went together to the library, ate their sandwiches side by side in the lunch room. They met nearly every Saturday. Sometimes they went to the movies, but more often they took the subway to Manhattan to museums and art galleries, and Lois, who had an allowance, unlike Rena, who had to baby-sit for pocket money, would buy them both lunch, exotic food neither of them had eaten before, in inexpensive foreign restaurants. With the coming of spring and warmer weather, they went often to the Bronx Zoo or the Brooklyn Botanic Garden, and once they walked across the Brooklyn Bridge and saw the sun set through the steel cobwebs. And they talked. For Lois, the world had opened wide. She soared on the wings of her expanded universe, heard sounds in new ways, watched people and wondered about their lives, felt herself growing, stretching, reaching. But best of all was being able to share it, to find words for it and tell it, each knowing the other would really listen and hear in order to understand the other's experience of what they were sharing and, through the differences as well as the similarities, compound the delight and wonder.

"I always thought when I got older I'd go live out West and raise horses," Lois said. "But now I don't know." It was a day in late May. They were at the Botanic Garden, sitting on the grass beneath the ranks of cherry trees, the air rich with the color and scent of the blossoms. "I was in my Zane Grey period." Rena pulled off her sweater and folded it over a package she had been carrying all morning.

"I don't think I could live anywhere but here," she said. "Everything is here. If you haven't got much money, and I probably never will, there's always something to do or see."

Not far from where they sat, a very young woman in blue jeans and a navy sweat shirt lay on her stomach reading a book. Two fat little boys, barely toddlers, one white and the other black, both of them gurgling with intensity, were trying to walk on her back. Idly, Lois watched, and though her mind was elsewhere she was charmed by the tableau.

"I'm never going to get married," she said. "I hate what happens to people when they get married and have families."

"It's true," Rena said. "I can't think of any married people I know who seem happy."

The young woman closed her book and rolled over onto her back, spilling the babies onto the grass. She swept them both into her arms and covered them with kisses, then got to her feet, kicked off her sandals, and began to dance. She was very beautiful.

"I think now I'd like to go live in different places," Lois said. "Paris, London, Rome, Venice. And just write poems."

"Let's do that," Rena said. "Why not? I'll have to work to go to college, but after that we could both get jobs for a couple of years and save money and then just go." They grinned at each other. Yes, they could do it; they could do anything. They really could.

"Paris first," Rena said. "I'll give English lessons and I can teach piano. Or maybe play in a bistro."

The young woman danced across the lawn, the children tumbling after, trying to catch her feet. She moved with unselfconscious grace, tossing her long, auburn, ponytail. Lois felt a stab of yearning, almost pain.

"That woman is lovely," she said.

"What woman?" Rena turned to look in the direction Lois was facing. "That one dancing?" She frowned. "Let's go, Lois. I'm getting very thirsty."

They got up and began to move off when they heard the woman call after them. "Hey, girls, you left something." They turned. Rena's package lay on the grass.

"I'll get it," Lois said, and running back swooped it up and brought it to Rena.

"It's yours," Rena said, "so you might as well carry it."

"Mine? What is it?"

"It's a present."

"But why? It's not my birthday or anything."

"I just felt like giving you something," Rena said gruffly. "Does it have to be your birthday?"

"Don't bite my head off," Lois said, tearing at the wrapping. "It's just that nobody ever... Oh, Rena!" It was a book, Chekhov's stories, bound in limp, tooled leather, a deep chocolate brown. "It's beautiful." Gently, she riffled the pages, fine as gossamer, and saw in Rena's clear, round hand the inscription on the flyleaf: "For Lois, just because she is Lois."

Moved beyond words, she threw her arms around Rena and kissed her cheek.

"Don't!" Rena said, pushing her away. "Don't do that."

"Why not?"

"Just don't!" Rena said fiercely. "Just don't ever do that."

Lois drew back, confused. Something, the beginning of fear, or the memory of another, ancient fear, pricked her.

When Lois got home, her mother was in the living room darning socks, one of her few concessions to domesticity.

"I don't know why you don't get friendlier with that nice girl up the street," her mother said. "Harriet."

"What makes you think Harriet's so nice?" Lois asked. "Nobody likes her."

"She's a lovely girl, pretty, well-mannered, and very intelligent. She's certainly more of a person than that Rena. And a lot neater."

"Neater!" Lois howled. "For God's said, I don't pick my friends for neatness. She's got a great handwriting, too. Am I supposed to like her for her handwriting?"

"Now Lois."

"I didn't say good. I said goody-goody. There's a difference," Lois said, feeling hopeless. "She's too good, It's phony."

"She has manners," her mother said. "Good manners never hurt anyone. I wish you were as well-mannered. As for Rena!"

"You only like Harriet because her parents have money and belong to your golf club. And because you think if I have friends who are like Harriet it makes me more presentable."

"Well it does."

"It does not! It doesn't change me one bit. If it makes you prouder of me because your friends can say, 'Oh, what sweet lovely girls,' then I must say you have terrible standards. Mine are different."

"Oh? And what are your standards?"

"You wouldn't understand," Lois said. She wasn't at all sure what her standards were. She was only beginning to discover what they were not.

"All I'm trying to say is that if you choose misfits for friends, you'll pretty soon be a misfit yourself."

"Rena is not a misfit!" Lois said, her voice shrill. "She's the smartest girl in school, a lot smarter than Harriet. She's a gifted pianist, almost as good as Philip even though she doesn't practice as much. And besides, she's interesting."

Misfits! What was that supposed to mean? Well, if it meant the people who didn't fit comfortably in the world, who didn't slide mindlessly through every day, who bumped into things and ideas and knew what was nonsense and rebelled against it, then Rena was a misfit and Lois hoped that she was, too. Her mother said that misfits were unhappy people and had unhappy lives, and Lois said that there could be different kinds of happiness and that, by God, she'd be much happier being thoughtfully unhappy than mindlessly happy.

She took her new book to bed with her that night and read for a long time. At first she was perplexed, the stories seemed so simple. But when she'd closed the book and was trying to fall asleep, she realized that the stories were not simple, after all, that the people in them had been very real to her, no matter how brief the stories, and that she had learned something important about them and about their lives. She took the book off the night table and put it under her pillow and thought about Rena. How awful if she had never gotten to know Rena. How empty and ugly her life had been before and how the scales were falling from her eyes. Then fear gripped her and she fell asleep praying to whoever was in charge to keep Rena from pneumonia, streptococcus, spinal meningitis, polio, and, if possible, even the common cold.

In the last days of school they were euphoric, despite the endless dreary preparations for graduation: finishing up the dresses they'd been working on forever in sewing class, posing for class pictures, remembering to bring money for class rings, practicing the dirge-like shuffle down the auditorium aisles to "Pomp and Circumstance." They were forever being lined up in size places. But, as it signified the end of an era, it was worth it. They were at last, unbelievably, marvelously, to be free of this dun prison where they had passed two-thirds of their lives. And would go on to the next stage.

"I think I'll invite Donny to Sidney's party," Rena said at lunch one day. Sidney Roper, the oldest boy in their class, was having a party the night after graduation in his finished basement.

"I thought the party was just for the class," Lois said.

"He said to bring anyone we wanted. He's having some girl he likes who goes to parochial. There'll probably be kissing games."

If Rena was going to bring Donny, then Lois would ask Leonard. She had had a dopey letter from him a few weeks earlier, which she hadn't answered because she had decided that he was immature. But if it was going to be that kind of party, she had no choice. She called him that night and he said sure, and how tall was she now? They talked about height for a while, and then he said he'd pick her up around 7:30.

The last days were interminable. Then, miraculously, they were shuffling out of the auditorium clutching their diplomas, in size places for the last time. Outside in the bright sunshine of the golden June day, ecstatically free, Lois thought: This is my first last time. She was almost thirteen and had grown two feet since, utterly terrified, she had first gone through those doors, and there wasn't a thing she had learned in the interval that she couldn't have learned in one year at home except how to endure monotony without fidgeting too much.

Promptly at 7:30 the next night, Leonard arrived. He was all dressed up in a navy suit and a red bow tie, and he smelled powerfully of cinnamon.

"You wearing cinnamon?" Lois asked him.

"After-shave lotion," he said haughtily, then grinned. It was a metallic grin; his teeth were covered with braces. Lois hoped there weren't going to be kissing games. They walked the three blocks to Sidney Roper's house, trying to make conversation. Leonard told a couple of jokes she'd already heard, and then they fell silent.

"I don't actually know anything about you, Leonard," Lois said after a while.

"Like what do you mean?"

"Like do you read books? Do you think about things?"

"Sure I think about things. I'm very mechanical-minded. I'm trying to invent a water clock."

"That's interesting, Leonard. I hope you'll tell me about it."

Mrs. Roper let them in and told them to go downstairs to the finished basement where the party was. It was a big, brightly lit room, and almost all the kids were there already. Rena hadn't come yet. A Glenn Miller record was playing, but nobody was dancing. The boys were bunched at one end of the room and the girls were chatting at the other. Everybody said "Hi" and Sidney Roper told them to help themselves to Cokes and potato chips at the bar. Lois had never yet had a good time at a party, and she was pretty sure this one wouldn't be any different. Most of a party was spent trying to get it started and then it was time to go home.

"You want to dance?" Leonard asked her.

She didn't really know how to dance. "Not if we're the only ones," she said.

"So am I supposed to go over there and stand around talking to the boys?" Leonard asked. 'I don't know any of them."

A few more kids came down the stairs and into the room and then Rena arrived. She was alone.

"Where's Donny?" Lois asked.

"He couldn't come. He had to go away for the weekend with his parents."

"Hey, everybody," Leonard said, clapping his hands. "How about getting together and having a party? Boys and girls together. Whaddya say?" Everyone looked up at him and grinned and a couple of the boys sidled across the room to where the girls were.

"That's Leonard," Lois said to Rena.

"He's cute," Rena said. "Is he going to be the life of the party?"

"I hope someone is. You'd think we were a bunch of lepers. You'd never guess we spent about ten thousand hours of our life in the same room."

"Everyone's self-conscious," Rena said. "We don't know each other this way."

"If nobody's going to dance," Leonard said, "how about some games?" In no time at all, he had them all arranged in a circle on the floor, boy, girl, boy, girl, and they were playing Spin the Bottle. Lois didn't mind the kissing; it made everyone friendlier and happier. But after a while, when everyone had kissed everyone else at least once, it began to be boring. They went on to Post Office and that was more fun. A dark closet was the post office and in private there was more scope to the kissing. The boys were more daring and it was interesting to see the variations in their approach. Some of them put their arms around Lois and kissed for a long time, some of them were quick and shy, and Sidney Roper even put his tongue in her mouth. Leonard had worked out a way to kiss so that you hardly felt his braces.

After a while, Lois noticed that every time Rena was It, she sent for Leonard and that, between turns, she would sit next to him and talk to him as though he were the only person there, touching his arm or taking his hand while she talked, and looking at him as though he were something delicious to eat.

"This is kids' stuff," Rena said, her hand on Leonard's arm, after they had been playing for a while. "Why don't we just put out the lights and neck?" Some of the girls gasped and one of the boys, closest to the light switch, flicked it off. There was some giggling and scuffling, but then the dark made them silent. Some boy, she didn't know who, had his arm around Lois. She excused herself, wriggled free, and groped her way to the stairs. She had to pass Mr. and Mrs. Roper on her way out so she forced herself to smile and thank them and then she was outside and running home.

It wasn't until she was in bed that she began to cry. A lot of bad things had happened to her in her life, bad and difficult and sometimes mysterious things, but this double betrayal made her feel worse than she could remember ever feeling, worse in a new and different way. She knew that what had happened wasn't as serious as her nervous breakdown when she was nine, or the time she'd had pneumonia and almost died, or the time she'd deliberately gotten herself lost at Coney Island when she was six because she was so angry at her father, and then, alone, had been so frightened. Fear and anger she had known, almost beyond endurance. And when Frank the chauffeur who had been so gentle and whom she had loved, had been fired, she had grieved for a long time. Many things in her life had been almost impossible for her to face and to accept --- the new puppy being run over in the street, Philip sleepwalking into her room in the middle of the night to tell her there was a horrible face at the window or the house was burning down, the man in the park who opened his coat and showed her his huge, purple penis, and the worst part of that had been the look on the man's face. Oh, life was full of dreadful moments against which she had railed and wept and trembled and thrown up.

But this latest was different. What had happened tonight was so complicated that she would never be able to sort it out. She was feeling so many things and she knew that there was nothing, nothing she could do about any of it --- the hurt, the rage, the outrage, the despair, the disappointment, the loss.

Rena, Rena.

Leonard called the next morning. "Where'd you disappear to?" he asked. "What was the idea of cutting out like that and leaving me?"

"I felt like going home," she said.

"Listen, Lois, I didn't know what to do. Honestly. I hope you don't think it was my fault. I told her you were my girl friend and then when I went to look for you, you were gone."

"That's okay, Leonard."

She was leaving for camp in a few days and she was glad to be going. The days were bleak and empty. She had to go shopping with her mother for a lot of last-minute things and help her pack the camp trunk, but there was still too much empty time in which to brood and feel as though a vitally important part of herself had been amputated.

The day before she was to leave, her mother called her to the phone. It was Rena.

"Lois? I have to see you."

She found that she was utterly incapable of

saying anything.

"Are you there, Lois?"

"Yes."

"It's important. I must see you."

"All right. Come on over."

"No. I don't want to come there. Meet me halfway, the corner of J and Bedford. In about ten minutes?"

When she got to the corner, Rena was there, slouched against a lamppost. She straightened up when she saw Lois. They stood for what seemed a long time, neither of them able to speak.

"Listen, Lois," Rena said at last, her voice shaky, "I've been feeling rotten, worse than I've ever felt in my life. I know I can't ask you to forgive me."

"That's all right."

"Don't say it's all right! It's not all right. I want you to understand something. Lois? Are you listening?"

"Yes."

"Well, then, listen. I was jealous."

"About Leonard? Him?"

"Not Leonard! I don't give two hoots about Leonard. And didn't the other night, either. Do you understand?"

"No."

Rena groaned. "Why must you make everything so hard? Lois, it was you, damn it. You. I couldn't stand it that you had a boyfriend. That you liked him."

Lois's heart began to pound and for a long moment she listened to it, knowing that she was scared. She felt that only by the most intense effort could she keep pieces of herself from flying off her body.

"Lois. Look at me."

She forced herself to look at Rena. Rena was crying.

"Lois, I've never felt this way about anyone."

"Oh, Rena!"

"I'm going now, Lois. I hope you have a good summer." She turned and Lois, trembling, watched her walk quickly away, her shoulders hunched against a storm, though it was a perfect day.,

"Goodbye Rena," Lois said softly, but Rena was already half a block away.

THE POWER

Prudence Dewhurst was fourteen years old when she became absolutely certain of The Power. It was growing in her breast just inside the rib cage and she could feel it opening like a flower, or uncurling like a fist. She had discovered during the past year that she was in direct contact with God, but only lately had she understood that this contact conferred a special power, palpable as a physical fact.

It made all the difference. It lit her pale face with small, secret smiles during French class and at night in her narrow corner of the dormitory she hugged herself to sleep feeling warm and snug and special. She no longer awaited the mail with anything like the old eagerness; it was, in fact, a matter of complete indifference to her whether her mother wrote at all. Packages, too, had lost their charm, for with the coming of The Power her needs had altered completely. She had entirely lost her sweet tooth and there were times when she would have forgotten even meals if the bell had not summoned so imperatively.

No, she was different, special. Not like the others at all. There was no question of it. She had The Power. The problem, though, was that she did not yet know what to do with it. If only she'd been born a Catholic! If only this were a convent! She would go, humbly, to the Mother Superior and confess the whole thing. At first they might suspect her of the sin of pride, but in time her humility and her sincerity would convince them. They would know that she had A Calling. They would hover over her, watchful and loving. They would pray with her, comfort her, they would bring her, at last, to fullness.

But, alas, Abigail Carruther's school was not a Catholic institution. Dr. Abigail was an agnostic and her school was run along more or less Ethical Culture lines. There was high purpose, there were lofty character goals, there were frequent expressions of a morality to which they all subscribed, there was a good deal of music and art, but of spiritual guidance and religious fervor there were none.

No, Dr. Abigail's school was definitely not a cradle for saints, and incipient sainthood, Prudence felt sure, was the nature of her infection. The fantastic thing, though, was that no one seemed to have noticed anything, no one at all, not the girls, not Miss Burney who taught mathematics and social graces, not Madam Delacroix, not Auntie Flo or Nurse James or even Miss Elfrieda whose sharp eyes could see through walls. Not even Dr. Abigail with all her prying, with her endless "Tell me your dreams, dear." It was past all understanding that something of such shattering magnitude, something that Prudence was so full of that she felt herself bursting at the seams with it, should escape all notice. Who could blame her, then, for not being able to hold it inside herself? It had been a difficult week and she was too tired, now, to resist the temptation to share her new importance. Besides, God had spoken to her during the night and she was worried. She had not understood Him. Austerity's face is clear but it speaks in distances. She could hear the voice, but the words came blurred through the echoing tunnel and the thick, curly beard.

In time, of course, she would understand. Why else be singled out thus? She was almost sure that The Power was there because she was going to do a miracle, but it seemed to her that if she was going to do a miracle she ought first to predict it. She was waiting for God to tell her the miracle and she was cranky and nervous and tired, and here was Marjorie Harkavy, who was not her best friend (Prudence had never been able to manage a best friend), but who, since their beds adjoined, might be said to be her closest friend. Prudence, too tired for volley ball, had begged to be excused and she sat, now, watching the game from the sidelines but not really seeing it, for the excitement of volley ball as a spectator sport is limited. And here came Marjorie Harkavy, ejected from the game because of the violent redness of her face and the unchecked fury of her play. Marjorie flopped on the ground beside Prudence and lay there like a drowning fish strangling on air.

"You give too much of yourself," Prudence said. "You really do."

Slowly, Marjorie's breathing regulated itself. Air, Prudence thought. How we use it and use it without even thinking about it. Like God. Die without it. Maybe air is God.

"I can't help it," Marjorie whined. "I play to win. I can't stand losing and I always play to win."

"Yes, but you overdo."

"I hate to lose. I'm a real competitor."

Ridiculous! How could air be God? Then God would have to be air.

"Anyhow, it's just my complexion," Marjorie said. "I can't help it if I have this kind of high complexion."

The air today was delicious. Though it came down snow-washed over the mountains, it held, this early April day, the soft promise of spring. Spring was not actually due for another month, for it came late to Dr. Abigail's little valley, which was tucked high in a corner of a mountain near Lugano, facing south toward Italy. Sitting as she was now, with the mountain behind her, Prudence looked across the playing field that sloped gently down to the line of somber firs, and knew that only the horizon and the limits of her vision prevented her seeing her mother, who was in Palermo, some six hundred miles due south and who was perhaps at this very moment standing at the edge of the blue Tyrrhenian Sea, looking north above the fishing nets and thinking with love, Prudence, Prudence. Fat chance!

Marjorie rolled over onto her back and looked up at the sky.

"How soft the ground is," she said. "Did you go for your X-ray this morning? Wasn't she a character?"

"Who?"

"The X-ray lady. Frau Stettenheimer."

But Prudence had not gone for her X-ray. She must have missed the announcement. Regular physical examinations were an important part of the school program, for some of the girls were delicate. But it was Prudence's opinion that the school's concern with their physical welfare was not only excessive but a calculated sop to the guilt of their parents who, free of their daughters, could not be accused of neglecting either their education or their health. There were the checkups and the therapy and the endless, idiotic injections and, if that were not enough, Nurse James was an expert in matters of diet, a great believer in wheat germ and berries and nuts. Furthermore, the school was expensive.

"Are you going home for the spring holidays?" Marjorie asked. Prudence paused before answering, waiting for a mental image to correspond with the word "home." She tried to review, chronologically, the long succession of pensions and hotel rooms and boarding schools that had been home. Once, a long time ago and dimly remembered, there had really been a home.

"My mother's in Palermo," she said. "I'm going there to be with her for the holidays."

Marjorie sighed. "You're so lucky," she said. "I'm going to have to stay."

Please, God, let me be lucky, Prudence thought. Let nothing happen to spoil Palermo. For something was always happening. Something had happened at Christmas and before that at Thanksgiving. She hadn't seen her mother since the summer. But then, of course, she was forgetting. It no longer mattered. Not now.

"Listen, Marjorie," she said. "I have something to tell you."

"What?"

"It's a secret."

Marjorie composed her face to assure Prudence that she was good at secrets.

"It's...it's not easy to tell."

"You've started to menstruate!"

"Oh, Marjorie, you know I've been for over a year."

"You've got a crush on Miss Elfrieda!"

"Please, Marjorie, it's nothing like that. And you don't have to guess since I'm going to tell you."

◆ 35 ◆

"Well, then, tell!"

"It's...you see...something's been happening to me. I've been having...well, visions!"

"Visions?"

"God, Marjorie, God's been talking to me. And something else. There's going to be a miracle."

Marjorie's face registered dismay.

"Oh, Prudence," she wailed, "you're such an oddball! You can't really believe the things you say."

Stung, Prudence said, "May God strike me dead on this spot if every word isn't the absolute truth."

Marjorie shook her head. "This religion kick," she said. "I don't know how you can be so serious about it. I mean, it's not as if you were a Catholic, or anything."

"Faith," Prudence murmured. "It's a question of faith. Either you've got it or you haven't. It's as simple as that."

Faith, faith. Once you closed your eyes and jumped, took that incredible plunge into faith's arms, then everything became possible. You could live there, in those arms.

"Well, anyway," Prudence said, "you'll see. Because there's going to be a miracle."

"What kind of miracle?" Marjorie said, her voice impatient with scorn. "I know! Dr. Abigail's going to get married. There's going to be man on the premises. A whole, real man."

"That's all you ever think of," Prudence said. "Sex. Sex and games."

"Come on, Prudence," Marjorie said. "Tell me what kind of miracle. I want to spread the word. Maybe I can drum up some disciples for you among those kooks on the volleyball court."

"You promised to keep it secret," Prudence said, closing her eyes. She had made a terrible mistake. She had wanted only to share her joy and instead she was being made to share Marjorie's scorn.

"Honestly, Pru!" Marjorie said. "Sometimes I think you're just plain crazy."

"Naturally," Prudence murmured. "Naturally you would think that."

Marjorie got up. The ground is cold," she said. "I'm going to see if they'll let me get back into the game."

Prudence did not open her eyes. Still, she could feel Marjorie withdraw, could feel herself alone again. From the playing field came the sudden, sharp sound of violent dispute and, without looking, Prudence knew that it was probably little Sally Manning who had been thrown to the ground and whose anguish now cut the air like a scythe. They were strange girls, ordinarily so well-mannered and quiet, sometimes too quiet, yet from time to time they erupted in such unexpected, bestial ways. Sally Manning was terrible at games; she couldn't keep her mind on them. Once, holding onto the ball, she had simply strolled off the field like a sleepwalker. Everything Sally Manning did enraged the other girls, and especially Marjorie Harkavy. It was probably she who had thrown Sally down.

It was all so revolting! Girls ought not to engage in team sports. It made them monstrous and hateful. Prudence couldn't bring herself to open her eyes, even when Miss Elfrieda's whistle shrilled and order had been restored. Through her closed eyelids, the sunlight wove shifting patterns. Light and dark, light and dark. Whatever could she have been thinking to have chosen Marjorie Harkavy for a confidante? Stupid! She would have to be even more careful. She was different. She must learn to withdraw even further from the society of those around her. She must learn better to live within herself. Deep in her eyes, the sunlight danced, dark and light, light and dark. Fatigue shrouded her like a mist and wound thus, she drifted for a while in the limbo between waking and sleep. Was the mountain coming down? It seemed to her that perhaps it was. And where the mountain had been a man stood, his cruel and handsome face lined with sorrow. Stood and softly called her name. Who was he? Was he after all her father? But her father was dead and she had never seen him. Tell me, she called to the man, tell me the secret. But the man only stood and softly called her name. Prudence, he said, and she saw that there were tears in his eyes. Prudence, Prudence.

She opened her eyes. Between her and the sun, Miss Elfrieda towered, laughing down at her.

"Prudence?" Miss Elfrieda said. "Are you awake?"

Prudence blinked. From this angle, Miss Elfrieda's legs in the black slacks she always wore, seemed impossibly long.

"What a funny girl!" Miss Elfrieda said. "Sitting so straight...and fast asleep." She held the volleyball in one hand, the furled net in the other. Behind her, Prudence saw, the field was empty. The game was over and the girls had gone. She looked up at Miss Elfrieda and blinked again. How handsome Miss Elfrieda was, her teeth so white in the healthy sunburned face, her short fair hair blown across her clear brow. She looked so physical, so vital, so overwhelmingly alive. Prudence wondered if it could be true, what Marjorie was always hinting about her.

Miss Elfrieda shifted the volleyball into the crook of her other arm and reached her freed hand down to Prudence. The whistle hanging round her neck swayed and caught the sun, a charm against evil.

"Come," she said. "Time to go back. You will catch your death sitting on the damp ground."

Prudence avoided the offered hand and got quickly to her feet. "I guess I was asleep," she said. "I didn't hear the girls go."

"You are a strange child," Miss Elfrieda said as they walked across the field. She turned on Prudence her grave, penetrating eyes and Prudence, meeting them, felt a slight chill and thought, perhaps she knows. "You are so quiet, so thoughtful. What deep sorrows you seem to be hiding. Is it so?"

"No," Prudence said and, turning to look over her shoulder, saw that the mountain was still there.

"How you have grown this year!" Miss Elfrieda said. "You know, I think you are going to be, very soon, a beautiful woman. Yes, I think so. Like your mother, eh?"

Beautiful? She, Prudence, beautiful? The idea was so preposterous that she was for an instant stunned by it.

"But too thin. And too pale. You must come more in the open air. I will teach you how to breathe."

"How to breathe?" Prudence said, aware that Miss Elfrieda was waiting for her to say something. She looked at the woman walking beside her and her spirits, so damaged by the encounter with Marjorie, began to rise. Yes, perhaps if she learned how to breathe.

They had reached the west terrace and as they crossed the flagstone the warm smells of lunch

reached out to them. An inside smell, Prudence
thought. Inside smells, outside smells, air, and Miss
Elfrieda to teach one to breathe it. She smiled at Miss
Elfrieda. But beautiful? Surely not, no, not like her
mother a beautiful woman, no. Not she.

Inside, she watched Miss Elfrieda's straight
back disappear into the shadows at the end of the hall
and listened to the girls, already assembled in the dining room, singing one of the invocations they had
learned to make them worthy of the impending meal.

> *"Faith, truth and lo-ove,*
> *Knowledge, health and beauty,*
> *To higher service*
> *Now we dedicate..."*

Prudence slipped into the dining room and,
taking her place, joined her voice to the others.

> *"Till our ideals*
> *Shall reign o'er all victorious*
> *And light of knowledge*
> *Guide us on our way."*

She was seated, this month, next to one of the
younger girls, an American named Harriet Melody.
Harriet was new at the school. She was given to
shrill nightmares and all day she talked gloomily and
everlastingly about The Bomb.

"In America they have grown quite accustomed
to The Bomb," was her unvarying prefatory remark.
"You see, once you have made the first compromise,
you are doomed."

Harriet kept a scrapbook in which she pasted
all the news clippings she could find relating to The

Bomb. On the cover of the scrapbook, she had elabo-
rately lettered in red ink, "LEARNING TO ACCEPT
THE DEATH OF THE WORLD: A CHRONICLE."

"They have developed a survival cracker,"
Harriet was saying as Prudence tore off a corner of
her roll and spread it with butter. "There are tons of
them in this shelter in Albany, New York, where five
hundred state employees, including the governor, are
going to survive. And then after they have eaten all
those crackers and survived, they will come out again
and go on governing the state of New York."

Prudence tried not to listen.

"The governor of New York State is an extremely wealthy man," Harriet said. "He is going to
have shelters with crackers in them at all his homes.
He has homes in the country and homes at the seashore and homes in the city and he plans to survive in
all of them. He is determined to survive. He has determined to be absolutely the fittest."

Although Prudence knew that, unlike some of
the wildly improbable fears so many of the girls in-
dulged in, it was reasonable to be disturbed by The
Bomb, Harriet Melody carried it too far. She was a
bright girl, Harriet Melody. Too bright, Prudence had
heard them say, too bright for her own good. Most of
them here at the school were too bright, too sophisticated, too something for their own good. Why else
had they been sent so far from home, to a place so
isolated?

"Once you accept any part of it, the first, the
smallest part of it," Harriet persisted, "then you have
opened the door to all of it. The whole thing. Total
destruction. It's like jumping off a cliff. You can't
just jump a little bit."

"All right, Harriet, knock it off," Marjorie

Harkavy said from across the table. "It seems to me we already had this sermon once today."

"And at least three times yesterday."

"I'd like you to see my scrapbook, Prudence," Harriet said, ignoring the others and the fact that Prudence had already seen it more than once. "I know you would appreciate it."

But Prudence had discovered a note at her place and she pretended total absorption in it, though it said only that she was to report without fail to Nurse James directly after classes at three o'clock. But by three o'clock she had forgotten. She went, instead, as was her habit, to the study hall to prepare her lessons for the next day. Many of the girls were gathered there, quietly studying. Prudence found an empty desk and, sitting at it, was annoyed to discover that she had neglected to bring her books. No matter; she would borrow one. She looked around at her schoolmates and was alarmed to see that none of them had books. They sat, dreamlike, staring into their laps, at their hands, into space.

"But where are the books?" Prudence cried. A few of the girls looked up, startled, and off in a corner, someone sniggered, as though Prudence had said something profoundly stupid. Confused, Prudence took paper and pen from the desk drawer and began a letter to her mother.

"Dear Mother," she wrote, "I have been meaning to write all week but I have been, as usual, terribly busy. I don't know where the days go."

Where do the days go, she wondered, biting the end of her pen. It seemed to her that she had spent a million days in this place and that they had all, after all, been only one day, this day. She stared at the sheet of paper, wondering what she could say to the distant blurred outlines of her mother. Today Miss Elfrieda said that I am going to be beautiful. That happened. And if she did not lie, what will I do with beauty? Will I spend it like the days? Miss Elfrieda says she will teach me to breathe. Perhaps if I learn to breathe. In and out. Oh, Mother, I have such a wonderful secret. I can't tell it, even to you. Especially not to you. In and out. There is a girl here who worries about atomic bombs. She says that when they made the very first bomb they killed the world She says you don't have to jump off the cliff; you can walk away. But once you jump, by God, you have jumped! Odd. In a way it was like faith.

It was hopeless. There was nothing in her life that she could say to her mother, nothing that would have any meaning for her mother. She put her head on her arm and closed her eyes. In and out. And if I learn to breathe, she thought, what then? What will change? She fell asleep.

She had no idea how long she slept. Someone was tugging at her arm.

"Get up P-Prudence. P-Please." It was Sally Manning and she looked frightened.

"What's the matter?"

"I've b-been trying and trying to w-wake you."

"Why?"

"They want you in the library."

"The library?"

"I think you have a v-visitor."

A visitor? She could not remember if she had ever had a visitor. There was some mistake, surely. She walked quickly towards the library but the corridor seemed endless; the double doors seemed to recede as she drew near.

She pushed the doors ajar and peered nervously

inside. The library was a long room. At its far end, through tall mullioned windows, the north light slanted obliquely in, diffuse and mote-flecked, making the high book-lined walls shadowy and unreal. Half in and half out of the shadows a woman stood looking out at the mountain. She seemed lost in thought, or perhaps it was only that she didn't hear Prudence. She stood motionless for what seemed a very long time while Prudence watched her from the door, listening to the beating of her own heart. She knew at once that the woman was her mother. She had caught her scent the moment she had pushed against the door, but she stood, nonetheless, immobilized by a premonition, frightened. It was so long since she had seen her mother. Still, with the holidays so near there was no reason for her to be here now, visiting this remote corner of a Swiss mountain. No reason, of course, unless... Think of God , she told herself and shut the door behind her.

Her mother turned from the window and, peering through the long shadows, tilted her head a little to one side, like a dog, listening.

"Prudence? Is that you?"

Prudence stepped inside. "Hello, Mother," she said.

They met in the center of the room and her mother leaned to kiss her. They were very nearly the same size.

"How you've grown," her mother said, sounding nervous. "Come, let me look at you. Why is it so dark in here?"

"They don't turn the lights on until five," Prudence said. Her mother took her arm and, surprised, Prudence felt that her mother was trembling. They walked together out of the shadows to the far end of the room.

"Yes," her mother said, studying Prudence's face in the cold light under the window. "You're changing. You're not a little girl any longer." She spoke wistfully, as though she were going to miss the little girl she had scarcely known. And Prudence, looking into her mother's face, saw changes, too. Her mother's beauty had edges that she'd never noticed before (perhaps they had not been there?) --- something around the mouth that was a little too fixed, too rigid. Something in the gray eyes that was both cold and pleading. For the first time, Prudence wondered what her mother was really like.

"Are you happy, darling?" her mother asked, fitting a cigarette into a long jade holder. Prudence, who did not know what happiness was, stared at her mother. Was she happy? Well, then, was she not happy? And then, as her mother lit her cigarette and puffed extravagantly at it, Prudence realized that the question was rhetorical.

"Yes," she said dully. "I suppose I am happy."

Her mother, holding the burnt match, looked about for a place to drop it.

"No ashtrays, I'm afraid," Prudence said. "They don't encourage us to smoke."

"That's all right," her mother said, dropping the match at the base of a potted rubber tree plant. "I'll use one of these ghastly trees. I'm sure they're entirely indestructible." Prudence smiled, remembering the long list of her mother's dislikes: potted plants, parakeets, things crocheted, military bands, umbrellas, sachet, Tschaikovsky, hairpins.

"It's a good place, though, isn't it, darling"? her mother asked. "They do treat you well?"

"Of course."

"And you're getting enough to eat? You don't look as though you're getting enough to eat."

"The meals are very generous," she assured her mother. "They serve far more than I can eat." Prudence sighed. She knew that her mother was playing at her notion of motherhood, but she wished she would show a little more imagination. God. Think of God.

"Tell me," her mother said. "What did you have for lunch today?"

"Lunch? Today?"

"For instance."

Prudence hadn't the vaguest recollection of what lunch had been. She thought very hard but she could remember only that, after Harriet Melody had been silenced, she had become aware that a Beethoven quartet had been on the hi-fi, and that she had strained to hear it above the clatter of cutlery. She looked at the eagerness shining in her mother's beautiful eyes, the eagerness to be told the luncheon menu. Prudence's mind was a total blank.

"Peaches!" she cried, at last, inspired by a sudden vision of row on row of golden canned peaches.

"Peaches?" her mother said, clearly disappointed.

"Yes, peach halves with raspberries and ice cream," she invented, carefully watching her success in her mother's face. "For dessert, of course. And let me see... what was the entree? Yes, chicken livers and mushrooms. They do that awfully well here." She felt terribly sly, rewarded by the relief that gradually softened the worried lines on her mother's face. "And hot biscuits," she added, "with scads of butter." Her mother was very nearly beaming. "And cocoa, too. We have cocoa with every meal, you know."

"Good!" her mother said. 'Oh, very good."

"You're not hungry, are you, Mother?"

Her mother laughed. 'Of course I'm not hungry, darling." she said. "I only wanted to know...to feel...a little more closely...how it is with you. How it is here."

She stared at her mother across the small space that separated them.

"Yes," she said. "I see. How is Palermo, Mother?"

"Palermo was charming," her mother said with sudden enthusiasm. "Dirty and ancient, and there's the most marvelous cathedral! But we've left Palermo, you know."

Left Palermo? We?

"That's why I'm here, darling. Peter has to be back in London next week and so we drove up to do a little skiing first. And, of course, to see you. The drive across the mountains was fantastic, darling. I can still taste my heart in my mouth."

"Peter?" Prudence searched her mind, but Peter was nowhere in it. "Who is Peter?"

"Oh, Prudence!" her mother said and laughed her small, delightful laugh. "Surely I wrote you. Of course I did. Don't you ever read my letters?"

Prudence shifted her feet, sorry she had asked. She wanted to spare her mother the need to tell her that Peter was her father's second cousin or Uncle John's baby brother, you remember Aunt Sophie, don't you, well... It didn't matter at all who Peter was. Only, she was mildly curious about what had happened to Alan. It had been Alan only last summer, hadn't it? Or had he been the summer before? Or ten summers ago? Was it possible that she was really only fourteen years old?

"Let's sit down," she said, pulling her mother away from the window to one of the dark corners where a huge leather sofa brooded. "I'm tired. We had volley ball this morning."

"Volley ball?" her mother said, trying to make her voice gay. The scarred, badly cracked leather creaked beneath them. "And how will volley ball prepare you for... for the future?"

"It sharpens the eye and strengthens the wrist," Prudence said, glad to be out of the light where she needn't feel so transparent. "A strong wrist is so important, don't you think?"

They both laughed and then her mother sighed and said, "Peter did so want to meet you." Prudence allowed herself to know, finally, that the holidays were off. She would not be going anywhere. She would be staying right here until the summer holidays. "Well, it can't be helped!" her mother said stoically. "It will just have to wait until June."

"You're going to London, too?"

"Yes, darling, I must. I'm so sorry. I can't tell you how disappointed I am."

Prudence closed her eyes and remembered God. It was nice to know that she did not even have to hate her mother.

"That's all right," she said, and her voice sounded perfectly normal. "It's only three months." Consoling her mother; how mature she felt. "Time goes so quickly here," she lied. "There's so much to do."

"Oh, I nearly forgot," her mother said, her voice tinkling with relief. "I brought you something. Now, where did I put it?" She got up and moved about in the shadows. "Damn!" she said, bumping against something. "Turn a light on, for God's sake, Pru. There's no reason to be stumbling about in the dark."

Prudence leaned across the sofa to where she knew there was a table with a lamp. She found the switch and pressed it. The small glow lighted the scarred surface of the table and little else, but it seemed to mollify her mother. "There it is!" she said, spying the small package that lay beside her gloves and handbag. She snatched it up and brought it to Prudence. "I hope you'll like it, darling."

"Of course I'll like it," she said, knowing that it would be expensive and beautiful, whatever it was, but that it would not be anything that she could care about. "Do you mind if I don't open it now? I'd like to save it."

"No, of course not, angel." Her mother glanced at her watch. "I've got to run, sweet. It gets dark so early in the mountains and I don't want to be caught. Not on these frightening roads."

She leaned to kiss Prudence, holding her close for a moment.

"And do try to write more often, Pru. I look forward so much to your letters."

"Yes, Mother," she said, surprised that there should be tears in her mother's eyes. "I was just beginning a letter when you came."

"And eat more. Try, darling."

"Yes, Mother."

Her mother moved toward the door. You needn't see me out," she said. "It's turned quite chilly."

"All right. Anyhow, it's against the rules..."

"Goodbye, darling."

"Goodbye."

"And Pru?"

"Yes?"

"You do forgive me, don't you?"

"Forgive you?"

"About the holidays. You do understand, don't you?"

"Yes, Mother. It's all right."

"Goodbye, darling."

She stood at the window and looked out at the gathering dusk. In a little while a car ... what was it, a Land Rover? ... wound past on the road below. There were two of them in the car. Peter, she supposed, who was so eager to meet her. She felt infinitely sad and at the same time unreal, as if the encounter with her mother had not really happened, though the scent of her mother's perfume was strong on the air. She looked up at the mountain, wanting suddenly to shout something at it. It stood there so solid, so smug, so eternal, so white and pure and lofty. She saw the lights of the Land Rover recede in an arc toward the edge of the mountain. In about five minutes more it would reach the pass and vanish from her view. Slowly, she counted, feeling The Power pulsing inside her, pounding, swelling, like a muscle screaming to be used. When she had counted to three hundred, she closed her eyes and clenched her teeth and whispered through them, "Now, now, now!"

NOW!

She heard it then, softly at first, a distant rumbling that gradually grew in volume. She opened her eyes and saw (surely she saw it?) the great blocks of snow tumbling down the side of the mountain, roaring as they grew into an avalanche. And then, quite suddenly, the thunder ceased. The mountain shuddered and grew still. It was over.

"Naughty girl!"

Prudence started and wheeled at the voice that was right behind her. Miss Elfrieda was standing there, shaking her head. "Naughty, naughty child," she said. "I have been looking for you everywhere."

Had she been there all along?

"I...I was here. I had a visitor."

"Oh?"

"My mother."

Miss Elfrieda's eyes, catching the last of the light, glinted. "Ah," she said sadly. "Then that explains it."

"Explains what?"

"Why you did not come again this afternoon for your X-ray. Nurse James is beside herself. She asked me to come for you to bring you back. By the scruff of the neck, if necessary."

The tightness in Prudence's chest eased; Miss Elfrieda had neither seen nor heard. Perhaps no one had. And if no one knew, Prudence thought, it would be days, even weeks, before they were discovered. Maybe they would never be discovered.

"Did you hear anything just now, Miss Elfrieda?" she asked. "Something like ... thunder, I thought."

"Nonsense, my dear. Too early for thunder. Come along now, we mustn't keep Nurse James waiting any longer."

"I ... one minute, please, Miss Elfrieda." Prudence felt, all at once, too weak to move. She was both exhausted and elated. The Power was real. The Power was hers. God had taken her hand and moved it with wonderful justice.

"You're trembling, Prudence!" Miss Elfrieda said and caught one of the girl's hands between her own. "And how cold your hand is. Are you all right?"

Prudence fought the impulse to snatch her hand away. The woman's touch, physical contact of any sort with another human being, seemed at this moment particularly vile.

"It's nothing," she said, drawing back from Miss Elfrieda. "Just a chill."

They began to walk towards the door. Miss Elfrieda looked at her sideways, appraisingly. "And your mother?" she said. "Is she well?"

Dead, Prudence thought. Crushed, smothered beneath tons of pure white snow, washed clean and virginal and innocent. This, her bridal night. Sleep well, sleep well.

"Yes, she's well," she said. When they reached the corridor, she saw that the lights had been lit. "But I don't want to be X-rayed," she thought wildly. "I need to be private."

"No," she said to Miss Elfrieda. "I won't go."

"Won't go?" Miss Elfrieda said, turning the searchlight of her dark brilliant stare on Prudence. "What's the matter with you, child? You know Nurse James won't hurt you. Has she ever yet hurt you?"

"I don't need an X-ray," Prudence cried. "I won't!" She must run, she knew, looking desperately about for a direction. But there was none. There was nowhere. There was only out into the cold, falling night. She could not run out. Not out there. "I don't need an X-ray," she said, controlling her voice, trying to sound reasonable. "I'm perfectly all right."

Miss Elfrieda's hand tightened around her arm.

"Of course you are, my dear," she said softly. "And in any case, it's too late for an X-ray. Frau Stettenheimer has already gone with her machine.

She could not wait for you forever, you know."

Slowly, they moved down the corridor towards the infirmary. It was all right, then, if there wasn't going to be an X-ray, if they weren't going to peer inside her.

"But all the same, we'll just go along and see Nurse James," Miss Elfrieda said firmly, her hand strong as a chain around Prudence's upper arm. "Just to please her."

Docile, Prudence walked alongside Miss Elfrieda, remembering that she had left her mother's present in the library and wondering vaguely if it was another wristwatch. How many would that make? Six? Seven? And she never wore a watch. She was afraid of time.

Inside the infirmary, the sudden glare of the white walls was, as always, startling. Too sterile, Prudence thought, too cold. The glare hurt her eyes. The door shut behind them and Miss Elfrieda let go her grip on Prudence's arm. Nurse James looked up from her desk and glowered at Prudence from beneath her heavy straight brows.

"Well! At last we have the pleasure of your company," she said. "So glad you could finally make it, Prudence Dewhurst."

"She has an excuse," Miss Elfrieda said. "Her mother came unexpectedly to see her this afternoon. So, of course, in all the excitement, she forgot."

Prudence saw the two women exchange glances, saw Miss Elfrieda shrug and grimace as though she were in some pain. In the next room, she heard someone moan. The baths were in there. Through the half-open door, she caught a glimpse of Marjorie Harkavy swathed in something white like a winding sheet, floating in the warm bath with her eyes shut. She saw with shock that Marjorie Harkavy's hair was shot with gray. She was not a girl at all!

Too light, too bright, she thought, watching Nurse James rise from her desk and go to the sterilizer. The needles, she thought. Too bright, too white. One sees too much. Her heart began to knock with terror and she knew that she was about to have a moment of perfect lucidity, and that in that moment she would see through her blind eyes what was real and what was fancied, for there was a place where there were differences like that and in that place those differences mattered. Oh, hurry, she thought, oh hurry hurry hurry!

"Take your clothes off, dear."

Faith. With faith everything once again became possible. There was order and system there within those arms and you could live with that. The logic and sense of a world where you could, conceivably, accept even annihilation in preference to other things, the logic and order of religion, of God, of The Power and, yes, the sanity, even the sanity within...

You had only to close your eyes and, at last, finally, to leap. She had leaped. She had long ago leaped. It was not fair to be called back. She would not let them call her back to their chaos and their terror.

"Take off your clothes," Nurse James said sharply, and Miss Elfrieda advanced to help her but Prudence struck away her hands and cried out as though she were wounded for in that instant she understood where she was and why she was there.

She watched Nurse James approach with the needle She closed her eyes and began, without words, to pray. She prayed, not to God who was absent, but to something, to herself, and, praying, she waited for the moment to pass.

THE MALL

"Watch it, Buster!"

He's talking to me. I jump out of the way of the wheelchair he's pushing. The toothless old man in the wheelchair has a long skinny neck and his head is hanging to the side as if it's too heavy. His eyes are looking at me but I can't tell if he can see out of them. There's nothing in them. I'm used to that.

The reason I didn't see them is, I was walking past The Jewel Box and my eye caught on a bright chain with blue stones. They must have just put it in the window. Sometimes I see something I wish I could wear. But, as she'd have said, that's out of the question.

I wasn't looking for her. I stopped looking for her a long time ago. She isn't coming back. When she was gone that's almost all I did, day after day, look in all the different places. I'd go from the Cookie Jar to Dalton's and then to Dream World, and so on all around Level A. Then I'd take the escalator down to Level B and do the same thing. The Locker Room, Hot Feet, McKendrick's, Waldenbooks, Aunt Marjorie's Potato Skin Heaven, one after the other, even The Rink, where I knew she wouldn't be because she can't skate. Then I'd start all over.

People don't notice me. There's always so

many of them and, though I've always been here, only a few salespersons act as if they know me. She used to say, "We're nondescript." I asked her what it meant. "We're inconspicuous. People don't notice us. We don't stand out in a crowd." That made me look at the shoppers in a new way and they seemed pretty nondescript, too. Sometimes there's one who's extremely fat, or tall, or in a wheelchair like the old man. You notice them.

"If you keep yourself clean," she said, "and learn how to dress right, you'll be okay." She taught me how. When my clothes get dirty or too small, I know what to change them for, what colors to avoid, what sizes to take. Then I go into a rest room and remove the tags and change into the new clothes. She showed me how to get rid of the old ones; it's easy. She taught me everything.

Then once in The Sock Drawer, a new salesperson asked me if I was lost. It was my third time in there that morning.

"No," I said. "I'm waiting for her. She must be lost." I shouldn't have said that, but she was lost. I was there, where I'd always been, and she wasn't. She was always there and then she wasn't there, she wasn't anywhere. She must have gone where all the shoppers and salespersons go at night, through the doors, where she said I must never go. Through the doors. I don't know what's out there beyond the cars.

I was afraid the salesperson in The Sock Drawer would ask more questions, so I said, "Oh, there she is now. Have a nice day," and left.

I'm not supposed to answer questions. I'm never supposed to tell anyone I live here. I've always lived here. We both did. Now she doesn't. Maybe she's dead. I know about dead. There are orange fish in The Wishing Well and sometimes one of them floats on its side on top. You can see its white belly. That's dead. Once, in the window of Personality Pets, there was a dead puppy. By the time they opened it was gone and a new puppy was in there barking, yap, yap, brown with white spots.

I hope she's not dead. She used to put her hand under my chin and look at me in a certain way. She looked sad when she did it, but I liked it anyway. She taught me everything. I don't know why she went away. I don't know what I did wrong. She was always here and now she isn't.

I walk around a lot, through Levels A and B, usually without going into any of the shops. I look at the shoppers. I look at their faces. I'm not looking for her any more. I don't know what I'm looking for. I can't find it, at least not so far. No one even sees me, hardly.

At the Wishing Well, I sit on one of the stone benches and watch the fish. It's not really a wishing well like I once saw in a picture book. It's just a little fishpond about five inches deep, with a rock at one end, water coming over it. A waterfall. You're supposed to throw in money and make a wish. My pocket's full of quarters and dimes. I don't bother with nickels or pennies. It was Bonanza Weekend and there were mobs of shoppers, so the Wishing Well was full of change last night. I never take more than I need, but last night I took six dollars.

She taught me money. She said I'd never survive without knowing money. Anyone can see it's the most important thing there is. Everything has a price. The shoppers go into the places and decide what they want. Sometimes the prices are marked down, like on Bonanza Weekend or Special Sales Days. The shopper gives the money for what he wants to the salesperson who puts the money in the cash register and wraps the merchandise and gives it to the shopper. Then the shopper goes away, maybe to another shop. At night the cash registers are emptied. I don't know where they take the money. There must be some way of giving it back so the shoppers can buy something else, or maybe the shoppers go to other places where they are the salespersons.

Sometimes I see a shopper take something when there's no salesperson around and put it in a pocket or under a coat, and leave without giving the salesperson the money. She said that was called stealing and if you're caught doing it you're in Big Trouble. Capital B capital T. Sometimes I have to do it when I need something like a new shirt that I haven't got enough quarters and dimes for. I do it at night after closing, usually in the K. C. Emporium, where I mostly sleep. Their shirts are the best, the finest long staple pima cotton.

There's a night watchman at K. C. Emporium. I see him every night, but he never sees me. Mostly he sleeps, and I know the times he makes his rounds. He has a flashlight and a gun. He gets up and goes to the Men's to pee and then he walks around the shop with his flashlight, waving it around. Then he goes back to sleep. I guess they pay him money to do it. You pay money for merchandise and also for services. The night watchman is doing a service, like the barbers and the beauty shop operators. Sometimes I think when I'm bigger they could pay me to do that service. I could do it blindfolded. I can get around every inch of the K. C. Emporium without a flashlight.

A man sits down on the bench next to me.

"Stand over there," he says to a woman. "In front of the waterfall. Take Riley outa the stroller."

The woman lifts the baby from the stroller and it begins to cry. It has chocolate on its face.

"Hush, Riley," the woman says. She stands in front of the waterfall, jiggling the baby up and down.

"Hold still," the man says, pointing a camera at them. "Smile."

The baby goes on crying and the man clicks the camera. A blank piece of paper comes sliding out of the camera. The man tears it off and looks at it. He keeps looking at this piece of paper and so I do. Gradually, it stops being blank. First there's like a shadow and then little by little you can see shapes and colors and pretty soon there are the woman and the crying baby and part of the waterfall. It's like magic. First there's nothing, and then it's there, the picture.

"How'd you do that?" I ask the man. He looks surprised.

"It's Polaroid," he says. "You never seen Polaroid?" I don't know what he means.

"No," I say, "I never have."

"Well that's how it works," the man says. "It takes the picture and develops it right in the camera. Ask your daddy to explain it." "I will," I say. I haven't got a daddy. I never had one. All I had was her. She could have explained it. She could have explained anything.

The man gets up from the bench and they leave without saying anything else to me. I've noticed that when people are together and one of them goes away, they say "Goodbye," or "So long," or "See ya." Salespersons always say, "Have a nice day," to shoppers when they're finished. She never said any of those things. I had no way of knowing she was going away. One minute she was there and the next minute she wasn't.

I sit a while longer, thinking maybe I'm like that piece of paper in the camera, before the picture comes up. But the man talked to me. Usually, nobody even sees me.

There's one person. She's a little like her, but not really. She's a waitress in The Pizza Oasis. She has her name pinned to her blouse. Millicent. I like to say it to myself. Pizza is my favorite thing to eat, but I try not to go too often. Millicent isn't there every day so sometimes I go when she's away, just to be safe. But that's where I decide to go today, even though I know she's there.

I take the escalator down and walk past Waldenbooks and Hot Feet to The Pizza Oasis. It's empty. Millicent is the only one behind the counter. She's leaning against the soda machine. I sit on a stool and try not to look straight at her. Waitresses don't wear the same kind of clothing as other salespersons. Millicent's wearing a frilly white blouse with a sort of red apron over it, with suspenders. The skirt is frilly, too, and so short that practically all her legs show. It's a uniform. If the other waitresses were here they'd be dressed the same, except for their feet. Millicent is wearing thick white tube socks and dirty pink sneakers.

"Hi," she says, smiling. "You here again? What'll it be?"

"The number one combo, please."

"Ya got it," she says, and shovels a slice onto a paper plate, then scoops ice into a paper cup and puts it under the coke spigot. When the cup is full, she puts it next to the slice and says, "There ya go."

They always say that.

"Thank you," I say, counting out the money.

I'm the only shopper there. After Bonanza Weekends the mall is always pretty empty. The shoppers come those two days to save and now they must be resting up, waiting until they want something else. Millicent has nothing to do so she stands there watching while I take the first bite of my slice.

"Careful," she says. "It just came out of the oven."

"It's okay," I say. "I like it hot."

She watches me chew a while then says, "How come you're always here alone?"

"I'm not alone," I say, though I'm not supposed to answer questions. "She's in The Linen Closet."

"Your mom? She works there?"

I make a noise in my throat, not really answering.

"Did you go to school today?" she asks. I nod. She used to say she wished she could send me to school but there's no way. Out of the question, she said. I don't officially exist, she said, there's no record. I was born in the custodian's closet. She showed it to me, a big closet, with brooms and mops and buckets and a big sink. "In that corner," she said, pointing. "What a night!"

I've gone back a couple of times and slept in that corner, but I don't like the way it smells.

"You come over to the mall after school for supper? Because your mom works here?"

"She doesn't care for pizza," I say. She's asking too many questions. I shouldn't have come. I have plenty of money, enough for a tuna melt or macaroni and cheese at The Red Oven. A Whopperoo at The Beeferia. I sneak a look over my slice at Millicent. She's still looking at me as if she has more questions. Half of me wishes she'd go on asking them, even if I can't answer. But then a shopper comes in, a guy in blue jeans can't be any bigger than a twenty inch waist size. He goes straight to the jukebox and starts it playing. The Barn Owls doing "Gonna Rock My Sleepin' Beauty Awake." I never play the jukebox. Sound is a funny thing to buy. It only lasts a few minutes and then you don't have anything.

The guy sits down at the other end of the counter and Millicent goes over to him. He says something and she laughs and says something back, I can't make out what. I sit chewing my slice, sipping my coke, slow as I can.

"You want another slice?" Millicent says, drifting back to my end. She leans over and whispers, "On the house."

"What do you mean?"

"For free."

I look at her, surprised. "I can pay," I say. "I don't have to steal it."

She laughs. "That's not stealing. If I give it to you, it's a gift."

I know what gifts are. The Gift Horse features them. Fancy soaps shaped like fruit or shells, silk flowers, candles. Things like that. But you still have to pay for them. She's waiting so I say okay and she smiles and gives me another slice. I thank her.

"Are you always so serious?" she asks. "Don't you ever smile?" I guess I don't. I never thought about it before. I try out a smile.

"That's better," she says, laughing. "What's your name? You're in here so much and I don't even know your name."

"Buster," I say.

"Buster?" She laughs again. I like making her laugh. "Okay, Buster."

She stands there and I want to say something but I don't know what. I don't even know why. Then I think of something.

"Nice day," I say.

"Whaddya mean, nice day? It's pouring buckets."

I'm not sure what she means. Sometimes shoppers come through the doors wearing sweaters and heavy jackets and hats and their ears and noses are red. She said that meant it was a cold day, like in The Rink, only more so. Other times, shoppers wear light clothes and come through the doors, their faces red and sweaty. That means it's a hot day. Hot like a slice right out of the oven. Then there's rain. Rain is water coming down. Maybe that's what Millicent means by buckets. Umbrellas are for rain. The rain falls on the umbrellas the shoppers hold over them so the rain won't fall on their heads. The shoppers come through the doors with the umbrellas folded and dripping. Here it's always the same. Pleasant, she said, no rain, no snow, no cold, no hot. "Climate control," she said. On hot days, some shoppers come through the doors just to cool off. On really cold days, they come to get warm. It must be terrible through the doors, all those different ways it can be. Here it's always the same. You don't need coats or hats or boots or umbrellas. I never needed any of those. If I decided to go through the doors, which I probably never will, I don't know what I'd need or how I'd carry it all.

"Yeah," I say to Millicent. "It's pouring buckets, but here in the mall it's always a nice day."

"You've got beautiful eyes," she says. "Anybody ever tell you that?"

"No," I say, "they never did."

"You've got to be kidding."

"No," I say, "I kid you not."

"Well, believe it, you've got beautiful blue eyes. Those long lashes, I wish I had them."

I feel something, her telling me this. I don't know what it is. It's good, though, it's something good.

"Did you really go to school today or did you play hookey? I bet you play hookey a lot." I don't know what she means. Once I played a Video Game. I didn't really know what I was supposed to do. A kid standing next to me watching kept yelling, "Get it, get it! Look out! Boy, you really suck."

"You'll be sorry some day if you don't get through school. God knows, I am. I'm probably stuck in this underground dump for life. If I'd of finished school I could of done other things."

"You could be a salesperson," I say. "Or an operator in The Beauty Spot. You could do manicures."

She snorts. "I mean something important, not shit like that. A secretary in an office downtown, maybe. Or better still, a veterinarian. That's what I wanted to be when I was little. I always loved animals."

"You could be a salesperson at Personality Pets."

"I can't stand to see them locked up in those cages," she says, sighing. "Waiting for someone to come along and love them. I couldn't stand that, all that waiting. How they look. So anxious and hopeful and sad."

The other shopper goes back to the jukebox and puts in another coin. Wah, wah, wah. Loud.

"I wouldn't be able to sleep at night, thinking about them," Millicent says. "I'd want to take them all home."

Home.

"I have to go now," I say, wiping my mouth.

"You want another slice? I'll heat you up another slice."

"No, thank you. I couldn't."

"Oh, come on. You're a growing boy. You can handle it. You're too skinny."

"I am?"

"Doesn't your mom tell you that? You got to put some meat on those bones if you want the girls to fall for you."

I can see she really wants me to have it so I let her give me another slice. The jukebox is so loud it makes the place less empty. The other shopper, the guy down the counter, calls Millicent over. He calls her Honey. She used to call me that sometimes. Honey. Sweety. The guy tells Millicent he wants another slice, this time pepperoni, and another 7-Up. I sit there thinking: I have beautiful eyes, I'm serious, I'm too skinny.

I've never sat here so long, and I never had so much conversation, not since she stopped being here. She should have said something, have a nice day, take care, see ya. I was size eight when she stopped being here. Now I'm a twelve. I stuff some more pizza into my mouth but I can hardly swallow it. I don't want to go. I want Millicent to keep telling me things. I want to keep on looking at her. But I force myself to get up off the stool. I put a dime down next to the paper plate with what's left of the third slice. I know about tipping. The dime doesn't look right, though, so I put another one alongside it.

"You going?" Millicent asks. "You didn't finish."

"I honestly can't," I say.

"Well, take care."

"So long," I say. "Have a nice day."

"This day is about over," she says, looking at her watch.

When I get back to Level A, I look through the doors and I see she's right, the day is almost over. There are only a few cars and it's dark. It's time to hide. Usually I go to the K. C. Emporium in one of the stalls in the Men's. I sit on the toilet seat with my feet up and hold the door open about two inches so it looks like nobody's in there. After the lights go out I wait until I know everyone's gone and the night watchman is probably asleep.

But I don't go to the K. C. Emporium. Instead, I go to Personality Pets and look at the puppies. They sold a bunch of them on Bonanza Weekend and half the cages are empty. The puppies still there are mostly asleep, looking like used dust mops. The two salespersons are covering up the parrots and the cockatiels for the night.

"Closing time," one of them says. I nod and head for the doorway, but when I see they're not looking, I duck behind a pile of 25-pound sacks of Purina Chow and Sta-Fresh cat litter and crouch down, listening to the last of the cockatiel's squawks and the thumping of a hamster on his wheel. Soon the salespersons are gone and the lights go out. I get up and go back to where the cages are.

One of the puppies is whimpering, sad little noises, not loud crying like Riley, sad little noises. I put a finger through the bars and the puppy licks it with his furry tongue, then flops down and falls asleep.

I'm sleepy, too. There's a big empty cage where they had two German Shepherd puppies and I don't know why, but I climb into it and pull the barred door closed until I hear it latch. It smells like newspapers in there, not a bad smell. I fold myself up on my side, my knees under my chin and my arms wrapped around my legs. I don't know why, but that's what I do. I go to sleep, thinking that in the morning when they come I'll just stay here and look out at them.

That's what I'll do.

THE BOX

Margo had been at it only a few minutes when she heard Primrose sniffling in the doorway behind her.

"Go blow your nose, Prim," she said without turning around. In the last weeks, Prim's runny nose had been chronic. Probably an allergy, damn it.

"That's Leo's underwear," Prim said.

"I know it's Leo's underwear."

What a sad, drab little heap they made, his socks and jockey shorts. Except for his sandals and boots, he'd been so uncaring about clothing that he'd never acquired enough of it for them even to have bothered with "his" and "her" drawers; he'd just dumped his stuff in among hers. And when she ran a wash she'd never separated their things, either, just put them back any which way. She'd gotten so used to his things being there among her slips and bras that she'd even stopped seeing them.

Until after the accident. After the accident, she could see nothing anywhere in the apartment that didn't scream "Leo" at her. Just opening a drawer to get at a pair of her panties was enough to give her the shakes.

"What are you doing with Leo's things?" Prim asked.

"I'm putting them in this carton."

It had taken her weeks to be able to do it. She'd tried doing it stoned, but, surprisingly, that had made it even harder. This morning, however, she'd awakened knowing that Goddamn it she was going to do it today.

"But they're Leo's things," Prim said. "They're not yours."

She turned to look at Prim. Christ, what a poor little waif she looked with her accusing eyes and her nose all runny. Her long pale, hair, needing combing, hung down half hiding her face, and she'd outgrown that crumby dress beneath whose frayed hem her knees were grimy knobs crisscrossed with bandaids. Why, I can cut her hair and get her blue jeans now, Margo thought. It was Leo who'd insisted on the long hair and the dresses. Leo, with his romantic hippy sensibilities, wanting Prim to look free and feminine, not noticing that mostly she looked neglected and uncared for. It was a hell of a way to raise a kid when you lived in a four-story walkup in a garbagy neighborhood because you weren't supposed to care anything about money. How many times a day could you comb a kid's hair? And how often could you change her dress when she only had two or three?

"Well they're not yours," Prim said again.

"Why, you little bourgeois materialist," Margo said. "Where'd you learn such things?"

"Why are you putting Leo's underwear in a box?"

"Will you for Chrissake go blow your nose?"

"No. I don't know how."

She got a tissue and, sighing, knelt and wrapped it around Prim's nose.

"Hold it," she said. "Now hold one side

closed. That's right. Now blow."

Pam blew. "Is Leo in a box?" she asked.

"Yes."

"The other side now?"

"Yes."

Prim blew again. "Why is Leo in a box?" she asked.

"I told you, Prim. Because of the accident. Now wipe your nose."

"Is the Honda in the box, too?"

"No."

"Why not?"

"Because they don't bury motorcycles. Jesus, Prim, will you go play somewhere? Go down on the stoop. Maybe Sandy's there."

"I was just there. It's raining."

"Then go fingerpaint or something."

Prim faded out of the doorway and Margo turned back to the bureau. The clothing would take only a few more minutes; it was the closet shelf she dreaded. The clothing was only cloth, she told herself, touching it, lifting it, impersonal, no longer warmed by Leo. Like me, she thought, also no longer warmed by Leo. The hell with him, little-boy poet with all his love-talk and free-talk, well, he was free all right, twenty-six years old and dead, so smashed-up dead they couldn't even give his heart away. Free, free, damn him. She'd call Tony later. Or maybe Andy.

"Are you putting things in that box to bury them?" Prim said.

"I thought you were going to fingerpaint," Margo said, wheeling around.

"I changed my mind."

"Well go do something for God's sake."

"Are you?"

"What?"

"Going to bury Leo's underwear?"

"No. I'm going to give it to someone who can use it."

What a laugh, that anyone could use this crap, that anyone could be that bad off. She'd be too ashamed to bother the Salvation Army with it.

"Isn't Leo ever coming back?"

"Look, Prim," she said, trying to keep control. "Why do I have to tell you the same things every single day, ten times a day? I know it's hard for you to understand, but dead means forever."

"Is forever the same as never?"

"Yes," she said, almost shouting. "In this case, forever is the same as never."

"I'll go watch TV," Prim said and vanished.

Okay, she thought, he's out of my drawers. She'd give Prim a long, hot bath tonight and get her to bed early. She was a thumb-sucker and good about falling asleep. And then she'd get Andy to come over. Or maybe Tony, if he was around, Tony had more serenity. Andy was too sensitive; she'd have to worry about his feelings, but Tony would just turn on and make love and go to sleep holding her and that was what she wanted. Andy would have to talk about it first, and he would talk about love, and he would talk about Leo, and he would talk about poetry, and he would talk about life, and he wouldn't say anything she needed to hear and didn't already know. Besides, he was too much like Leo, a pale, faded copy of Leo. Free, was it? Well he was free, all right. And she knew a thing or two about freedom herself.

The closet was warm and dark. She stood for a moment without turning on the light, just feeling the warmth and the dark and the silence, breathing the close air, the warm dark smell of shoes and camphor. She was not going to shed one more tear for him, the lousy bastard, tootling around the countryside on his bike, his head probably full of acid, thinking up poems that probably weren't any damn good, grinning like an idiot, telling himself how free he was and how good it was. Well, hail to thee, blithe spirit, bird thou scarcely wert.

"Is Leo my daddy?"

She pulled on the closet light. Prim was leaning on the doorjamb, her lower lip pushed out, ready for defiance if it was needed.

"Of course Leo was your daddy," Margo said. "You know that."

"Then why do I call him Leo? Everybody calls their daddy daddy."

"Leo wanted you to call him Leo."

It made him feel freer, of course. Daddy is a word that binds. He was a great one for the power of language, never a mumbler, but what did he think ... that if you took away the words there'd be nothing there?

She yanked the pants off their hangers, three pairs of them, and tossed them over Prim's head into the carton. The sheepskin jacket next. The single suit, his father's, left over from his father's funeral for which he'd borrowed it, never worn since. Nothing now but the box on the shelf. His treasure trove. His poems and the things he'd treasured in his short life. His mind, his soul, his memories, his self. She pulled it down. She would just chuck it in the garbage and not even look inside it.

"Well, if he was my daddy, why didn't he love me?" Prim asked. Her nose was running again.

"Who said he didn't love you? He was nuts about you."

"Then why did he go away?"

"He didn't go away, baby. He had an accident. Go get another tissue, we've got to blow your nose again."

Damn, damn, damn, she thought. I'm twenty-two years old and I've got this kid, this person, needing everything from me, asking all these bloody questions that I'm still asking myself and can't answer, and he's free, he's out of it, damn his hide, I will not feel sorry for myself. And I'll look in his Goddamn box, I'll look at every bloody thing in it, read every bloody gorgeous word, and then I'll throw it all away.

Prim was back with the tissue. Margo knelt to help her with it but Prim backed off.

"No," she said. "I'll do it myself."

ERIC AND MAX AND JULIUS
AND ETHICS

Eric Golden came home from college in June and made straight for his grandparents' apartment on Park Avenue. He was tired and apathetic and, though he would have liked to believe that he had mononucleosis, something definite and subject to medical prescription, he was pretty sure it was some kind of emotional crisis he was having, something to do with identity; who he was sick of being, who he was going to have to become.

It was the mid-sixties, and it had been a hard year. He'd sat in, sat down, marched on, carried placards, shouted, wept, jeered, sung, been beaten up and, briefly, imprisoned. Violently nonviolent, he himself had not laid a hand on anyone. Committed and alienated, he'd rested up in coffee houses, listening to protest songs, feeling as bitter as the espresso. He'd made love to girls with long hair and dark glasses and squatted in a desert with Indians, chewing peyote and having visions. He'd walked away unscathed from the scattered wreck of a Honda, defying his mother's monotonous forebodings relayed to him bi-weekly by airmail. Still, he'd managed to get to class often enough to pass everything.

One more year and he'd be a bachelor of arts

complete with diploma, nontransferable, nonnegotiable, good for absolutely nothing. He hadn't a clue about what he wanted to do with his life. He declined invitations from his mother, abroad on sabbatical, and his father, who was in Chicago with a new wife, making another new start. On impulse, he wrote to his grandparents asking if he could stay with them. Their New York apartment had an extra bedroom that doubled as a "den."

"Come, come," Grandma Tess wrote by return mail. "The pleasure is ours."

He had planned to sleep for two weeks straight but the telephone woke him the first morning before eight. He opened his eyes to see his grandfather stride into the room to the desk, a few feet from where Eric lay, and take charge of the telephone. A den was supposed to be a private place where you could repair to lick your wounds, but Eric saw that he wasn't going to have any privacy and that his borrowed chamber was not a den but an office.

"Two o'clock this afternoon, Fortunoff," his grandfather bellowed, swiveling in the chair and looking at Eric with distaste. "They'll come to your office."

Those big feet, must be a thirteen at least, sticking out of the sheets, hanging off the end of the sofabed. Eric. How he had loved that kid! Pink-cheeked, big-eyed dynamo, exploding with energy, full of importance. Smart. Two years old and he could tell you the name of every car on the street, though he couldn't read. "Ford, Pontiac, Chevrolet," he would chant, mispronouncing as the cars went by. "Plymouth, Dodge, Cadillac." He went wild at the sight of a Cadillac. Of course, cars were easier in those days, but still. And look how he'd

*turned out, this overgrown galoot with the black
beard and the long hair, looking like some kind of
halfbreed, and sleeping in his underwear.*

"In addition to the usual, I want to know what
percent if any their business fell off since the new
motel opened across the Throughway. Listen, Fortunoff, you know what I want, I don't have to tell
you." He slammed the receiver down.

"I thought you were retired, Grandpa," Eric
said, pulling himself to a sitting position and planting
his feet on the carpet. "Christ, the carpet's softer
than the bed. How come you sleep on rocks?" Their
health. They thought a lot about health. "No kidding,
Grandpa, I thought you retired years ago."

He'd been a manufacturer of ladies' ready-to-
wear almost all his life. Five years ago he decided
he'd had enough. He wanted to spend his declining
years in play, sport, and travel. But cards bored him,
golf made him angry, and although he loved to dance
and did so crossing a number of oceans, travel finally
made him restless. Once you got there, what was
there to do but look at *shvartzes* with baskets on their
heads, eat food that gave you gas, or run with Tess to
shops and watch her buy junk she didn't need or
really want. In Leningrad he never even got off the
bus; he could see that they were all slaves and that
the guide was trained to tell only lies.

He stayed home, looking for a hobby. He
found one. He took to knocking down beautiful, old
estates and building on their ruins drab garden apartments which he subsequently sold, taking back mortgages. He had expected his fortune to diminish with
his retirement, but instead it kept growing and he was
faced with the problem of investing his new money.
He formed corporations and acquired partners, men

like himself who also didn't know where to put their money, but he was the manager. He had never allowed anyone to make a decision for him, although he liked to think of himself as "open to suggestions." Before long, what with scouting investment possibilities, exploring all the angles, figuring on long pads of multilined green paper, talking to lawyers, accountants, builders, and bankers, and keeping his partners abreast, he was busier than he'd ever been.

"You don't sound retired," Eric said. "Why don't you play golf?"

"Put some clothes on," Grandpa Max barked. "What are you going to do, lay there all day like a lox?"

"I'm up, I'm up. Seriously, Grandpa, you've got more money now than you can use. How come you don't take it easy?"

"Responsibilities," Max said, pushing his anger down. "But what would you know about responsibilities, your generation?"

Why get angry with a kid? Some kid! Six three, two hundred twenty pounds. What did they need them so big for with the world getting so crowded. Big and sloppy, all that hair. Tess said, "Even so, he's beautiful." Leave it to a grandmother to find beauty. Furthermore, this kid was some kind of anarchist. "I worked hard all my life. I slaved. One year of high school was all the education I got." A trust fund for their education. But he had been happy to send him to school, proud.

"I sent him to school to get educated, not arrested. The trust fund is for tuition, not bail."

Tess said, "They're all getting arrested nowadays. It's nothing to be ashamed of. It's a stage."

A stage. A phase. When I was his age, who

had time for stages? I was already in business for myself. I worked fifteen, sixteen hours a day. I slept on the cutting room tables, too tired to go home at night. My mother came to The Place with hot soup in a jar. I knew what I had to do, I was in a rage to do it. Nineteen years old, working all my life, but now it was the real thing. Other people's money rode on my back. Five hundred dollars from Mama from the store, fifteen hundred from Tante Etta's hocked jewelry. And I paid them back in a year. One year. With interest.

"What do you mean, Grandpa? If you already have all the money you need. What kind of responsibilities?"

"You think the money just sits there? You have to invest it. That way, the money works for you. You use the income and you still have the money, the principal."

Eric nodded.

"It's a lot of work, finding where to invest it. A safe investment, a good return. It's not easy, even with money getting so tight."

Eric grinned. "Grandpa, I feel sorry for you."

"What would you know!" He was angry again. "When I was your age, I didn't have time to lay around all day in my underwear."

"It's not even nine o'clock," Eric said, getting to his feet and scratching his chest. "I'm tired. Maybe I've got mono."

"Mono?" Max said. "What's the hell is mono supposed to be?"

"It's a disease, Grandpa. Mononucleosis. Makes you tired all the time."

They even had new diseases, this generation, as if the old ones weren't bad enough. Fancy names for laziness. In my day, if you were sick, by God you knew it: T.B., pneumonia, influenza, we didn't kid around with sickness.

He picked up the phone and dialed the garage, watching Eric lumber toward the bathroom.

In the shower, Eric shampooed his hair and beard, feeling the weariness in his arms. What if he really did have something slow and serious? Imagine having to languish, perhaps die, in a Castro Convertible! And it would take more than his dying to keep the old man away from that desk. He would die listening to the old man shouting into the telephone about amortization and interest rates. Who was Grandpa Max to treat Eric's health so lightly, just because he was big, as if size had anything to do with disease, except that there was more of him vulnerable to attack. Both his grandparents were always saying, "The most important thing is your health." They had lived a long time and they had measured. The medicine chest was crammed with pills, the faintest symptom sent Grandpa to a specialist, and both he and Grandma made regular pilgrimages to spas where they dieted, took the baths, were massaged. They were both proud of how much younger than their years they looked. It was one of Grandpa's great pleasures to tell new acquaintances his age and then listen to their expressions of disbelief. Grandma, more modest, claimed it was all facade and that inside things were going to pieces right on schedule.

When he came out of the bathroom, Eric could hear his grandfather still on the phone, and he could smell coffee. He made for the kitchen. Grandma, dressed and finishing her breakfast, gave him a bright smile.

"Good morning, sweetypie," she said. "Did

you sleep well?"

"Yes," he lied, pouring himself orange juice.

"Would you like to come to the club with me and play golf?"

Their club was in upper Westchester and, weather permitting, Grandma was there every day, a calm, steady, dependable golfer who never made a spectacular shot or score, but never lost a ball, either. She had her good days and her bad days, but only she could tell which was which.

Eric declined. "Maybe in a day or two, when I've had a chance to rest up." Why worry her with his fears about his health? He sat on, finishing his coffee when she was gone, listening to Grandpa's voice rising and falling in the next room. He suddenly felt happy. It was the first time in months that he had absolutely nothing to do, nothing to think about. He pushed away the empty coffee cup and stretched, then wandered into the living room. The windows overlooked Park Avenue and he stood for a while watching the traffic course uptown and down, separated by an island of tulips. He heard the doorbell ring, and, knowing that Grandpa wouldn't hear it over the sound of his own voice explaining and explaining into the telephone, he went to answer it. A small, dapper, old man stood there.

"Where's Max?" the man said, striding into the foyer. "Who are you?"

Eric told him.

"The grandson! I remember you when you were an infant. How old are you?

"Twenty."

"Frances is fifteen, my granddaughter. A terror. Fat." He fixed Eric with a sharp, calculating eye, daring him to deny it. "I sent her last summer to a fat girls' camp. Special. Two thousand dollars, laundry and transportation extra. Camp Sparrow Dell, you heard of it?"

"No," Eric said.

"She dropped sixty-five pounds, thirty dollars per pound. She gets mad at me, she eats Hershey bars. Already she put back twenty-two pounds, all spite. Six hundred and sixty dollars!"

"Hello, Julius," Grandpa Max said, coming into the room. "Eric, this is my uncle Julius." Eric nodded. He had seen Uncle Julius years ago, but his memory was not of such a small and ugly man.

"Is there coffee, Eric?" Max asked. "You'll have coffee, Julius?"

"I don't mind."

Eric went into the kitchen and lit the burner under the coffee. He found cups and saucers and brought them out to the dining alcove.

"In my day, believe me, I've hated plenty of people, but never like that *shmuck* Weill," Julius was saying.

"You shouldn't let him bother you," Grandpa said.

"A know-it-all who don't know beans. Every time I have to talk to him it rubs me the wrong way. Let's get rid of him."

"He's a partner," Max said. "We can't get rid of him. You don't have to talk to him. I'll do the talking."

"Telling me, 'They don't do things like that today.' What, I don't know how they do things today? I didn't get where I am laying in a stupor while time marched on."

"Ignore him."

"Inherited money, third generation money, is

what he's got. If he had to go out and actually make a dollar he'd be dead. All he's ever had to do is be on boards --- temples, homes for the aged, hospitals. He makes me sick to my stomach."

Eric brought in the coffee and poured it. He poured himself another cup, too.

"And while we're on the subject of sick," Julius said, "I'm going into the hospital this afternoon."

"Why?"

"Gall bladder. They're gonna cut tomorrow."

"I didn't know you had a condition."

"Neither did I. It never even bothered me."

"So why are they cutting?"

Julius spooned sugar into his coffee and stirred it. "The condition showed up when I went last week for my regular routine checkup. I use Shapiro. You know him?"

"No."

"A top man, the best! I've been using him for years. I say to him, Shapiro, what's the difference if it never bothered me? He says, Julius, you're not a young man, you're eighty-two, suppose it starts to act up two, three years from now? So I'll have time to worry two, three years from now, I tell Shapiro. By then it may be too late, he says. At that age it could be too dangerous to operate, but it's your decision, Julius. I say, Shapiro, if you advise then what's to decide? You're the doctor."

"You're sure you're doing the right thing?" Max asked, shaking his head.

"You think I want trouble, special diets, when I'm an old man?

"You're not exactly a spring chicken now Julius."

"I'm in the pink." He finished his coffee and pushed back his chair. "Keep me advised. Physician's Hospital." He got up."

"Let me know if there's anything I can do," Max said. "I'll come visit you in the hospital."

"Thanks for the coffee," Julius said to Eric. "Why don't you get a haircut?"

Max walked him to the door. "I almost forgot what I came to tell you, Max. I made you my executor."

Max looked as though Julius had made him a declaration of love. Embarrassed. he coughed. "You'll outlive us all," he said. "You're too stingy to die."

"I didn't know he was a partner," Eric said when the door had closed behind Julius. "I thought nobody talked to him."

The break had come years ago when Max's mother, Anna, had loaned Julius, her baby brother, five thousand dollars, "a fortune in those days," in return for an IOU, which she gave to her husband Jacob to put in the vault. Jacob was a soft-spoken, gentle, trusting soul who left all practical matters to his hard-headed wife, ran errands, offered fruit to the company, and studied the Talmud with his buddies. He was careless with papers and records, believing them to be superfluous. He carried promises in his heart and stuffed IOUs, deeds, and other trivia in his sweater pocket. After his death, the box in the vault was found to contain nothing but birth certificates, a marriage license in Yiddish, and an expired fire insurance policy. Julius was prospering by then and Anna, aging and supported by her sons, asked Julius if he couldn't find it in his heart to begin paying back the loan. Julius knew that there was no IOU and, therefore, no legal claim on him. He insisted that he had repaid the loan.

"What? When?" Anna gasped. "Not one cent!"

He had given it, he swore, to Jake.

"Jake? Who ever gave money to Jake?" Anna screamed. "Money fell from his hands like oats. Nobody ever gave money to Jake."

Julius stuck to his story. Anna clutched at her breast, promising to die on the spot.

"God should strike me dead," Julius lied.

"Help, I'm dying," Anna moaned, swooning on the sofa. "Somebody get the salts."

It had been a terrific scene. Max had leaped to his mother's side and offered to punch Julius in the nose. Anna, her voice never stronger, bellowed, "Don't hit him, Max, he's your flesh and blood, I'm dying." Max, who had never hit anyone in his life, restrained himself with relief, Julius departed, Anna got up off the sofa, and a little while later everyone went in to dinner.

"We didn't talk to him for years, the bastard," Max said. "You think he cared? Then five years ago when Grandma and I took that South American cruise, who should be on the ship sitting at the very next table? He sent over a bottle of champagne. What could I do, ignore him?"

"Bygones are bygones," Julius had coaxed. "Flesh and blood are thicker than water."

"They live upstairs," Max said. "They just moved in, a ten-room duplex penthouse apartment. They're spending a fortune decorating."

"Who's they? I thought he was divorced."

"Sophie. His second wife. Come on, the car should be downstairs by now."

"Where are we going?"

"There's a piece of property I want to look at in Briarcliff. I was up half the night with heartburn and I don't feel like driving."

Eric had never driven a Cadillac, but Max showed him what was where and then, surprisingly, sat back and trusted him.

"I hope nobody I know sees me," Eric mumbled.

"What's the matter, you ashamed to be seen in a Caddie? You used to be wild about Cadillacs when you were two, three years old. I don't know what's with your generation. You have no values."

It was a beautiful day, one of those rare days when the New York sky is really blue and the river, even bluer, defies you to believe it is polluted. Max lapsed into silence, except for an occasional sigh. When they were well out of the city, the soft, early summer countryside began to heal him.

"Who needs it!" he said.

"Needs what?" In spite of himself, Eric was enjoying the feel of the car. It was like driving a cloud.

"Not that I didn't have plenty of aggravation in the dress business," Max mused. "But there, at least, I was my own boss. I made a decision and that was that. But with all these partners I have to be a diplomat, a nursemaid, a psychiatrist."

"Why do you do it then?"

Max shrugged. "Force of habit. I worked all my life. I had my first job at the age of five. Did I ever tell you that? Carrying pots of *cholent* to the bakery oven for neighbors."

"What's *cholent*?"

"A stew. A piece of meat, carrots, potatoes,

beans, cooked very slow for hours, the longer the better. Where we lived on the lower East Side, most of the Jews were orthodox. They couldn't light matches on the Shabbas, so they couldn't light the stove to cook. A baker in the neighborhood let them use his oven. They'd fix a big pot of *cholent* and it would sit in the baker's oven overnight. I had a regular cholent route, a nickel a round trip. Those pots nearly broke my back." He chuckled. "And every nickel I made, I gave my mother. I was paying my own way and even at the age of five it made me feel like a *mensch.*"

Eric had grown up in New Rochelle. He thought of his friend Lenny who delivered the evening papers. In bad weather his stylish blonde mother drove him in the family Lincoln Continental, pausing in front of each house long enough for Lenny to hurl the papers through the car window."

"A couple of years later I could write," Max said. "I could write not only English but Yiddish, so I invested in some stationery, got a folding chair and an orange crate, painted a sign, and set up shop on Second Avenue. I wrote letters for immigrants to their people in the old country." His customers were mostly prostitutes, faded beauties with tears in their eyes, dictating in Yiddish to Max, assuring the old people that everything was hunky-dory in America, and enclosing a dollar.

"I got three cents for a short letter, a nickel if it went over a page. I was seven years old and I wasn't a laborer any more, I was a white collar worker."

Eric thought of the lemonade stands of his own childhood. Frozen lemonade and paper cups supplied by his mother. Ten cents a cup and the proceeds were clear profit, spent almost at once at the local toy store.

"I had all kinds of jobs in my day," Max said, motioning Eric to turn off the parkway at the next exit. "When I was twelve, I spent a whole summer delivering orders for Julius. He had a delicatessen then. I worked fourteen, fifteen hours a day, mostly for tips. It wasn't easy to get tips in those days. Most of the time you didn't even see the people you were delivering to. You sent the orders up in a dumbwaiter." He laughed. "I used to send up notes with the orders. Little poems. I hope the pastrami brings you joy, but don't forget to tip the boy."

Eric laughed.

"That summer was the first time I kept any of the money I earned. I kept half. I wanted a bicycle."

"Did you get it?"

"I did and I didn't," Max said. He was silent for a moment, remembering. "By the end of the summer, I had enough money. The bike I wanted was in a store way over on the West Side. A beauty, I'll never forget it. I rushed over after work and bought it. I'd never ridden a bike but it didn't look hard. The minute I got on it, I fell off. It took me hours to get home because I made up my mind to ride the bike the whole way, not to walk it one step. I must have fallen a hundred times but by the time I got to my street I'd learned how to ride, though I was still wobbly and the streetcar tracks kept getting in my way. I was late getting home and my mother was worried. She was hanging out of the window looking up and down the block for me and when she saw me she gave a yell, you could have heard her in Canarsie. I guess I looked terrible, my knees bloody, my clothes torn and dirty. She took the bike away and I never saw it again. Later I found out she'd sold it. I never saw the money, either."

Though it was hard to believe that Grandpa Max had ever been a little boy, Eric was moved almost to tears. "She must have been a terrible woman, Great-grandma Anna," he said.

"She feared for my life," Max said, making allowances. "I was her first born, the oldest. My father wasn't going to be able to provide for their old age so it was up to me. Turn here. It's just ahead."

They spent the next hour looking at a piece of land, most of it covered by a sprawling motel. Since he owned the motel, Max must have been familiar with the property, which was leased to the people who operated it. Still, they circled it slowly three times.

"How come you own the motel and not the land?" Eric asked. "What good is the land if someone else owns what's on it?

"The people who run the motel pay rent for the land, but we should own it for protection. If I can pick it up at the right price, it should yield eleven, twelve percent. A safe investment."

They drove from there to a bank in the village where Max talked for twenty minutes with the bank president, an austerely solemn man, as suavely self-effacing as a funeral director. By contrast, Eric noted, his grandfather's vitality seemed like an act of aggression, inexplicable since Max was as conservatively dressed, as neatly barbered, his voice only a fraction more carrying. The atmosphere of the bank, ignoring the trend toward friendliness, was hushed and forbidding, but Max wasn't at all intimidated by it as Eric might have been, and although his grandfather had said he had come for information, as far as Eric could see it was Max who did all the talking.

Through some mysterious process, however, he came away in possession of the facts he wanted.

Julius was operated on the following day. He nearly died. Eric went with Max to see him a few days later, by which time he was very much alive. The operation had shrunk him somewhat, but there were spots of color on his cheeks and his eyes were beady with anger. His wife Sophie was at his bedside. Much younger than Julius, she was a small woman of fading prettiness with graying, fair hair. She seemed stupefied with weariness.

"He's impossible," she groaned to Max. "Everybody in the hospital is his enemy. He thinks they're all out to kill him."

"You saw with your own eyes," Julius rasped. "They turned me over like I was a bag of sand."

"If you weren't such a bastard to everyone maybe they'd treat you more gently."

"It's their bounden duty to treat me gently no matter what kind of a bastard I am. They took an oath."

"It's your imagination."

"And the food is poison."

"It's the best food in any hospital, as good as a hotel."

"They wake me up all hours of the night with their thermometers and their blood pressures and their specimens. What's the matter they can't take care of those items in the daytime? I'm a sick man, I need my rest."

"Impossible. The doctor says it's a good sign." Sophie sighed. Clearly, if she had ever had the stamina for Julius, it had long since drained away.

Max changed the subject. He told Julius he had gone to see the motel land and that he thought they should try to buy it.

"So buy it," Julius said.

"I talked to Higginbottom at the bank," Max said. "Six people own the land jointly and they're all willing to sell except one, a woman named Scribner. They're trying to come to some kind of terms with her."

"Go see her," Julius said. "Talk to her."

"Let's wait and see how her partners make out with her. We don't want to be too anxious."

"Sophie, show Max the card from that *shmuck* Weil," Julius said, his anger coming to a boil again.

Sophie shuffled through a handful of cards on the bedside table and handed one of them to Max. Eric, peering over his grandfather's shoulder, saw a crude cartoon of a man lolling in splendor and luxury, surrounded by a harem of shapely nurses in low-cut uniforms, sipping a highball through a straw. The message read: *"We're slaving in the market/ While you have yourself a ball/ You may have lost the bladder/ But you haven't lost the gall."*

Eric and Max laughed.

"Give it to me," Julius snarled, thrusting forth a naked, gnarled arm. He grabbed the card and tore it to shreds.

Without Eric quite knowing how, the days slipped by, assuming a pattern entirely unplanned by him. Max had appropriated him. There was never any discussion about it, nor any official recognition, but after that first day, he had become a sort of factotum to Max, making phone calls for him, typing letters, sorting mail, chauffeuring him, running errands. Though he knew he wasn't really of much use, Max seemed to like having him there, a perpetual eye and ear, to heighten his sense of himself. Perhaps he was lonely. He had, after all, spent half a century surrounded by a small army of employees, many of whom had been with him throughout his career. Eric fell into his role with no resistance, partly because Max's energy had infected him, and partly because he was becoming fascinated by a way of life, of seeing it and living it that, though it had spawned him, and though he would finally bury it, was entirely alien to him. He grew increasingly more curious, amused, puzzled, and in a way he couldn't define, uneasy.

About a week after Julius came out of the hospital, Grandma Tess asked him and Sophie to dinner. Julius seemed fully recovered, but Sophie looked even more frayed than she had at the hospital, and there were dark circles under her eyes. She had two stiff drinks before dinner.

"He's still convalescing," she confided. She had a peculiarly flat voice, devoid of all energy. "It's awful having him in the house all day. With the painters and the carpenters and all kinds of mechanics in and out all day for him to yell at, I'm going out of my mind."

"It'll be over soon," Grandma Tess consoled. "He looks marvelous."

Eric tried to imagine how Sophie would have been acting at that moment if Julius had died. He could see nothing in their attitude toward each other that faintly resembled what he thought of as love. He had assumed that what bound Sophie to Julius was his money, but Max had told him that only a small fraction of Julius's fortune would go to her, not enough to keep her for more than a few years, and that Sophie knew it. Max, shocked when he'd learned this, had told Julius that it was shameful, but Julius was adamant. "It's not like she's my own flesh and blood,"

Julius had said. "When I met her she was a total stranger."

"You've been married more than twelve years," Max reminded him.

"If I leave her my money how do I know she won't marry some gigolo, some young son of a bitch who'll take it away?" The thought of the unknown adventurer, handsome and gentile, racing his Jaguar through perfumed nights to gambling casinos where he would lose, drinking champagne and seducing beautiful starlets, courtesy of Julius by way of the foolish Sophie, made Julius livid. "Nothing doing!" he screamed.

"You have to trust somebody," Max said.

"Who said so? Human nature is human nature, even Sophie's."

Julius dominated the conversation at dinner. He'd had his first outing since the operation that morning, just a brief one to try out his strength. His man, Benjamin, had driven him in the chocolate and mocha Rolls to the chiropodist.

"He couldn't believe my feet," Julius said, deftly spooning grapefruit. "Just to look at your feet, the chiropodist says to me, you could be a boy of fifteen. Not a bunion, not a corn, not even a callus."

"A nice topic for the dinner table," Sophie said.

"Then why do you go to a chiropodist?" Eric asked.

"Maintenance."

"Weill thinks he knows the Scribner woman," Max said. "He's going to talk to her about selling the motel property."

"Weill!" Julius said. "You know I can't stand him. If he's in on the deal, count me out."

"Of course he's in on it," Max said. "It's the corporation that's buying the property.

"The least said about that Weill the better," Julius muttered.

It must have been then that Julius resolved to do what he did the very next morning, though they didn't find out about it until the end of the week when Max had Eric dial Higginbottom at the Briarcliff bank.

"Higginbottom?" Max said into the phone when Eric handed it to him. "They making any headway with the Scribner woman on the Open Arms property?" There was a brief pause and then Max barked, "What do you mean sold? Sold? ... When? ... Why didn't you call me? You knew I... What do you mean you thought I knew? Who? ... Impossible! ... That dirty lowdown ... What do you mean, for me? ... No, naturally I didn't know." There was a longer pause while Max's face turned from pale to purple. His eyes were wild but he was silent, listening. At one point he pounded his fist on the desk with such force that all the pencils and paper clips jumped. Eric jumped, too. Max began to bellow and his anger was so naked, so pure, that it scared Eric out of the room. He tried to disappear into a corner of the living room sofa but in a few minutes Max stormed in and began to pace back and forth.

"Take it easy, Grandpa," Eric said. "You'll have a heart attack."

"That dirty double-crossing son of a bitch!"

"Calm down. Think of your health."

Max's hand went to the heart side of his chest. You're right. Nothing's worth that." He stopped pacing and sat down across the room from Eric, breathing heavily. "The bastard. He pulled the whole deal off in about three hours. First he saw Mrs. Scribner. It took him about half an hour to convince her. She thought he was charming."

"Julius?"

"Some people are charmed by snakes, remember. Then he rounded up the other partners, the lawyers, had the contract drawn and signed and gave them a check. The crook!"

Eric thought he detected a hint of admiration buried in the anger in Max's voice.

"What's more, he paid eighteen thousand less than we were prepared to offer."

"Can he do that?" Eric asked.

"What do you mean, can he do it? He did it."

"I mean aren't there any ethics in business? Can people in the same corporation bid against each other?"

A light came into Max's eyes. "Ethics," he said, and the word was like a revelation to him. "Ethics. You know, Eric, I think you might have something there. Go fix me an Alka-Seltzer."

By the time Eric had the bromide fizzing, Max was on the phone with his lawyer. He took the glass from Eric and drained it. "Sorry, Irving," he said, turning aside to burp. "Go ahead, Irving. You were saying?"

What Irving was saying was that the corporation could sue Julius and probably win, but was Max sure that he wanted to sue his own uncle. He certainly was. Full speed ahead.

"We'll get that bastard," he said when he'd hung up.

"It's a game," Eric said, seeing it all clearly.

"This time he really went too far. He thought he could put one over on me. Well, I've got the same blood in my veins."

"It's Monopoly," Eric said.

"What are you talking about?"

Blacks were being slaughtered, babies na-
palmed, good men assassinated. The air was foul,
fish were dying, food was slowly poisoning them all.
Thousands of people were drowning in tidal waves,
being sucked into earthquakes, suffocating under
mountains, starving in arid lands, being held hostage
in airplanes or gunned down in airports, while Julius
and Max played Monopoly over a piece of land that
wasn't even there.

"Listen, Grandpa. This business... all this with
money, buying and selling and being shrewd, it's just
a game to you, isn't it?"

"A game?" Max shouted. "What are you,
crazy?"

But even so, Eric thought, was it any less valid
than anything else? Money, power, philosophy, glass
beads? What difference did it make? Once you had
gotten through the business of arranging the conditions of your life, your survival, weren't you stuck
with the game? Perhaps the means swallowed the
end. Perhaps there was no end.

A few days later, Julius's mail brought him the
news that he .was being sued. The complainant was
the corporation but it was at Max's door that he instantly presented himself, his little monkey face dis-
torted with suppressed rage.

"What's this all about?"

"It speaks for itself," Max said.

"I want to hear it from your own mouth."

Max shrugged. "As a private party you bid
against your own corporation. It's unethical. The
corporation is suing you. A, B, C!"

"You're actually suing me?"

"The corporation."

"Your own uncle?"

"You're a double-crossing son of a bitch."

"After all I did for you?"

"What did you do for me?"

"I gave you a job. You were just a little snot-nose kid."

"I worked for you," Max yelled. "Like a horse, fifteen hours a day, delivering your lousy delicatessen, sweeping your floors. For practically nothing."

"It wasn't easy to get jobs those days, especially for little kids."

"My feet were already bigger than yours. You were wearing my outgrown shoes."

"I gave you advice. I was like a father to you, a big brother. I taught you."

"You robbed my mother, your own sister. Now me. You'd rob yourself if you could figure a way to make a buck out of it."

Julius hunched his shoulders, then composed his face and said, "Listen, Max, let's be reasonable. Bygones are bygones. I only wanted to cut out Weill. I bought that land for you, too, fifty-fifty."

"I don't want it," Max shouted. "You think I could take it?"

"Suit yourself," Julius said. "I can't stand here and argue all day. I'm a convalescent."

"Why don't you just sell it back to the corporation," Max said, his voice a little calmer, "and save us all a lot of heartache."

"Over my dead body. Why don't you just drop the suit and forget it?"

"I'm managing a corporation," Max said. "I

have to consider the best interests of that corporation."

"Okay, Max, okay. I'll see you in court." He began, briskly, to leave. "By the way, Max," he said, pausing at the door, "how much is two and a half percent of three million dollars?"

"Seventy-five thousand," Max, the computer, said. "Why?"

"If I'm not mistaken, two and a half percent is the standard executor's fee at this time," Julius said, closing the door behind him. Max swore at the closed door.

"What did that mean?" Eric asked.

"He was telling me that if I sue I'm no longer executor of his estate and that I'm out seventy-five thousand dollars. He was trying to bribe me."

Slowly, the mills of the law began to grind. The days went by. Max had a new proposition, a shopping center, that took him and Eric to New Jersey several times a week. Then, late one afternoon, Sophie appeared hesitantly at their door.

"I want you all to come to dinner tomorrow night," she said firmly.

Max just as firmly refused. He and Julius were no longer on speaking terms. Sophie persisted. Tears came to her eyes. "I can't do a thing with him, God knows," she said, "but I can't allow this to happen." Tess, too, coaxed Max.

"I can't have dinner with someone I'm suing," Max shouted.

"Be big."

"To celebrate the apartment," Sophie said. "Here we have all this beautiful new furniture, it cost a fortune, and who can we invite?"

There was no mistaking that the apartment had

cost a fortune; every penny of it showed. Eric wiped his feet on the doormat for a long time before allowing himself to cross the threshold. The walls were either paneled or antique-mirrored, the white carpeting ankle deep from wall to wall, and there was a fireplace with a real fire in it though air conditioners throbbed away to make it bearable.

"Welcome to my humble home," Julius said.

The first awkward minutes were passed touring the rooms with Julius as guide, detailing origins, ingredients, even prices. Eric, stumbling along in his grandparents' wake, was overcome by a sense of unreality, as though he had wandered out of his own life, whatever that was, onto the set of a 1940's movie. He listened while Max and Tess politely admired everything, but was relieved when Max finally took exception to the mammoth white Steinway grand piano.

"What do you need it for?" Max asked. "Nobody plays."

"Need, shmeed," Julius said. "At my age, a man doesn't have to need."

During dinner, which was simple but good, Eric could sense beneath the strained small talk, the growing tension, and he waited hopefully for the obligatory scene. It came with the blueberry pie and coffee when, solemnly, nervously, Sophie said, "Listen Julius. Max. I want you to iron out your differences."

"Mind your own business," Julius said.

"Whose business is it if not mine?" Sophie said. "They're my family, too. Who've we got, God knows?"

"So why should I be any different?" Max asked. "Nobody talks to Julius. Not even his own daughter, I hear."

"Shhh!" Tess said.

"It's no accident," Max said. "What does he care about friends or family? He only cares about money. He's not a nice man. Even you have to admit it, Sophie. What he lacks, he has no ethics."

"Ethics!" Julius snorted.

"You think that's not important?" Eric felt called upon to say. It was he who had supplied the word in the first place. "If people have no ethics, no morals, they might as well be animals."

Julius turned to look at him briefly, as though trying to remember who he was.

"Ethics," he said again, turning back to Max. "Where your mother and I came from, Max, they didn't have much in the line of ethics. Pogroms they had. Dogs attacking us they had."

"That was a long time ago. It was a different world."

"Maybe for you it was a different world. For me it was my world. When I came to this country, just a little kid, I was over three weeks in the hold of a stinking ship like cattle herded together, pigs in a pen. And I was hungry all the time."

He held up his hand to stave off interruption. "If I didn't steal I'd have starved to death on that ship. You know how I made it? I went where I smelled vomit, that's how. From that person, who was too sick to need it, to care, I stole food. I had to steal because nobody gave, not even to a little kid and, believe me, scared. Your mama came here first, Max, two years before. She sent me the ticket and the fifty cents to take the taxi wagon from the boat and the address written on a piece of paper to show the wagon driver. With her new name. Because when they got to Castle Gardens and your papa gave his name to the officer to fill out the papers, the officer didn't have the time to listen so good so he wrote out some other name. You know that, Max? You know that you haven't even got your own name?"

"I know, I know," Max nodded. "So what's in a name?"

"Ethics! Dozens of people crowded scared to death in a taxi wagon with their scraps of paper and their fifty centses and not a word of English and all of us dumped like a load of garbage practically in the same block. The streets were supposed to be paved with gold, but right away I saw they were paved with dreck. It was a jungle. And what was I? A little shtunk, weak and ugly. If I walked in the next street they threw rocks at me and beat me up and called me kike and sheeny. What did I have to fight my way out of that jungle with? Ethics?"

He paused and looked lovingly around the room at the gleaming crystal chandelier, at the silver glowing behind the leaded glass panes of the cherry-wood breakfront.

"Others came out," Eric said, frightened to find himself speaking. "They came out decent."

"It was a jungle for me, too," Max said.

"Listen, Max," Julius said. "I am what I am. I'm eighty-two years old. I'm on top of the world. You know what you can do with your ethics."

In the end, there was no lawsuit. The corporation bought Julius out, but he kept the land beneath the motel and he reverted to what he had always been and should have remained, a lone operator, unencumbered by partners or affiliates. As Max said, "A hawk doesn't fly in flocks."

When the summer was over, Eric went back to

school. Though he still didn't have any idea who he was, he was beginning to understand why.

Doggedly, he went on with the search for his own life.

DEATH IN NEW ROCHELLE

When the two peacocks fell off the truck in front of his house, Marvin Newton was raking leaves in his yard and thinking of Adelaide, who had left him four and a half months earlier after twenty-four years of marriage. He had spent a lot of time since trying to figure out why. She would always think of him affectionately, she had said, and hoped that they would be friends, but for her the marriage was over. Hurt, he had told her that he didn't know if he wanted her for a friend. He had been a good father to Clara, off now digging up ruins in the Southwest, and he had always thought of himself as a dependable, considerate husband to Adelaide. There had been some good moments in the marriage and not many bad ones. He didn't know many people who could claim as much.

Occupied as he was, it took his mind a while to catch up with what his eyes were telling it: that two peacocks had fallen off a truck and, after a stunned moment, were picking themselves up and brushing themselves off.

"Hey, you lost something," he shouted after the truck, but it had already turned the corner. Meanwhile, the peacocks marched onto Marvin's property and were inspecting it with apparent approval. There was nothing he could do but watch them, and after a while, seeing that they meant to stay, he went inside to practice. He was first violinist for a second-rate opera company, so the occasional screeching of the peacocks was no distraction, but before long the telephone rang. It was Adelaide.

"I just got back from Juarez," she told him. "Mexico."

"Oh? I hope you had a good time," he said, rattled by the sound of her voice. It was his first direct contact with her in two months.

"I didn't go for a good time," she said. "I went for the divorce. The papers will be coming through in a few days. I thought you ought to know."

"Yes, well, thank you."

"It was a squalid and dispiriting experience. I'd like to describe it to you in some detail."

"That's all right. No need."

"I think there is a need," she said. "After all, it was your divorce, too."

"But it was your experience," he countered.

"It was the end of a twenty-four year marriage." There was exasperation in her voice. "In which, in one way or another, we were both involved. I'll send you an account of it. In writing."

He had barely hung up the phone when the doorbell rang. He opened the door to a statuesque young woman in granny sunglasses and a very long coat.

"There are two peacocks on your garage roof," she said.

"Yes."

"I thought perhaps you didn't know."

She was a very young woman, he saw, and although he felt that their exchange had come to an end, she apparently did not. She was carrying a huge handbag open at the top so that he could see that it was stuffed with papers and notebooks. Assuming that she represented some obscure religious sect and was on the verge of proselytizing, he thanked her and made to close the door, but she was already inside.

"I'm sorry, I'm an atheist," he said, hoping that would end it. She gave him a long questioning look and began to unbutton her coat.

"I'm an agnostic," she said, walking past him into the hallway. "I believe in possibilities. I believe in magic and mystery. I don't like closed doors."

He began to feel a little afraid. She had taken off the sunglasses and was looking about with open curiosity.

"But I haven't explained myself, have I?" she asked, turning to face him, her eyes wide and luminous. With her glasses off, her beauty stunned him. "I live in the neighborhood and I'm doing a dissertation on the impact of suburbia on the decay of middle-class morality. Would you mind answering a few questions? It won't take long." She slid out of her coat and, throwing it across a chair, walked ahead of him into the living room, leaving him to decide whether he was more disturbed by her presumption or her figure. The latter, despite the bizarre clothing that covered it from neck to ankles, was obviously equal to her face.

"I should think you'd have more sense than to come barging into a strange man's home," he grumbled. "To say nothing of better manners."

"Anyone could tell at a glance that you're harmless," she said. The insult unsettled him, but did not prevent her from settling onto the sofa. She foraged in her bag and drew forth notebook and pencil.

"Now. How long have you lived here?" she

asked, opening the book to a clean page.

"Nineteen years."

"How many in the family."

"Just me, now."

"You live alone here?"

"Yes. My wife .. that is, I'm divorced. Recently. And my daughter's just out of school and working in the West."

"And you go on living here?"

"Yes, why shouldn't I?" he said, taking a chair opposite her.

"What sort of work do you do?"

"I'm a musician. Violinist."

"Did your wife work?"

"No. Before Clara was born she was a copywriter for a few years. Then she stayed home to raise Clara. She sometimes talked about going back to work, but she never did."

"Why do you think that was?"

He thought for a moment, wondering at the ease with which he had fallen into answering this strange girl's much too personal questions.

"Well, we didn't really need the money," he said. "She hadn't liked copywriting and she wasn't really trained for anything and, as she got older, I guess she lost confidence in herself. She wrote a little poetry."

"Anything published?"

"No. She did have two poems accepted by a projected quarterly, *The Jaundiced Eye*, I think it was called, but the magazine never materialized."

"What was the reason for your divorce?"

He stared at the girl. The look she returned was level and impersonal. "I don't know," he said, and watched her expression change to one of disbelief.

"Surely you must have some idea?"

"None. Not really."

The girl stabbed out her cigarette. She was obviously in a rage.

"Now see here, Miss..." he said, beginning to be angry himself.

"Joy. My name is Joy."

"Well, Joy, that's the best answer I can give you. I spend half my time trying to figure it out. We were married for twenty-four years and I would have said we were happy."

She was scribbling away furiously in her notebook.

"You lived for twenty-four years with a woman who suddenly divorced you and you have no idea why?" she said. "Was she in love with another man?"

"Not that I know of. I doubt it."

"Were you unfaithful to her?"

"Never. Well, once. On tour. She never knew about it."

"Did you quarrel?"

"Rarely. Never seriously."

"Do you have any bad or annoying habits? Drinking? Gambling?"

"No, nothing immoderate. What school do you go to?"

"Barnard."

"Master's or doctoral?"

"Doctoral."

"Social work?"

"City planning," she said, and grinned. One of her teeth had a corner chipped off. He wondered how she had done it.

"Sex?"

"What do you mean, sex?"

"What was your sex life like?"

"Now, see here, Joy. What has our sex life got to do with city planning?"

"There's nothing personal about this, Mr. ... um," she said gently. "No, don't tell me your name. Think of yourself as an anonymous cipher. Was your sex life all right?"

"It was fine. So was my wife's."

"Did your wife achieve orgasm?"

"She did not achieve it," he said, trying to control himself. "It came to her naturally in the natural course of events."

There was a pause. The girl was squinting at him. "You know, I don't think you're lying," she said. "She never complained, your wife? About the sex?"

"No. Yes. She sometimes said she wished I'd talk."

"You never talked to her during lovemaking?"

"What was there to say?"

The girl scribbled in her book. "Just a few more questions and I'll be finished," she said. No, he had never smoked grass. Yes, he had said he was a musician. No, he'd never committed any crime. Yes, he had served in the Korean war but hadn't seen action. No, he was not particularly political, though he voted, and yes, he would describe himself as a liberal, and, yes, as a younger man he'd been more active. Yes, he read, he played some tennis, his health was excellent, he had never been in psychoanalysis, he had no hobbies, he liked crossword puzzles and poker, he had no immediate plans of any kind. Goodbye, Joy.

He watched her down the path and out of sight,

glad to be rid of her, sorry to see her go, then went into the garden to see if the peacocks were still there. They were not only there; their manner implied that they had never been elsewhere. Strictly speaking, only one of the birds was a cock. The other, smaller, nosier, and plain as a turkey, was a peahen, and it was lucky they had fallen off the truck simultaneously since they were obviously used to each other. Though not opposed to birds, Marvin had never particularly fancied them. These, so large and ostentatious and uncommon in New Rochelle, made him nervous. In the next few days he did what he could to trace their origin and to determine their destination, but his efforts were fruitless. When the peacocks had dined on all the tulip and hyacinth bulbs Adelaide had planted the previous autumn, Marvin felt he'd better learn what he could about their care and maintenance. He went to his branch of the public library.

"What have you got on peacocks?" he asked Miss Chaspee, the librarian at the desk.

"Thomas Love Peacock, English poet?" she said. "I played with you 'mid cowslips blowing when I was six and you were four?"

"No, no, not the poet," Marvin said. "The creature."

Grain, snails, frogs, insects; these were their diet. Since grain-and-feed shops were as uncommon in the suburban neighborhood as livestock, it took considerable driving about before Marvin was able to procure a sack of feed. The peacocks would have to forage for the rest on their own.

The peacocks throve, which was more than Marvin could say for himself since Adelaide's defection. Having been a woman of repressed literary urges, she had unburdened herself of her creativity in the kitchen. Marvin had never had reason to do more than press the lever on the toaster or peel a tangerine. In recent months, though often acutely hungry and obsessed with fantasies of haute cuisine, he had dined chiefly on canned soup and liverwurst sandwiches. However, not long after the arrival of the peacocks, his telephone rang one night.

"Hello, Mr. Newton?"

"Yes."

"This is Sylvia Mermelstein. A neighbor of yours? I don't know if you know who I am? The beige house with pink shutters on Barbara Lane?"

"Oh, yes," he lied.

"I saw your peacocks the other day? In fact, I've walked by several times just to see them. We had some friends visiting on Sunday and we all walked by. I must say it's terribly interesting of you to keep peacocks. They change the whole tone of the neighborhood."

"Do they?"

"Even their screaming is rather, well, exotic. Sidney and I were wondering if you'd care to come to dinner Sunday night? Nothing fancy?"

"Why that's very kind. I'd be delighted."

Because his house was located in a development, its streets dotingly named for the builders' progeny, and because Sylvia Mermelstein's invitation was merely the opening gun in a barrage of calls from neighbors whose borrowed pride in his peacocks seemed to have given them a sense of heightened status, he began to dine, on nights when there was no performance, in a succession of split-level and ranch-type homes tucked along Steven Street and Kenny Close and Ricky Road. And though he was invariably warned that dinner would be informal, nothing fancy, he saw that there was always some touch a little more festive than he guessed his hosts were accustomed to, a rare wine, the good silver, double damask napery, a uniformed woman brought in to serve. Before long, single women, divorced, widowed, spinstered, began to appear at these dinners, their conversation animated, their eyes sparkling, their manner as brightly polished as the silver. As he was obviously the target for their shafts of gaiety, it was impossible not to respond, to feel himself warming to all these proofs that he was desirable, perhaps even interesting. Although he had gone that first night to the Mermelsteins in an old sports jacket and spent most of the evening in his habitual nonperforming posture, slumped onto his spine, he began to change. He found himself sitting straighter, talking with more vivacity, collecting and dispensing anecdotes and witticisms, and employing gestures he'd never used before.

It was at the home of the Barrons, the fifth of these dinners, that Joy reappeared. The Mermelsteins were there, and a recently widowed sister of Gertrude Barron, Grace Something, a thin, nervous woman with nice eyes who talked a great deal, her conversation consisting almost entirely of information digested with breakfast that morning from the *Times*. Over cocktails, after Grace had deplored the wanton slaughter of baby seals in the Bering Sea, Gertrude Barron remarked that she hoped Joy would arrive in time for dinner. She had said she'd be there, but you never knew.

"Yes, she still has the apartment on 116th Street," Wilbur Barron said in answer to a question from Sylvia Mermelstein, "but she comes home whenever she needs a bath. Or, to be more precise, whenever she thinks she needs a bath. The plumbing there leaves something to be desired. Such as hot water." Wilbur Barron was a building contractor and plumbing interested him. He would have gone on with the subject, but his wife interrupted to remark that in her opinion the problem wasn't the lack of hot water but of clean towels, since Joy was notoriously negligent in the domestic department. This led to a flurry of comparisons. The Mermelstein's boy had always been tidy, Grace's twins were impossible, and Marvin's Clara probably did her washing in muddy streams if she did it at all. After they had agreed that none of this was important since, thank God, their children weren't making bombs in the basement, it was time to go in to dinner.

Marvin had failed to connect the Barron's Joy with the strange girl who had burst in on him, so that when she appeared halfway through the lobster bisque, glowing and a little breathless, but not at all apologetic, and took the empty place across from him, he was startled to feel himself reddening.

"How are the peacocks?" Joy asked him at once.

"Oh, you two know each other?"" her mother asked.

"Joy used me as a subject," Marvin said. "She interrogated me at length one morning."

"I hope she wasn't rude. Joy can be very rude."

"More ruthless than rude, I'd say," Marvin said.

"Speaking of ruthless," Grace said. And off they went to the Middle East, to terrorists, to Yugoslavia, to Cuba, straight through the soup, the pot roast and potato pancakes, the salad, chocolate roll, coffee. Marvin, who knew his Thoreau and could still invoke Socrates if he had to, talked easily, aware that he was trying to impress Joy. Whenever he looked across at her, which he tried not to do too often, he found that she was staring at him. He tried to imagine what was in her head and failed.

The next morning, Adelaide's letter describing her trip to Mexico arrived in the mail. He couldn't bring himself to read it until almost a week later. Then, one night after a particularly good dinner on Linda Lane, he took it to bed with him.

She had spared no detail, not even the weather. She described the flight to El Paso, most of her fellow passengers bent on the same errand as she, and her surprise at finding that most of them were middle-aged men, though there was one young girl who cried all the way; the bizarre unreality of sitting in the hotel lobby in Juarez the following morning among the other silent ones awaiting lawyers they had never met to come and fetch them; the trip with her lawyer to the courthouse; the flock of ragged children who surrounded the limousine on its arrival, fighting to open the doors, begging for pesos. And then the seedy courtroom with its bilious green walls and fly-specked windows, the bored judge who spoke no English, a Mexican flag at one side of his desk, an American flag at the other, signifying that by their divided homes these two nations were united. One by one, they were called before him. When her turn came, she was asked, through her lawyer, whether she was Adelaide Newton, she admitted to this, she signed a document, the judge put his seal on it, and that was all. It was over.

But that was not all. She went on to describe her feelings afterward, her need to be alone, so that when she left the courthouse she declined the lawyer's offer of a lift back and walked instead in the glaring sunshine, feeling that she had been processed in a mill so devoid of human feeling, so commercial and bureaucratic, that she felt not only cheated but soiled, as though her whole life had been a mockery. She had gone only a few blocks when she saw that she was being followed by an Indian woman with a baby and small girl in tow. The woman kept pushing the little girl in Adelaide's direction and the child kept demurring and hanging back until, at last, the woman slapped the child across the back of her head and pushed her so roughly that she almost fell upon Adelaide. Then, her hand outstretched, the girl whined something in Spanish.

"Inglés!" the mother hissed and "Mawnee," the child whined. "I looked into the child's face," Adelaide wrote. "It was unprepossessing, the mouth sullen, nose runny, eyes glassy with hate, and I felt my heart contract with fear. The simplest thing would have been to give her a handful of coins and end it, and although they pursued me almost to the border, where I escaped in a taxi, I was so enraged, so unwilling to make the mother's exploitation of that miserable child a success, that I couldn't bring myself to do anything but refuse. Above all, I was terrified at the depth of my own anger. Had the child not had the sensitivity to hate what she was being made to do, had she not been so obviously fighting to hang onto some shred of dignity, and no more than eight years old, and had I not myself just gone through an experience so devoid of feeling, I could never have held out, but it became a contest between me and the woman. I felt that I was fighting for the child and whatever decency she might salvage from her miserable life. Once in the taxi, I wept all the way across the bridge to El

Paso and back to the hotel."

Thus ended Adelaide's account. Marvin put the pages aside, moved because Adelaide had revealed an unfamiliar side of herself and mystified that she had chosen this time, when the marriage was over, to do it.

The next morning before he began to practice, he spent some time outside looking at his peacocks. The male was certainly a beauty and full of conceit, and it amused Marvin to watch him preen and strut and spread his marvelous fan while his dowdy mate swooned and trotted after him. No question who ruled this roost, and by virtue of nature's gift of splendor to the male. In this lower species beauty was not an arbitrary ethnic decision, subject to change by the whimsical dictates of stylists, but a very real distinction implanted as surely in the cock's tail as in the hen's eye. Still, beneath his plumes, the peacock was a scrawny, silly bird indeed.

Marvin went inside to practice. He picked up his violin to tune it and then put it down. He had been playing Puccini and Verdi for so many years that he knew he could do anything in the repertory in his sleep. He put his violin away and went instead into the city to a shop in Greenwich Village that he frequently passed on his way to the store where he bought his music. He spent the next two hours and what, to him, seemed a fortune, blissfully selecting, trying on, and at last purchasing an entire wardrobe, brightly colored, highly styled, so fashionably haute monde, he was assured, that he would be noticed with appreciation and respect on any of the great boulevards of the Continent.

When he got home, Joy was just turning away from his door.

"What have you got there?" she asked, while he groped for his keys. "Here, let me hold some of that for you." She took one of the big boxes and, when he had unlatched the door, marched inside with it.

"What are you doing here?" he asked. "More questions?" She was already out of her coat and undoing one of the boxes. "It's just clothing," he said, embarrassed, dumping the rest of the packages onto the floor. When he returned from hanging their coats away in the hall closet, she had undone all the packages and had everything spread out on the living room floor.

"Coo," she said, standing back to admire the panorama, "you're changing your image."

"Don't be silly."

"Try them on," she said. "Here, these. Let me see."

"No." He snatched the things from her and threw them across a chair. "Time for a drink," he said, and went into the kitchen for ice. She was right behind him. "Scotch? Martini?"

"No, thanks, I've brought my own."

"Your own what?" he said, banging the ice tray against the sink.

"Grass. Want to try it?"

He poured himself a drink and she followed him back into the living room and began to burrow inside her huge handbag, emerging at last with a yellowed, misshapen cigarette.

"Here," she said. "Why don't you start?"

"No, thanks. What are you doing here anyway?"

"I came to turn you on."

He sank onto the sofa and took a long swallow

of his drink. "Is that part of your research?" he asked, watching her light up.

"Not as a rule. You know, usually I get housewives. They're only too delighted to talk to me. You'd be surprised how quickly they get down to the nitty-gritty. Actually, you're the only man I've ever found at home. How did you like Aunt Grace?"

"Aunt Grace?"

"She was quite taken with you. Probably been sitting next to the phone ever since. And you'll never call, will you?"

"I'm not up to that sort of thing yet," he said. "I haven't really thought about it." He watched Joy take a long drag. "I wish you wouldn't do that," he said. "Here."

"What do you do about sex?" she asked when she had finally expelled what remained of the smoke.

"Ignore it. Hope it will go away."

She held the joint out to him. "Come on, try it. It won't hurt you." He took it, meaning to put it out in the ashtray, and then put it to his mouth instead and tried to smoke it as he had seen her do. He coughed on the first try but the second one was better. Between puffs, they passed the cigarette back and forth, smoking now in silence. Soon there was nothing left of it.

"Satisfied?" he asked, returning to his drink. "Nothing happened."

She leaned across and very gently kissed him on the mouth.

"Don't do that," he said, though it seemed the most natural thing in the world for her to do. "Now what are you doing?" But he could see very well what she was doing. She was taking off her clothes.

"Don't do that, either," he said. "Listen, Joy,

you're just a child to me. You're not much older than my daughter. For me it would be incestuous. I'd never forgive myself, really. Joy, stop that, please, put your things back on and go home this minute."

She was laughing at him and he knew that she was not a child, that at this moment he was in some important way not quite as old as she. In no time at all, she was out of her clothes, looking exactly as he had feared she would look, and then she was undoing the buttons of his shirt. He told himself that he was seeing things through the eyes of his generation, now extinct, that at her age she'd been taking the Pill and having sex for years, that for her it was no more than a handshake, a sneeze, hadn't he read that everywhere? They began to make very slow love for what seemed a very long time, giving careful attention to the details, and it was nothing like either a sneeze or a handshake. Outside the window, day turned to dusk and dusk to night. Afterward, sprawled across his new clothes on the living room floor, she raised herself onto an elbow and looked down at him.

"What did you feel?" she asked. He closed his eyes against her question and took a deep breath.

"Intense," he said. "Oh, my God, intense." He heard her sigh.

"Do you know you talked the whole time?" she said. "I swear I don't know what makes you people tick. Come on, now, show me how you look in your new duds."

For the next half hour he was in and out of one outfit and then another until hunger drove them to the kitchen, where it took all their combined ingenuity to scare up a passable meal. He promised that in the future he would keep a better-stocked larder. But he had no way of knowing if there would be a future. When it came time for her to leave, he asked if he would see her again.

"Of course, stupid."

"Can I call you? Have you got a phone?"

She patted his cheek. "I'll call you," she said. "Or just appear. Bye-bye, sweet." And she was gone.

Awakened the next morning by the telephone, his first thought was of Joy. It was Adelaide.

"There's something I want to discuss with you," she said. "Could we have dinner tonight?"

"I'm playing, but we could meet afterward. Is anything wrong?"

"No, just an idea I have. But I can't go ahead with it without your cooperation."

He was distracted all during the performance that night. The company's repertory was as limited as the gifts of its singers, and by the time Mimi was coughing at the gates, he felt that if he had to go through another season playing nineteenth-century music for two-hundred-pound consumptives to die to, he'd go berserk. He yawned across the pit at Otto Belsky, the percussionist, who had been with the company as long as Marvin. They had occasionally discussed the possibility of breaking away and doing something else. Tonight it came to him that he could electrify his violin and, with Belsky and a couple of other good men, form a rock group. During intermission he mentioned it to Belsky.

"Rock?" Belsky said, horrified. "At our age?"

"Why not? Rock's been around a long time, now. We could stress our ages. Call ourselves The Seniors, or The Rock of Ageds. We're better musicians than a lot of these kids."

"But rock!"

"I like rock," Marvin said. "And there's nothing to it. The rhythm you know. We build the melodic line on modes, Dorian and myxolidian, mostly. Listen to the Gregorian chants, it's all there. I'm still not sure about harmonic progressions, but I'll analyze them, and as for phrasing, anything goes." He felt his enthusiasm growing; he hadn't thought about music in years.

When he got to Downey's, Adelaide was already there. She was a tall woman, no longer willowy as she had been when they'd married, but she was still handsome. The familiarity of her after the months of separation jolted him. Did he love her? It was a question he hadn't put to himself in twenty years. Stabilized in their marriage after the first years, he had taken their feelings and their commitment to one another for granted.

They were shown to a booth and after a few strained exchanges about Clara and about how well the other was looking, they fell upon their menus with relief.

"I'm starved," Adelaide said, and when the waiter brought their drinks she began at once to tell him what she would have, not siphoning her order through Marvin as she had always done. She was, he saw, already accustomed to her separateness. He wondered if she would insist on paying her half of the check.

"Now, tell me how you've been managing," she said.

"I've been doing fine." He sipped his Scotch. "Of course, it's taking some getting used to."

She looked at him over her glass with a hint of smugness, as though he had confirmed something she had known all along. He had a flash of intuition: she had known he wouldn't suffer much; she thought him deficient in feeling.

"And you?" he asked.

"I've got a job," she said, her face lighting. "I'm doing public relations for Upsex."

"For what?"

"The feminist organization," she said, launching into a spirited and lengthy explanation of her organization's part in the movement. It always shocked him to be reminded that women still didn't feel equal; he had always thought them at least that. "Yes, that's true," he said from time to time, and "That sounds like a valid approach." Far from reacting defensively to anything she said, he found her news pleasing; he felt powers accruing to him by virtue of his sex that he'd never imagined were his. When she interrupted her lecture to complain that her steak was overdone, he summoned the waiter and, with unembarrassed authority, sent it back for another.

"But what I wanted to talk to you about," she said, at last, "was the divorce."

"Yes, I read your paper."

"What did you think of it?"

For a moment, called upon for a critical judgment, his mind went blank. He nodded his head gravely, stalling for time to ward off platitudes.

"It moved me. It didn't sound like any you I ever knew."

She smiled, vindicated once again on some private point.

"I can see how awful it must have been for you," he said.

"Can you understand, then, how unfinished it left me feeling?"

"Unfinished?"

"It wasn't enough.   Something more is needed."

"What do you mean?"

"A divorce after a long marriage is a major event." She broke off a piece of roll and buttered it. "It's as momentous a part of life as marriage, birth, death. There are rituals for those events, but not for divorce. I want to have a, well, a sort of party."

"A party?" he cried, horrified.

"Not exactly a party. Maybe more like a wake. Damn, there just isn't any word for it. I want to invite people and formalize it."

Their waiter drifted within range and he signaled to him. "Two very large beers," he said in a loud voice. "Adelaide, you must be out of your mind. You want to celebrate the divorce?"

"You don't understand a thing I've been trying to tell you," she said, her eyes misting with frustration. "I want to observe it. The whole thing so far has been so empty, so impersonal, that I might as well have been selling off a few shares of stock. I want to feel the seriousness of it." She was so close to outright weeping that, automatically, he handed her his handkerchief.

"Let me get this straight," he said. "You want to have a sort of gathering. At the house?"

"That would be most appropriate, I think."

"And who's to be invited? Are they to bring presents? Is it to be catered? Do we dance, or what?"

She sighed and nibbled at the piece of roll she'd buttered. The waiter set down their steins of beer and, still breathing heavily, Marvin blew the foam off his glass. It missed Adelaide by centimeters, evaporating somewhere behind her.

"I don't know why you're getting so excited,

Marvin," she said. "You'd think I was proposing something obscene."

"Obscene," he said. "Yes. You don't go around advertising a failed marriage."

"Nonsense. Death doesn't necessarily mark a failed life, just a life that's come to an end. Sometimes a marriage simply comes to an end."

"You choose a divorce. You don't choose death. If you do, it usually means a failed life."

"Calm down, Marvin. I've never seen you so overwrought. And I don't mean to advertise it, just to have a few people in who cared enough to come to our wedding, or to send gifts when Clara was born. To round things off."

He tried to recall who had been at their wedding: relatives, many of whom had passed away; friends, many of whom had drifted away.

"And then there's your mother," Adelaide said.

"My mother!" His voice crashed across the noisy dining room, creating, in its wake, a momentary hiatus of silence. His mother was eighty-two years old and lived in Pipestone, Minnesota, and furthermore, her arthritis was very bad. Her reaction to being summoned to New Rochelle to attend a celebration of her only son's divorce was beyond imagining.

"No, I suppose it would be too much for her," Adelaide conceded, sliding a sheet of paper across the table at him. "Here, I've drawn up a list. You can add anyone you like, of course."

"Spare me," he said, shoving the list back without looking at it.

"Then there's this," she said, handing him a printed card. "The invitation."

He stared at it. "Adelaide Fowler Newton and Marvin Newton request your company at the observance of their recent divorce, to be held Sunday, May 16th at 4:00 P.M., 32 Alvin Boulevard, New Rochelle. Informal. RSVP."

May 16th was only three weeks off. His anger subsided into a feeling of helplessness.

"The *fête*," he said drearily, "seems to be *accompli.*"

In the following days, except for an occasional sickening stab of dread, Marvin kept busy and tried not to think about the impending event. Once or twice he thought about trying to call Joy, from whom there'd been no further communication, but in the end he argued himself out of it. She had been playing with him and, though he was grateful for the experience, common sense cautioned him against being a fool. The paths of their lives were utterly divergent, he knew, and it was only through some perversity that they had crossed at all.

On an impulse, he invited Otto Belsky and borrowed Sylvia Mermelstein's cleaning woman to give his house a thorough going-over the day before the event. Late on the morning of the sixteenth, he awoke feeling surprisingly happy. Perhaps it was simply that the barometer was rising. It was a perfect spring day, dry and cool and golden. Outside the bedroom windows, the peacocks were making raucous, savage love.

He dressed with care, taking a long time at it, and was just knotting his tie when he heard a car drive up. He looked out to see Adelaide alighting from a spanking new 1976 yellow Chevy convertible, its rear seat piled high with bundles. He bounded out to help her.

"My word, Marvin, you look sharp," she said.

"That's a nice car," he said, wondering.

When they'd carried all the bundles to the kitchen, he helped unpack and sort them. She'd thought of everything, from canapes to petits fours.

"You ought to go into the catering business," he said, peering into casseroles. "There's enough food here for an Italian wedding."

She walked through the dining room and into the living room, running a finger over surfaces. Sylvia Mermelstein's cleaning woman had done a good job.

"The house looks good," she said, a little wistfully. "You are managing well. What's that awful noise?"

"What awful noise?"

"In the garden. Cats? No, it isn't cats." She was at the window, peering out. "There's a big, fat, brownish bird out there, Marvin. What is it, a turkey? My God, Marvin, and there's a peacock. There are peacocks out there, Marvin! And they're copulating!"

He stood next to her at the window and looked out. "So there are," he said. "And so they are."

"But what are they doing here?"

"They live here. They're my peacocks."

She turned from the window to stare at him. "What are you doing with peacocks, Marvin? How strange." She turned back to the window, frowning. "Peacocks. He's splendid, isn't he? But why not a dog, Marvin, if you were feeling lonely? An Airedale. You always liked Airedales."

"The truth is, Adelaide, I didn't exactly choose to have peacocks. They just sort of happened."

"How do peacocks just sort of happen?" she asked, looking at him uncertainly.

"Like anything else. These fell off a truck. Let's set up the bar."

When they had finished this, and set the dining-room table for the buffet, it was nearly four o'clock.

"They'll be coming soon," Adelaide said, lighting a cigarette. "I hope this won't prove to be embarrassing to you in any way, Marvin. I don't mean it to be."

But how could it not be, he wondered.

"Tell me something, Adelaide," he said. "Have you been ...seeing anyone?"

"I have a lover, yes," she said, and looked away. He was stunned; it was the last thing he expected. His mind roared and blundered through his confusion, trying to sort it out. Was he hurt? Yes, of course, but why? Come back to that. Shocked? Yes, he couldn't imagine it. For the first time, really, since she'd left, she had become palpably, concretely, a stranger. Fleetingly, he recalled what it was like making love with Adelaide. Would she be different with her lover, then? How could he know? But he knew. She would be different, changed, no matter how slightly, as it had been different for him with Joy. But what did that mean? Then his mind took hold of something and all the rest fell away.

"Then that was why," he said.

"That was not why," she said. "I only met him a month ago."

The guests began to arrive. They straggled in, embarrassed and reluctant, unsure what demeanor was appropriate to the occasion: Berny and Beatty, with whom they had taken a few trips; Howard and Rhoda, with whom for a long time they had played bridge on Monday nights; Allan and Julie, old friends of Adelaide's from college days; Otto Belsky; Adelaide's father; an Ethical Culture leader whose name Marvin couldn't recall though he had officiated at their wedding (how had Adelaide managed to dig him up?); Milton and Sally, cousins of Marvin's he hadn't seen in years; and, finally, Sidney and Sylvia Mermelstein, invited the previous night by Marvin on some confused impulse, instantly regretted, to connect his present with his past.

As each of the guests arrived, the greetings ranged from strained to excessively jovial. Marvin buried his discomfort in the business of making and serving drinks, accomplished with such alacrity that before each guest had quite retrieved his hand from being shaken he found it holding a glass. But what next, Marvin thought with mounting panic. Well, it was Adelaide's show. Her composure was total. She beamed and kissed and clasped hands and graciously accepted compliments on how well she looked, exactly as though she were the mother of the bride. She had never met the Mermelsteins, but she welcomed them warmly.

Marvin was at the bar mixing a drink for Mr. Fowler, Adelaide's father, when Joy made her entrance.

"It looks more like a rapprochement," Mr. Fowler was saying wistfully, "but I don't suppose from the invitation it's that. I always liked you, Marvin."

Marvin looked across the room in time to see Adelaide take Joy's hand with some bewilderment.

"Only a woman could have thought up anything as harebrained as this," Henry Fowler said, shaking his head. "And only a woman like my daughter. She always had this nutty, humorless streak. I don't know where she got it from. Her mother was a very sensible woman."

"Excuse me, Henry," Marvin said, thrusting Mr. Fowler's drink into his hand. He strode across the room to where Joy and Adelaide stood, hands still clasped.

"Joy Barron," Joy was saying. "A friend of Marvin's. I don't think I know you, either."

"This is a neighbor's child," Marvin cut in. "She's doing a study on suburbia and she sometimes pops in to ask me personal questions. Joy, this is my wife. My ex-wife."

"Oh, I am pleased to meet you, Mrs. Newton. I feel as though we're old friends."

Marvin grabbed her firmly by the arm and led her away. "What the hell are you doing here?" he asked.

"I was passing by and I saw all these cars," Joy said. "So I thought, oh goody a party. But then I watched some people go in and they looked so miserable that I thought maybe you'd killed yourself. I'm so glad you're all right."

"Joy, you'll have to leave."

"Why? It is a party, isn't it? But why is your wife here? Have you made up?"

"I can't explain now. I'll tell you about it another time."

"But I'm not going," Joy said sweetly. "It would look awfully peculiar and suspicious if I were to leave the minute I got here. Do you mind if I take notes?"

Marvin groaned and, turning his back on Joy, went back to the bar. Otto Belsky was making himself a drink. Marvin took it out of his hand and downed it in one gulp, then made them both fresh drinks.

"You don't look too good, Marvin, old buddy,"

Otto said. "Is it going to be some kind of roasting?"

"How the hell do I know! No, I don't think so." People were beginning to settle into chairs and sofas and all around him there was a hum of uncomfortable small talk. The Ethical Culture leader, a short, elderly man in a black silk suit, stood at the window, his back to the room.

"There are peacocks out there," Marvin heard him say softly.

"I've got an electric fiddle," Marvin said to Otto. "And a Fender Blender. I've written a tune. I'll play it for you later."

The room grew still. Marvin looked up and saw that Adelaide had signaled for attention.

"I want to thank you all for coming," she said in her clear, carrying voice. "This is an unusual occasion and I imagine some of you must be feeling imposed upon, so a few words of explanation are in order." She clasped her hands, pausing to collect her thoughts. "Those of you who knew Marvin and me at all well saw us as a reasonably happily married couple, as we were. We had problems, as everyone does, but for the most part our life together was serene. I believe we were, and are, genuinely fond of one another and I think that is a kind of love. But sometimes a marriage outlives its reasons. One stays in it simply because one is in it." She paused again. Outside, a peacock screamed and everyone turned toward the open window. Adelaide waited a moment and then went on.

"When a marriage of any duration comes to an end, for whatever reasons, there is always a sadness. Sometimes there is anger and often there is pain, but I think the end of this marriage is marked by neither of these. For me, the most painful thing about the end of my marriage was the mechanics of it. Marriages end in lawyers' offices with the negotiation of matters that have to do with money and property, the only tie apart from the children that remains and is recognized by society. It's precisely because of this, because I find it shameful and undignified, that I've asked you here to be present at a divorce service I've asked Dr. Ashley to conduct." She nodded across the room to Dr. Ashley who, rubbing his hands, now came forward. Adelaide sat down in the only empty chair, next to Joy who, Marvin saw, was wide-eyed with disbelief.

For a moment, Dr. Ashley merely looked at the faces in the room while he polished his glasses with a handkerchief. When his gaze reached across to Marvin, it lingered there speculatively and, it seemed to Marvin, who faltered beneath it, a little sadly. Marvin felt his anger begin to gather.

The old man replaced his glasses carefully, cleared his throat, and began.

"As Adelaide Fowler Newton has so painfully discovered, there is no ceremony for divorce. Ceremonies are formal ways of joining together to express our deepest feelings --- happiness at the coming together of two who have pledged to share their lives, joy at the birth of a child, sorrow and the need for comfort at the loss of a loved one." He removed his glasses again, and held them up to the light. He had missed a smudge, which he again attacked with his handkerchief. Since he was not reading from a text, Marvin wondered with annoyance why he had to see so clearly, then realized that he must be at a loss.

"But what is a divorce?" he continued. "It is a cancellation, a nonevent. And what do we feel about it?

There is no community of feeling; our attitudes toward divorce are as confused and varied at the personal level as at the religious and state levels.

"When a divorce occurs soon after the marriage, then the marriage was simply a mistake. A few year later, a divorce usually means that there has been some change that could not be assimilated. But the end of a long marriage is more complex. After all the years of sharing their joys and sorrows, burdens and laughter, bodies and friends and children, what happens that two people decide that their life together is no longer tenable? Unlike marriage, which is a single unifying event, every divorce is two experiences; the parties to it become more dramatically separate than any other two people at that particular moment. Why? What has happened? I wonder if I could trouble you for a glass of water?"

The room was totally silent while Marvin carried out this mission. The doctor took a few dainty sips, cleared his throat again, and continued.

"We are often little more than children when we marry," he said. His voice had risen and its resonance filled the room. "As children, we marry in a kind of innocence. What have we become, in our forties and fifties, after the long years, when we decide to unmarry? Have we lost our innocence? It has often seemed to me that those of us who come to this do so out of a yearning to regain that lost innocence, that lost youth. Men often seek it in a new and younger love that brings them to a pitch of feeling beyond what they believed they could ever again feel." Marvin glanced across at Joy. Oh, blah, blah, blah, he thought.

"Women, most of their lives concerned with their children and home," continued the Ethical Culturist, "their identities bound up in the success of their husbands and children, often feel when their work is in fact over, tragically robbed of their own lives and, if they have the strength for it, they may strike out to discover who they really are. But the common denominator in every marriage is this: a day comes when we understand that time is running out and that the way it is is the way it is going to be."

He paused again and closed his eyes behind the spotless glasses. There was a gentle stirring in the room and the sound of Joy scribbling in her notebook.

"So, then, the change, the restlessness, if you will, that arises in these years can be seen as an affirmation of life, a second spring, no matter how foolishly it may be acted upon. Or it can be seen, as it so often is, as disloyalty, immaturity, selfishness, a refusal to accept one's responsibilities, to grow old and make one's peace. Where, then, does the truth lie?

"Frankly, I don't know the answer," Dr. Ashley said, his voice softening. "I would like to see if we can find some answers from the two people who are responsible for this gathering. Adelaide?"

Adelaide's answer, clear and ringing, came without a moment's hesitation.

"The truth of whether we are behaving foolishly or wisely," she said, "lies in the degree to which we understand ourselves."

Marvin leaped to his feet. "My God, Adelaide, what are you saying?" he shouted. "That all conscious behavior is wise?"

"If we're people of good conscience, yes."

"Ah, but how can we be sure of that?"

"If we take the trouble to understand ourselves, then we have to take our own honor and moral sense on faith."

"Bullshit!" Marvin said. "Literature and history books are filled with people who thought they understood their motives, who thought themselves right, and who nonetheless behaved foolishly, even evilly. Think of Hitler, for one."

"Just a moment," Dr. Ashley said, raising a hand. "We're getting rather far afield. I think we need to get back to specifics. Adelaide, this is a personal event. We want to know your particular feelings, to know what motivated you. Obviously, you called for an observance of your divorce not only out of some need for symmetry, which is, if I may say so, sentimental, but because you didn't feel entirely finished with your marriage. The fact that you needed Marvin to share this experience with you would indicate that there is still something you want from him."

"That's true," Adelaide said, her voice a little less sure.

"It's only the compulsive housekeeper syndrome," Marvin said, bitterly angry. "Women can't bear the messiness of loose ends."

"You asked about my feelings," Adelaide said. "Marvin and I spent more than half our lives together and, of course, I'll always have feelings for him and for that part of my life." Here her voice nearly broke.

At this point, Joy raised a hand and without waiting for acknowledgement said, "I think if you examine the question of what kept the marriage going, you'll find the answer to what it was that broke it apart." Adelaide looked startled. Marvin, from the perch he had resumed on the windowsill, was startled, too, then pleased. "My observation, for what it's worth," Joy said, not waiting for Adelaide to collect herself, "is that too many marriages are like the suburbanite's dream of the one perfect shopping center, where everything is available at discount prices and the parking is easy."

Adelaide's face lit slowly with a broad, appreciative smile. "Yes," she said. "Exactly. Convenience. Comfort. Habit. And finally, alas, boredom." She paused as the smile left her face. She might have been alone in the room. "In the last years, I felt that I was drowning in the marriage and would die, and I saw that Marvin had long ago died."

"Speak for yourself!" Marvin shouted. Adelaide looked at him across the room.

"He was perfectly content," she said, not taking her eyes from his face. "Everything he did was exactly what he had been doing for years. He was entirely predictable. And with me, it was the same." She took a deep breath. "But I became frightened. I needed to discover if I could still feel. I wanted to dare something."

She sat down . She was finished.

"And did you?" Dr. Ashley asked.

"Yes."

Marvin, turning his back to the room, looked out the window. He wanted to ask why she couldn't have changed within the marriage; he would have permitted her anything. But not here, not among these strangers. Strangers? Adelaide was the stranger; he had never really known her. Perhaps that was the answer to his question.

Outside, the peahen was perched on the roof of the garage, blinking her eyes. Below, the peacock slowly spread his incredible fan into the dying sun, its orange light reflected like hindsight in the eyes of the cock's plumage. Like the peacocks, like Joy, like Adelaide's leaving, like the dinner invitations, Marvin thought, the things in his life were unchosen, things that happened to him. He restrained an urge to leap through the window and kick the peacock to death.

But then he understood that what had happened to Adelaide had begun to happen to him as well. One of them had had to break free to free them both. The arithmetic of change, as Dr. Ashley had implied, is that sometimes one equals two. He turned back to the room and looked across at Joy. Did he want her? He didn't know. Did he want Adelaide back? He didn't know that, either, but he knew that if he did, what would win her would be whatever vitality there might be in his newly emerging self.

"Marvin," Dr. Ashley was saying, perhaps for the second time, "would you like to say anything?"

"No," Marvin said.

RALPH

"Ralph," she said. "Ralph."

She wasn't saying his name as injunction but as rhetoric. It was a sound in her mouth, a new thing she was trying though she had spoken it a thousand times. Abstract Ralph. She contorted her mouth into the grinding little leap from the rearguard guttural R forward to the flat A, up and up to the L and landed, finally, in exaggerated safety, all the way forward, blowing the PH through her lips as long as her breath held, so that the sound, his name, died like a wind.

"Raaaalph-ph-ph... What a silly sound."

He was half asleep. The sun, baking his back, was a yellow blanket snuggling him to the sand. He was nothing, a slice of Ralph, a sliver of meat in a nature sandwich.

"Nobody names their children Ralph anymore," she said.

What could be more innocent, since it was true? Still, he stirred uneasily, digging his toes deeper into the sand. Is there anything drier than dry sand? Can you proceed through drier to driest, or have you gone all the way when you've arrived at dry? She was going to be vicious; he could tell. The finality of dry. It ought to be a superlative, like excellent. It was wrong to proceed from dry to drier to driest. Once something was a little bit not dry it was something else. Moist. Damp. Dry was dry. It would be better to say nothing. Still, nobody named their children Herbert, either. Herbert was her husband's name. He'd bet there wasn't a Herbert on the beach under the age of twenty. So what?

"What kind of parents would name their only son Ralph?" she wondered, her voice idle, free of contempt. But he knew, he knew. He had the kind of parents who would name their only son Ralph. She'd never met his parents; there was no reason for her to attack them. But he didn't expect her to be reasonable. She was trying to diminish him; any means would do.

"I cherished and honored my parents," he murmured on the crest of a breaking wave.

"What kind of vision could they have had to connect with the sound of Ralph?" she persisted. "What could the sound of Ralph have conveyed to them? Did they think it poetic? Noble? Dignified? Cute? Courageous? It's such a nothing name. Didn't they have any imagination at all?"

They had named him for an uncle, his mother's brother, who had died in childhood.

"I might name a dog Ralph," she said. "Though only as a joke. Preferably a female dog."

He was tempted to mention Herbert. And they had named their sons Robert and Richard, a total failure of the imagination as far as he could see, a disgustingly arid affectation. But peace. He was nothing, a Ralph washed up by the sea, stranded, sundried. She was a gull, pecking. It was in the nature of things.

"I'm pretty sure there was never a president named Ralph," she said.

Herbert? he thought. Yes, Hoover. She could have Herbert Hoover.

"For that matter," he couldn't help mumbling, "I've never had a friend named Grover or Woodrow."

"A scientist? I can't think of a single scientist."

She was silent for a while. Perhaps, satisfied, her mind had moved elsewhere. Perhaps she'd seen something, someone she knew. That songwriter and his wife who were always standing on their heads. Yoga. His mother had had a drawer full of Christian Science literature. She had taken something called Dr. Von's Pills for an imaginary ulcer. He hadn't thought of that in years. Fads. Names were faddish.

"Not one. Can you think of a scientist?"

"Ralph Hippocrates," he said, "Ralph Euclid, Ralph Archimedes, Ralph Copernicus, Ralph Newton, Ralph Kepler." Herbert Galileo, Herbert Darwin, Herbert Einstein... His stomach muscles were tense. He had inherited, or learned, his mother's stomach. He could get up and throw himself into the sea, wash himself clean of his Ralphness, polish his skin, settle his stomach. But when he climbed out again she would be there waiting to finish.

"What time is it?" he asked.

"You're the only man I ever met who doesn't wear a watch. Even Dick and Bobby have been wearing watches since they were seven."

He groaned at this new charge against him, against his manliness. There was a time when she had considered his watchlessness part of his charm.

"Nevertheless," he said, "what time is it?"

"What do you mean, nevertheless?"

"I mean even so, or notwithstanding. I mean other considerations aside, what time is it?"

She wasn't going to tell him. She was going to punish him for his unadorned wrist.

"You have plenty of time," she said. "Your boat doesn't leave until four."

He knew when his boat left. He'd been taking it every Friday of the summer. He left on the four o'clock boat and Herbert arrived from the mainland on the six o'clock boat. On Mondays, they each reversed themselves. It was a simple arrangement. Herbert worked from nine to five at some business having to do with leather goods. Ralph had arranged his life so that he would never have to be anywhere at nine o'clock. He felt that this was a crucial difference between them. Herbert had a lot more money but Ralph's time was his own. He sometimes had deadlines, but they were dates on a calendar, not hours on a clock. He could cope with calendars.

"Saints? Generals? Kings?" she resumed.

"Long line of kings," he said. "From Ralph the Ready to Ralph the Twelfth."

He had met Herbert only once at a big party on someone's sundeck. Ralph would probably not have noticed him at all, and he certainly wouldn't have judged him, had Herbert been anyone but her husband. Instead, everything that was Herbert, even his chunky good looks, had become instantly distasteful. It had taken Ralph a long time to get used to the idea that she had no intention of leaving Herbert to marry him.

"But why should I leave Herbert?" she had asked. "It's a perfectly happy marriage."

"Oh, you idiot," he had said gently, in his innocence. "How can it be a good marriage if you need me?"

"Statesman? Athlete?" she went on. "Oh,

yes, there was that pitcher, wasn't there? The one who cried?"

He could tell her that Ralph was the name of a ghost once thought to haunt printing houses, but would that help his cause? He rolled over onto his side and squinted at her through his eyelashes. She sat with her chin on her knees, supple as a cat, every line of her perfect. She was one of those women who cannot make a graceless movement. She was a wonder at tennis, a tireless dancer, absolutely faultless in bed. Every part of her worked precisely as every part of the human body had been meant to work. She was totally physical and he wished to God she would shut up.

"What are you trying to say?" he asked.

She scooped up a handful of sand and let it run slowly through her fingers. "I'm not trying to say anything. I'm just musing."

It was because she was so physical that she took lovers. Making love was as free and necessary to her as breathing and had nothing to do with morality. She had always had lovers and, he knew, she always would. He had made the mistake of falling in love with her.

"Why don't you say what you mean?" he asked, though he was in terror that she would. "Why don't you stop and think what it is you're really trying to say?"

She was tired of him; she had used him up. He had been too compliant and failed to provide her with enough drama. He shouldn't have fit so easily into her schedule. But no. In the beginning he had made scenes, protested, wanted her to leave Herbert, wanted to confront Herbert himself. But she had prevailed. There were the boys. She was happy in her marriage. And she was careful to protect Herbert from any knowledge of Ralph, not because she felt guilt but because she knew it would give Herbert pain and she had no need to punish him.

"I'm not really trying to say anything," she said, not looking at him, prostrate before her, brown and thin from his summer of love, but at a point beyond him in the middle distance. "How clean the air is in September. The light is so different." It was. The days all week had been sparkling, brilliant. He closed his eyes again, lulled. There had been so many pointless, unfocused quarrels in the last weeks. Perhaps this one was over. They had become so domestic together. That was it, of course. She saved the petty domestic quarrels for him. It was he, Ralph, who kept Herbert and his marriage serene.

"I was only hearing the name Ralph in a new way," she said, "and it struck me, suddenly, as a terribly insignificant sound. I'm merely trying to think if there's ever been anyone of any real consequence named Ralph."

"You think people are condemned by their names?"

"Shaped, maybe. But can you think of anyone? An artist? Millionaire? Poet? Philosopher? Writer?"

"Emerson," he said.

She was silent. Thank God for Emerson!

"That doesn't count," she said.

He sat up, startled, and stared at her.

"Why doesn't it count ?"

"It's Ralph Waldo Emerson."

"So what?" he shouted, enraged. "What if it's Ralph Waldo Emerson?"

She thought. She had still not met his eyes.

"Well, take John Fitzgerald Kennedy, for instance," she said. "And Jacqueline Bouvier Kennedy. They're people with well-known middle names. But you can still say John Kennedy. And Jacqueline Kennedy. But you never heard anyone say Ralph Emerson, did you?"

He stared at her for a long time. He hated her, but he saw that she was still beautiful. She would never grow old. One day one of her lovers would kill her. Push her off a boat or something. She was unrelentingly cruel, but he knew that it would be a long time before he stopped loving her. He knew that he was a fool and that wisdom required a death of the heart. He could already feel, undigested in his stomach, the long bleak days ahead.

"You win," he whispered, getting to his feet. He brushed the sand from his chest. "I'm going."

She looked up at him. Because of the sun, he was unable to read her eyes.

"Goodbye, Ralph," she said.

"Goodbye, Shirley," he said.

THE CHASTITY
OF MAGDA WICKWIRE

Magda Wickwire spent her birthday alone, feeling feverish and close to hysteria, which was the way literature had led her to believe brides often feel. It wasn't her bridal day, merely a birthday, of which she felt she'd had a few too many, But it happened that this birthday coincided with the day when a young man named Arlen Abbington was being graduated, without particular distinction, from a small New England college where he had majored in political science. Now, suitably equipped, he was presumed to be ready for the world.

Magda had never met Arlen Abbington, but it was upon his readiness for the world that her own had come, in the last decade, to depend. The moment Arlen's young hand closed on his diploma, the last obstacle to Magda's happiness would be removed. The last except for the divorce, but there was no reason why that shouldn't be accomplished swiftly, and certainly no reason for them to wait for it to be final. She had spent so much time waiting! Waiting had become a second heart, beating like a clock inside her breast. The waiting had never completely unnerved her, however, for she had the gift of patience; but it had made the years so slow, so long, filled though they were with the endless details and duties of her academic life. And hadn't she, after all, a glorious fulfillment to be waiting for, and the solace that Harold was waiting, too? It was not that she was like so many of the faculty women she knew, women who were waiting for a miracle that would never happen, or in whom all hope had long since died, turning their hearts to stone. She had love, she had Harold, she had a date, marked on calendars everywhere, when her waiting would come to an end. The tenth of June. The day of Arlen Abbington's graduation.

Arlen was Harold Abbington's third and youngest child, and Harold, a fastidious father, felt obliged to subordinate his own happiness to the needs of his children. He would not cut his moorings until his children were launched. He had escorted one daughter into marriage and another into a career as a librarian. Now, at last, Arlen, who had taken so long about it, being an indifferent student, had achieved his education and set Harold and Magda free. Magda, who had come to hate Arlen, though she knew him to be innocent, gave herself the special birthday present of forgiving him and, having done so, regretted not being in a position to send him a graduation present. She would have enjoyed the quiet irony of giving a gift to Arlen, and she knew exactly what it would have been: an expensive wristwatch.

Time. How sluggishly the ponderous years moved while her life, her youth, flew by. She bent herself with vigor to rebuffing the physical incursions of age. She watched her diet, creamed her face with hormones, submitted her flesh to a masseuse, and slept in chin straps. Twice a week she went to a modern dance class where, in leotards, she writhed, painful and contorted and martyred. It wasn't vanity that drove her. Time had cheated her; why, then, shouldn't she cheat time? If love was late, it would find her young. She would keep herself supple and smooth for Harold. For that, she would gladly suffer.

It was during a two-week seminar at Crabapple Hill that Magda and Harold discovered they were hopelessly in love. They had met several times before on similar occasions when their academic duties had brought them together, but her memory of their earlier meetings was vague, and this, because of the intensity of their newfound love, was a puzzle to her, one that she often contemplated. How close she had come to missing the focus of her life; how marvelous that she hadn't missed it after all!

Harold Abbington was a middle-sized man with reddish hair and a rather romantic moustache. He wore tweed suits with leather elbow patches and favored solid color knitted ties. He smoked a pipe that went out often enough to keep him busy at it: to knock out the dottle against the heel of his loafers (outdoors, of course; indoors he used a folding, three-pronged tool and was careful not to miss the ashtray), to draw from his pocket an oilskin pouch, to stuff the pipe's bowl with fresh tobacco, to tamp it down, to light endless matches, to suck and puff, and all the while to manage to look absorbed, not in what he was doing, but in something far graver or more amusing, as if the business with his pipe was a function of his body in which he was not really involved.

If Magda had noticed Harold on those earlier occasions, she had failed to notice anything to set him apart. This, too, became a source of wonder, for once she knew that she loved him, she saw that he was unique. How had she missed noticing the whiteness of his teeth, the sensitivity of his long, delicate hands, the charm of his nose with its boyish scattering of freckles, the nobility of his gently sloping brow, the flat perfection of his small ears, the solemnity of his gray eyes? He became entirely beautiful to her, and her failure to discern this beauty at once distressed her. It indicated a lack of perception that was entirely at odds with her character, which was poetic. She had had three poems published in highly respectable quarterlies with small circulations. These poems were hardly enough to give her a reputation, but they had helped to forge her sense of herself as a woman of taste and sensitivity.

Their love was unfolded to them one morning over breakfast. The oatmeal was tepid and gluey, but she had eaten it anyway, hoping it would give her strength for the morning lectures which she dreaded. She was a woman who didn't hit her stride until midday, when the sun was at its zenith.

Magda had always thought of herself as a "sun" person and it wasn't until Harold that she became a "moon" person.

She ate her oatmeal, alert to the conversation of the people at her table, none of whom was more than slightly acquainted with another, since they had gathered from universities and colleges all across the eastern seaboard.

"Academically, this was a rich year for me," Harold Abbington said, in answer to an expression of boredom from a fierce little Sarah Lawrence woman named Potter. "I was asked to give a colloquium course and I found it consistently exciting."

"Rot!" was what Magda, who was closer, thought she heard Miss Potter grunt, but Harold Abbington must have heard it as "What?" Encouraged to go on, he said, "I was compelled to read straight through the major classics. It's quite an experience to see how well they stand up."

Magda rested her spoon in the oatmeal, where it slowly sank, swallowed as if by quicksand. She looked at Harold Abbington, seeing only his moustache, and thought about how well the classics stand up. What else would make them classics?

"But some of the implications are disturbing," Harold continued. "Aeschylus and Thucydides were aware of most of the things that we are aware of today."

"I've always meant to take on Thucydides," Magda said shyly. "And Tacitus, too."

"Well, good Lord, do!" Harold Abbington commanded, and Magda's gaze moved from his moustache to his mouth, which was pink and firm and which he promptly parted to soften his injunction with a smile full of white, even teeth. "It's so frightening to realize that the classic historians knew so much and that, in all these centuries, it's done so little good."

"Yes," Magda breathed, deciding to abandon the oatmeal entirely. "After all the wisdom and warning of the period of the great tragedians, the Greeks went right ahead in the Peloponnesian War and did everything they'd been warned against."

"With the unhappiest consequences," Harold said, and they looked at each other and smiled.

"Pass the sugar," Miss Potter said in her deep, angry voice, and both Magda and Harold reached at once for the sugar bowl, which lay midway between them. Their hands touched. Magda was the first to withdraw, for she had felt more than accident in that touch. A current of sympathy, she was sure, had passed between them. Miss Potter was given the sugar.

"Great literature enables us to contemplate life richly," Magda said after a moment, reluctant to leave the subject that was binding her to this man, "but it doesn't seem to affect our behavior much."

"Or even to afford permanent purgative satisfaction," Harold added. Magda raised her gaze to Harold's and, a little embarrassed, they contemplated one another. His eyes were gray and clear. They were regarding her with interest. They had agreed on doom and found love. She flushed and bent to her coffee.

That afternoon, when the day's lectures were over, they met again by chance. She was strolling back to the women's dormitory, enjoying the sunlight now that she was able to feel, with relief, that she had acquitted herself well. There had been a ticklish moment when she'd been unable to remember a questioned line of Gerard Manley Hopkins, but then it had flooded back and thereafter she'd been in complete control. Now, like an omen of luck, a regal fritillary fluttered by, its wings like flames in the sun, and there was Harold Abbington walking toward her.

"Miss Wickwire," he said, placing his pipe between his delightful teeth, "I believe I've read one of your poems."

"Oh?"

"Yes. 'Witchburning.' In the *Pachysandra Review*."

"Ah."

"I found it immensely affecting."

"Thank you."

"Delicate and fragile as a wildflower."

She smiled modestly.

"And yet so deeply felt. You are, if I may say

so, a woman with rare insight."

"Oh, it's such a small poem," she sighed, glowing.

"I wonder if you'd care to have a cocktail with me before dinner."

"I'd love to."

"They've favored me, Lord knows why, with a room of my own. Since it's more studio than, ah, sleeping room I'm sure we can meet there with perfect propriety."

She was a woman who had given careful thought to the differences between lust and love. She had led a cloistered life, guarded into her majority by a minister father who treated her with such gentle love and who was so clearly afraid to fail her (her mother had died early) that she, of course, could not fail him. She remained pure. In her earlier twenties she had fallen in love with a distant cousin who had gone to war and died of an intestinal ailment before their love, which had grown passionate by airmail, could be consummated. She had tried to remain true to his memory. After her father's death, a time came when it was no longer clear to her to whose memory she was being true, and she began to suspect that the dead were tyrants, albeit against their wishes. She was ready to give herself again in love, but by this time the opportunities were few. She taught at a small girls' college where the men on the faculty were either intensely married or clearly uninterested in women. An instructor in the Romance language department had approached her once, but he had been impossibly obese.

Harold Abbington didn't strike her as a lustful man. He was thoughtful and intelligent and had responded to her poem. His socks were held up as carefully as his tie was knotted. He handled his pipe and his speech with thoughtful restraint. She felt no compunction about meeting him in his studio. He described to her where it was, and they parted.

She spent a long time deciding what to wear. Recently, she had begun to favor flamboyant clothes and had collected several richly embroidered flaring skirts and scoop-necked blouses that went well with her Mexican jewelry. In the end, however, she decided on an understated sleeveless black cotton (her arms were good) and her cultured pearl necklace. Because it was still early, she stood in front of a mirror staring at the white oval of her face. Her eyes were large and dark and a little mournful and perhaps the feature that most inspired men to protectiveness, or maybe it was her height, for she was barely five feet tall. Her hair was pulled back a little too severely and she tried to soften it. A face, particularly one's own, stared at objectively for any length of time begins to lose its meaning, becoming a blur of orifices and excrescences --- an arbitrary pudding --- and Magda had to turn away from the mirror, thinking how ridiculously and functionally our selves are encased. Possibly there was a poem here.

When she got to Harold Abbington's room, she saw that he had already mixed a small pitcher of martinis and laid out a plate of crackers. She was pleased that he was masterful enough to assume that she would drink whatever he provided. They sat opposite each other, their knees only inches apart, and sipped their martinis.

"Magda," he said. "May I call you that?"

"Please."

"A beautiful name. It suits you perfectly. You have a special glow."

She could feel herself blushing and she tried to hide it by coughing, but Harold, apparently not noticing, began to tell her of his college and of the associates he had been privileged to know and, in some cases, to supersede in his rise in the academic hierarchy. He spoke with a combination of wit, enthusiasm, and modesty that she found delightful. During their second martini, he asked her about her own career, and by the end of the third martini she felt that they were old friends. They came to a pause in the conversation, a comfortable silence in which they smiled happily at each other. Then, a look of sadness clouded Harold's face.

"Magda, I feel I must tell you this," he said. "I have a wife."

"Oh," she said, her heart sinking, her voice rising in an effort to keep her sunken heart from showing. "I thought you might. You look so well cared for."

"And three children," Harold said gravely.

"How nice. What are they? I mean, boys or girls?"

"The two oldest are girls. The youngest, who's thirteen, is a boy."

She smiled in a way, she hoped, that would tell him how lovely she thought it that he had two daughters and a son who was thirteen. She could think of nothing to say.

"I tell you this at once," he said, "because I've fallen in love with you."

"Oh," she said again, her heart rising and her voice sinking, "how dreadful."

"But it isn't dreadful at all," he said. "Though, of course, it is. I've fallen in love in a way that I no longer believed was possible for me. I've fallen in love --- joyously."

The martini trembled in her glass.

"You hardly know me," she murmured.

"I have known you always," he said. "I have known you and waited for you since the first moment when, as a small boy, I was moved by beauty."

Her eyes filled with tears. "You're terribly romantic," she said.

He put down his glass and leaned toward her. "But time has cheated me," he said. "It's brought you to me too late."

Too late. She was no longer a girl. He had all that family. But she was prepared to negotiate.

"Time has cheated me, too," she said.

"Tell me."

She told him her life. He listened, his eyes solemn and adoring. When she told him about the distant cousin, she saw that he was disturbed, and so she came quickly to his death, anxious to spare him. She tried to keep her voice steady, but she knew that, in telling him her life and the way in which she told it, she was letting him know that she consented to his love and was equal to it.

When she had finished, he put down his glass and, taking hers, put it down beside his own. Then, leaning forward again, he kissed her chastely on the brow. It was not what she wanted. She wanted him to sweep her into his arms, to crush her, to kiss her with passion. She wanted an embrace that would bury her self-consciousness. She had no idea how to bring it about.

He drew back and stared down at his hands, which lay forlornly in his lap.

"What are we to do, Harold?" she said. It was the first time she had said his name.

"I don't know. I can't leave my wife. The children."

It was no more than she expected. How could she love him if he were not an honorable man, a responsible man. But still...

"Perhaps we shouldn't meet again," she said with courage.

His look was despairing. "I don't think I could bear that," he said. She reached out and touched his cheek, feeling bold, and said, "I'm glad. I couldn't bear it, either. At least, not yet." And now he did take her in his arms and kiss her, though it was difficult, for she was sitting and he was half leaning out of his chair. She hadn't been kissed much, and never before by a moustache, and she was distracted from the meaning of the kiss by the combination of the softness of his mouth and the toughness of his bristle. The sensation was peculiar, and she was just deciding that she didn't mind it when the dinner bell rang and he withdrew.

In the days that followed, they met as often as possible without risking gossip. They couldn't afford a scandal. They met at meals and when the day's seminars and lectures were over and the afternoon still bright, they took long walks up and down Crabapple Hill. They gathered wildflowers and Harold sang old English ballads in a pleasant tenor voice. When they felt they were entirely alone, he would take her hand and swing it gaily as they walked. Often they would sit in a meadow, or if the sun was too bright, under a tree, he with his head in her lap, and they would talk and talk and talk. They had endless things to talk about. They had shared so much in their separate lives, books and music and plays. Their tastes were so similar, their passions so parallel, it was hard to believe there were all those years when they hadn't even known each other. There was so much to discover about each other and in that discovery they found they were rediscovering themselves.

"In love we're so increased," Magda said, and it was true. She was the sleeping princess, and his love was returning her to life. More than an object of love, he was a mirror in which she saw herself anew. The reflection given back to her, colored by his love, was one in which she found it possible to love herself. And it was the same for him.

***

Their two weeks were almost at an end. The weather, conspiring in their idyll, had been exceptionally fine, and on this day the cloudless sky was so serenely blue that it was impossible to believe that there could ever again be, anywhere in the world, storms and anger and violence. She sat with her back against a tree. His head was in her lap, and she stroked his hair, marveling at its silkiness.

"Your hair is so fine," she said, "and your moustache so bristly." She was almost completely happy. A bee droned in the tall, dry grass, and overhead, in the tree, a bird trilled a sudden lovely note.

"C sharp," Harold said. He had perfect pitch. She smiled down at him adoringly.

"Oh, Harold," she said, "it's almost over."

"It will never be over."

No, she wasn't completely happy. Two things stood in the way: he would be going back to his wife, and, also, she wanted more than his tenderness, his gentle kisses and his held hand.

"I'm a passionate man," he said, "but I won't

sully you with my lust."

She demurred. This was noble, surely, but in the circumstances, a little foolish. In love, one isn't supposed to be sullied by physical passion. The body has its voices, too, and they must be allowed to speak. She wasn't quite bold enough to say this, perhaps because she was a little afraid of her body, unsure of its voice.

"You mustn't put me on a pedestal," she murmured.

"I haven't put you there. You are there."

"I'm not so pure," she said. "I want our love to have its fullest expression."

"You are pure, my darling, the purest thing I've ever known. I won't violate that purity until I have the right to do so."

"The right?"

"When I can belong to you entirely. Only then will I feel I have the right to take you entirely." His voice trembled.

"But Harold."

They hadn't discussed his wife. Magda had tried not even to think of her. But it was useless to deny her. She existed. She was at the seashore with the children, but her head was as much in Magda's lap as was Harold's. Magda felt a sudden chill and bravely tried to imagine this shadowy woman who called Harold "my husband," who had borne his children, whose years of intimacy, now, admitted to Magda's consciousness, threatened to obliterate the beauty and reality of this moment. Harold belonged to his wife, not to poor deluded Magda. Still, she trusted Harold. He had given her every reason to trust him. He had asked nothing of her but to be allowed to love her, taking nothing but her heart. That he'd come so quickly to their love, to this need of her, could only mean that his wife had failed him. As though he'd read her thoughts, he bagan to talk about his wife.

"We were so young," he said, "and the children started coming almost at once. I thought I loved her then, in the beginning. I was more innocent than Amelia. She had a way of deciding things. I needed that then, being so unsure of myself. I was a lonely boy. I can't remember my mother, I was terrified of my father, and other boys made fun of me."

"Poor Harold."

"I was a dreamer and bad at games."

"Dearest."

"Amelia literally swept me off my feet. She was so firm and sure and practical. I know it sounds brutal and unkind, but it has come to be like living with ... well, a certified public accountant."

"My poor darling."

"We've grown so far apart that, if it weren't for the children, we'd have separated years ago."

Relieved, Magda continued to stroke his hair with a hand that was, thank heaven, small and pale and delicate.

"She's not my true wife," he said. "You are my true wife."

He lifted his head from her lap and was about to fold her in his arms when they spied Miss Potter briskly bounding toward them. They leaped apart. Harold found his pipe and put it between his teeth, and Magda contemplated the horizon as Miss Potter charged forward, oblivious of them, though they sat directly in her path. Her target was the shade of their tree, and not until she had stumbled across Harold's feet did she realize that it was occupied.

"I'm nearsighted," she apologized, sitting beside them. "I suppose everyone here is. But I can't bear to walk with my glasses on because the landscape is so ostentatious."

"Oh, do you think so?" Magda said. "I find it rather gentle."

"So damn much green!" Miss Potter said, drawing a banana from the folds of her voluminous skirt and beginning, methodically, to strip it. "Give me a dirty gray city any day. Country makes me nervous." She offered to share her banana with them, and when they declined, she took a huge bite of it. "All those trees! Just standing about. What do they want?"

It was an unanswerable question. They sat and watched Miss Potter eat her banana while the afternoon dwindled.

***

Harold's first letter to Magda assured her that, although sixty miles separated them, in his thoughts they were as one. Besides, the new superhighway made it possible to bridge the gap in little more than an hour. His second letter told her that he couldn't live without her, that he had given much thought to their situation and had reached certain decisions. In order to discuss these decisions, they arranged to meet for lunch at a town midway between their campuses.

On the appointed day, Magda drove to their rendezvous with a heart that managed to soar and flutter at the same time. Away from Crabapple Hill and back in more familiar surroundings, the shape of their romance had seemed to alter. It wasn't that she doubted their love; it was that in retrospect it seemed too perfect not to have been dreamed. She was afraid it would slip away and be lost, as dreams do --- that it wasn't tangible enough to endure.

Her first sight of Harold reassured her. They met at an inn in a small village, the perfect and appropriate kind of place that only someone as remarkable as Harold could have had the luck to find. The inn was dark and cool, all mahogany and copper, burnished with time. Harold was there, waiting for her. She slipped in quietly and was rewarded with a moment in which to view him before he saw her. He was smoking his pipe. He looked troubled and tragic, and her heart went out to him. She wanted to take him in her arms and soothe him. He saw her then, his face brightening, and they crossed the room quickly toward each other. For a moment, she was sure he was going to kiss her, but he only clasped her hands.

"Magda, Magda," he said.

They had a martini before lunch, and the lunch itself was excellent: an omelet, fried potatoes, wilted lettuce salad. Only the placemats marred the atmosphere, scalloped-edged paper doilies with a map showing their exact location on Route 82. A tablecloth would been so much nicer, for the place mats were insubstantial islands separating them, reminding them that they were transients.

He had missed her. She had missed him. He loved her. She loved him. He couldn't live without her. Nor could she live without him. Life had become meaningless. Life, she now saw, had always been meaningless. Could she wait? If she must, she could wait. For how long? Forever, if need be. Not forever, they didn't have forever. He had fixed a time. The very night of the day Arlen was graduated from college, he would come to her; they would never be apart again. Yes she could wait the nine years he reckoned it would be. He would make it up to her. They wouldn't, after all, be so old. The years that remained would be the best years, the mature and ripe years. It would be an adventure, a new life. What were nine years against the eternity of a love like theirs? Yes, yes, yes.

But meanwhile...

"Oh, Harold," she said, suddenly inspired. "it's Saturday. We don't have to be back until Monday, do we? Let's stay here. It's such a charming place. Do let's stay and make this our place."

He stared at her. Then, taking her hand and clasping it, he said, "Magda, you have great courage, my darling. But no, you must help me to be strong. It's a struggle for me, but we mustn't debase our love. We must keep it pure or it won't keep."For a moment, she thought she might hate him and was tempted to say something that would truly shock him. But she could think of nothing, and the moment passed. He was there, with his clear eyes and his gentle hands and his beautiful flat ears, and she was back in the Victorian novel of her life, where she would have to find a way, for nine years, to remain.

She drove back to school and plunged herself into the affairs of her college. She lectured ferociously. She gave difficult assignments so that she would have endless papers to grade. She took on extra duties. She helped decorate the new Meditation Lounge, making trips to the city to choose suitably inspirational fabrics. She gave little teas for her better students, where they chatted about how to combine marriage with careers and which courses would best fit them for their newly emancipated lives. She went to all the faculty meetings, many of which she was asked to chair because of her rare tact and her intricate knowledge of parliamentary procedure. She worked and studied and had four more poems published, and she was so assiduous that she became head of her department. Meanwhile, though she met Harold twice a month for lunch, her stack of letters from him grew and grew, moved from a desk drawer to a shoe box to a hatbox and, finally, to a huge corrugated cardboard box in which her winter coat had been delivered.

***

Today! The day of Arlen's graduation. Ten years it had taken. Ten years ground in the mill of the past. Still, there was plenty of time for life, she told herself. Over and over that day she ran to her mirror, assuring herself that time hadn't much damaged her. A hundred times she looked at the clock. Harold was coming that night, directly from Arlen's college, his bags packed the previous night, his wife informed some time in the past week. Over and over she tried to imagine the encounter between Harold and his wife. Amelia could hardly be expected to mind, Harold had often assured her. She would probably be relieved, it was so long since there had been any pretense of love between them. She might be wounded, of course, to know that Harold had nurtured a secret love for ten years, but then she would be forced to recognize the sacrifice he had made for their children. She would respect that. She knew that he had never been really happy, that she had been unable and unwilling to give him the kind of love he needed. It had come up again and again in earlier years, in arguments she invariably won unfairly by dismissing his need as fantasy, adolescent nonsense. In a way, though he knew it was ignoble, he looked forward to the moment --- really, he could hardly wait --- when he told Amelia he was leaving her and why.

It was three days since Harold's last letter, the letter that told Magda, aside from the usual assurances of his love, that he couldn't predict the precise hour of his arrival, since that would depend on the length of the graduation ceremony. It was a letter filled with subdued gaiety, sparked by the kind of boyish excitement that is, without much success, being held in check by a man who doesn't dare allow himself the luxury of outright joy. The letter had brought tears to Magda's eyes. How she loved him! She would set him free, exactly as she'd waited all these years for him to set her free.

It was after seven at night. The apartment was filled with the smell of roasting meat and of the cake she had baked earlier. Baking was another of her recent accomplishments, learned in anticipation of Harold, since it had always seemed wasteful and indulgent to bake for herself alone. The cake had succeeded; it was a magnificent cake. She had bought a pastry tube and spent hours frosting and decorating the cake, inscribing upon it in large Gothic letters, HAPPY BIRTHDAY, HAROLD AND MAGDA. This birthday belonged to both of them. This was truly, in every sense, a birthday.

A dozen times she went to the window, which was opened wide to the soft June twilight. Over and over, she examined the rooms of her apartment, trying to see them as they would appear to Harold, who, for fear of compromising her, had never been there. She had straightened and dusted and polished, and it looked perfect; there was nothing to add or subtract. She would have preferred it to be winter, with a light snow falling, so that there could be the added cheer and coziness of a fire burning on the hearth, but there was enough romance in this warm spring evening with its promise of a moon to offset that loss.

There was nothing more to do but wait.

She sat, sipping sherry, jumping up at intervals to check the roast, to admire the cake, to look out the window. She tried to read, but it was impossible to focus her attention. She put a Mozart sonata on the record player and told herself that before it was over, Harold would be there; but she should have chosen something longer. She followed the Mozart with a Schubert quartet and sat listening to it with her eyes closed, listening beyond it for other sounds, growing a little tipsy. At intervals, cars approached in the street outside her window, and her heart leaped and sank as they passed. Then, at last, a car approached that didn't pass, and she sat, frozen, unable to go to the window, listening to the sound of the braking, the motor being cut, the car door slamming, a step, another, a sound at the door below and, finally, the pealing of her doorbell. For a moment, she sat in terror, unable to rise from her chair to press the answering buzzer that would admit him. In that moment, all the years of waiting crowded upon her, paralyzing her. She gulped the last of her sherry and, with an effort, rose and went to press the buzzer.

She heard him coming slowly up the stairs. It wasn't the step of a man bounding joyously to a long-deferred future. It was a slow and heavy step. But then she remembered that he would be weighed down with baggage, and she flung the door open to him.

He was not carrying bags, only his hat. He

stood at her threshold, trying to smile, and she saw at once that he was frightened. Well, why shouldn't he be frightened, she was frightened, too. She stepped aside to admit him and, closing the door, watched him carefully set his hat down on a table. It was a hat she hadn't seen before, a courageous hat with a gaily colored feather in its band.

"How nice," he said. "What a lovely room." He seemed surprised, almost relieved, and she wondered what he had been imagining. Had he thought it would be a pigsty, that she lacked taste, that it would be bare as a convent cell?

"I try not to become too attached to things," she said. "But I suppose it's unavoidable. One gathers possessions and, in spite of oneself, they become dear and familiar."

Why were they being so formal? It was as though they had just met, not at all the way it ought to be. Perhaps Arlen hadn't been graduated after all. She spurred herself to the sideboard and poured out two glasses of sherry. She handed him one and said, "You must be tired. Did it go all right?"

"The graduation? Yes, but it's been a long day."

She urged him to sit, offering him the deepest armchair, sitting across from him on the divan with her feet coiled beneath her, trying to show him that they weren't strangers.

"It's been a long day for me, too," she said. "The waiting. And I've been preparing our feast. Are you starved?"

He looked down at his glass. "No," he said. "Yes."

"Shall we eat right away?"

"Let's wait a bit," he said. "That's nice, the

Schubert. I've always been fond of it."

He was mumbling. She had never known him to mumble.

"Especially fond of it, I mean." he said.

"Are you all right, Harold?"

He looked up and for the first time, his eyes met hers. "Magda, I have something painful to tell you."

She felt herself turn pale. "You haven't told Amelia!" she said.

"Yes. That is, I started to tell her but she cut me short."

"What?" Magda said. "Why?"

"I don't know how to tell you. It's so difficult."

"Try," Magda said. "Inarticulateness has never been one of your problems."

"Well, you see, she's not, as you know, a young woman. Amelia. Do you have any whiskey? I think I'd prefer it to sherry.,"

She's ill, Magda thought, going to fetch him whiskey. She's going to have a painful, lingering illness.Years of operations and hospitals and invalidism, damn her. Her hand shook as she poured the whiskey. She poured quite a lot of it. Then, turning to bring it to him, she saw that he was suffering, too. Poor Harold.

"We never believed," Harold said, taking a long swallow, "---that is, we thought she was past all possibility of that kind --- that sort of thing."

She stared at him. "What sort of thing?"

He gulped more whiskey and coughed. "But it sometimes happens," he said.

"Harold, what are you trying to tell me?"

He drained his glass, and his face turned very

red. "She's going to have a baby," he said.

The Schubert was finished. Stunned, Magda sat listening to the lengthening silence, fumbling for a reaction to match the monstrousness of Harold's news, staring at him, waiting for him to look up so that she could find in his eyes the answer to her horror.

"You mean, you did that?" she said, at last. "All this time, you were, you've been...?"

He looked up, surprised. "It meant nothing, Magda. It was perfectly meaningless."

She sat transfixed, unable to do more than echo him. "Meaningless!"

"Habit," he said. "The habit of years. It had nothing to do with us. How else could I keep you pure? Surely you know that a passionate man ..."

"Passionate!" she said. "Pure!"

They sat in silence, listening, now that the Schubert had died, to the clock ticking on the wall of the kitchen where the roast was burning. Time, time, she mourned, and, looking at Harold, she saw that his hair was almost gone, that his chin was weak, that his ears lay too flat against his head, that his moustache was ridiculous, that his feet were small. He had taken his pipe out of his pocket and was filling it with tobacco when she rose from her chair and, crossing to where he sat, began to beat him about the head with her pale and delicate fists.

THE SOUND OF COMEDY

The pale young man's name was Howie and when he left the Institution there was no one to meet him. It was a fine September morning with the wine-like smell of rotting apples strong on the orchard country air. He stood for a moment outside the gates and then began to walk down the road, his short legs carrying him quickly, although, having nowhere very special to go, he was in no hurry. During the preceding days he had thought occasionally about what he would do when, to use his own word, he was "uncommitted." Well, the doctor had uncommitted him and here he was, in every sense of the word, uncommitted.

If I had been met, he thought, it would only have been by the circumstances of my own denouement. The thought, although he was not sure that he understood it, cheered him. He had been in and out of the Institution before and he knew that sooner or later, no matter what resolutions he made, he was going to have to return to his mattress. His mattress held everything, all his resources.

"Dispose of my effects as you see fit," he had written in the note to Madame Markowska, his landlady, "but please keep my mattress safe." He had gone on to appeal to her in the only area where he knew her to be sentimental, the supernatural, implying that he hoped to return from time to time in whatever form was available to him. He wondered now what instinct had led him to be so provident. Surely, he hadn't planned to come down from the water tower any way but head first.

Or, as Dr. Krieger had repeatedly suggested, had he?

The doctor was no fool, but one can communicate in depth only in one's own tongue and, if the listener doesn't speak it, what can he make of the sounds that reach his ears? True, the walls surrounding the doctor were lined with guidebooks, but it is a sad fact that too much is often lost in translation. Howie had learned, through this doctor as well as all the others, to mistrust intuition.

"You can intuit all you like," Howie had shouted, "but you'll still be limited by your own experience. You aren't omniscient."

He seemed always to be encountering in others a lack of humility. Humbly, now, he paused at the side of the road and, undoing his fly, urinated into a clump of fading Queen Anne's lace. The yellow arc seemed a symbol to him of his unquenchable mortality; how fitting that, for the weed that served as target, it should hasten the coming of the season of death.

For one thing, the doctor wasn't Jewish and how could you ever convey to him the peculiar smell of Russian Jewish poverty? Go put it into words ... the stale, sweet and sour remnant that clung to walls and bedding ... amalgam of onions and pickles and tea and chicken fat and rising dough and honey and stewed prunes and burning candles and kosher soap and sweet wine and vinegar-rinsed hair — the thousand separate facts of close living alchemized into one nameless nostalgic nothing go name it.

"The smell is not important."

"Not important?" When it was always there?

"And what about the dusty walnuts?" Howie had shrewdly asked. "I suppose they aren't important?"

"The what?"

But it was too tiring. The doctor would have to be reborn to understand all the symbols of Howie's life.

"Try."

"The dusty walnuts. There's this table, you see, with the crocheted lace cloth. Maybe not lace, exactly, but fringed, certainly. Not white but sort of colorless, faded, a little dingy. Pride. And in the center is this bowl ... not really a bowl but an old soup plate with all its hard old arteries showing. And in the bowl are those unshelled walnuts which were never meant to be eaten. Also pride. Symbol of hospitality? But nobody dusts walnuts, you see. I mean, it's that kind of pride ... the walnuts have to be there, but they're covered with ... Listen, doctor, I don't want you to misunderstand. My mother boasted that you could eat off her kitchen floor, and you could. She scrubbed it raw. So it wasn't that not dusting the walnuts made her a slob or anything like that..."

Thank God the doctor had finally given up and decided that Howie's bed was more urgently needed by someone else. He fingered the railroad ticket in his pocket. It was nice of them to consider his transportation. It showed that their feeling for him extended beyond the gate. It showed faith. It was like mailing a letter; you put a stamp on it and when you drop it in the mail slot you don't want it to die there, you expect it to go where you send it, and of course he would go and weren't his feet going along the road in the direction they had indicated.

Go back to New York Howie and see if you can get your old job back and don't despair you need some defenses you are young love or something will come to you you are too raw and in time you will find a way to cover your skin who knows you might still be the first Jewish president and when you visit the grave you will say hello Ma it's me Howie and I'm the first Jewish president from CCNY. Or maybe someone terribly sexy some movie starlet would say Howie you are wonderful I love you Howie you are too thin eat something for me Howie eat at least a pear.

Making vital Cabinet appointments kept him amused all the way to the station. As he approached the ticket window, he grinned through the cage at the stationmaster's wizened, squinting face.

"When does the next train to New York come through?" he asked with a chuckle, pleased with the way his government was shaping up.

Beneath his visor, the old man peered at him through the dust and gloom of the years that separated them. For a long time he did not speak, did not consult his timetables, did not turn to look at the clock. He merely peered at Howie, his face void of expression. At last, he cleared his throat.

"You made maybe a mot?" the stationmaster asked, his pronunciation impeccable.

"I beg your pardon?"

"A witticism?"

Howie's heart sank. "Oh, my God," he said. "I never heard of a Jewish stationmaster."

"Because to tell you the truth, sonnyboy ..."

The clash and clank of a train cut off the latter half of the old man's truth, pulverizing it beneath grinding wheels.

"I don't know what you're talking about," Howie shouted, close to panic. "All I said was..."

"...with smiling. And with laughing. Like a funny joke on the musical comedy stage." He leaned forward and crooked an authoritative finger at Howie. "A simple question should be asked in a simple, direct way, with an appropriate lack of emotional folderol."

"I'm sorry," Howie said. He knew, without turning to see, that there were people behind him and he could feel the accusation of their impatience burning his back. "I only wanted to know when..."

"I am aware what you only wanted to know," the old man said with enormous forbearance. "The words I heard. It's the manner of ..." Again, his voice was swallowed by the louder noise of a moving train, gathering speed.

"Listen," Howie said, when he judged the stationmaster to have reached the punctuation, "I didn't mean to offend you. My mind was somewhere else. It was a long walk here and while I was walking I made myself think of something funny and I was still thinking of it when I got here and asked you that question about the next train to New York. I certainly intended it to be a harmless question, nothing personal."

"All right sonnyboy, all right. Enough with the long speeches, I accept the apology. Now, what can I do for you?"

Howie sighed. The bright, clear day seemed to be dimming, along with his fragile sense of reality. With an effort, he forced himself to repeat his request. The old man peered at him through faded, narrowed eyes.

"You just missed it," he said. "It just pulled out."

"You mean... that was it? While we were standing here talking?"

"Correct."

"Oh, my God," Howie said. "Did we need all that conversation? We could have corresponded instead. I'd have been happy to write you a letter of apology."

"The next train is in an hour. But cheer up, sonnyboy, it's an express." The old man's face splintered into the thousand fragments of a smile. His pride restored, he was making Howie this gift: an express.

"Thank you," Howie said doubtfully. "I'm certainly grateful to you." He turned to leave the window, but the old man wasn't finished with him.

"Just a minute, young fella. I'll choose to overlook the sarcasm in your last remark because you're an excitable young fella obviously not too responsible. But haven't you forgotten something?"

Howie stood uncertainly, staring at the old man. What could he have forgotten?

"To say goodbye?" he asked tentatively.

"A ticket! A ticket!" the old man shouted, jumping up and down. "Ain't you gonna buy a ticket?"

"I already have a ticket," Howie said with relief. "But thank you very much all the same."

He lurched away from the window and out, he hoped, of the old man's life. The absurd episode had depressed him and the hour ahead seemed endless. It was exactly as he had tried to explain to the doctor.

Whenever he emerged into "real" life he was forced to communicate with people on levels of their choosing. He crossed the waiting room and stood uneasily in front of the newsstand, reading the patchwork of headlines and paperback titles. He fingered the five-dollar bill in his pocket, generously supplied by the Institution, and vetoed the temptation to break into it for reading matter. He would read the latrine walls instead. They would be as entertaining as anything here and they were free.

But the men's room smelled of fresh paint and whatever literary jottings its walls had held were buried forever beneath a tabula rasa of shiny buff. Howie stared at the clean walls, instantly overcome by the temptation to violate them. It would have to be something uplifting, some truly inspiring message, a word capable of changing destinies between trains — for when would he ever have so fine an opportunity?

But the word eluded him. And, besides, he had no pencil. Sadly, he left without availing himself of any of the facilities. Back in the waiting room he found an empty pew. Sitting on its hard, body-polished surface, he clasped his hands in his lap and thought about praying.

The word, he realized now, was "Life." If he knew how, he would pray to Life and ask Life to make him worthy of It. But he was afraid that what he meant was that Life was not worthy of him and he could not change it he would have to change himself so please dear Life help me to care more or else not to care so much and I will go back and start all over again with the same defective equipment pretested and tried and true and guaranteed to fail. There must be a trick to it and maybe this time I will find out what the trick is it looks so easy when other people do it.

He wasn't sleepy, but he must have slept because someone was shaking his shoulder. He opened his eyes and saw the stationmaster. The old man, away from his post, seemed considerably diminished, an ordinary small old man.

"You better go wait on the platform, sonnyboy. Your train is coming."

He was touched to think that the old man hadn't forgotten him, that he should have concerned himself. He jumped to his feet and clasped one of the old man's hands between his own.

"Thank you," he said, vibrating with gratitude. "It's awfully nice of you to ... I mean I really do appreciate..."

"Again with the speeches?" the old man said, his voice rising. "You dying to miss this train, too?"

"I'll keep in touch," Howie called over his shoulder, running across the waiting room toward the exit to the platform. "Honest." He hated to leave the old man who was his father, perhaps, but a moment after he had boarded the train the old man was forgotten.

The train was a wheeled capsule, a continuum, a vacuum, a horizontal rocket staggering through life. Highly improbable, Howie thought, terribly chancey. For a while, hypnotized, he watched a fly commute between the baggage rack and a gay garden of a hat perched atop the gray head of a straight-backed anonymous woman. How much did the fly know about its own flight? Did it know that it was moving due south at sixty miles an hour? Did it know that its own flight was as nothing compared to the greater transportation in which it was involved? And what about the spinning ball upon whose surface the train moved? Or was it all here, between hat and baggage rack, all that counted to the fly, and to Howie, of reality?

Lonely, Howie quit his seat. He made his way slowly to the club car at the rear of the train in the dim hope that its atmosphere would indeed be clubby and that he would be invited to join. There were only four people in the car, two of each sex. They were all young. One of the girls was asleep, but the other girl and the two men looked briefly at Howie as he entered and away again, as though of all things on earth he was the least promising. Rumpled and self-conscious, he sank into the corner of a settee, pretending that he had come for the landscape.

But these four people were all he had. On them, as far as he could tell at this moment, his whole future depended. They were suntanned and attractive. They were connected. They were obviously traveling together.

"Positively my last year," the plump man said. His bow tie was a shade too bright, his teeth a shade too white.

"Ah, go on, Jack,." the other man said, as though they had had this conversation many times already, and as though it would never cease to engage his full participation.

"No, I mean it, Al," Jack said earnestly. "I've really had it. I'm sick and tired of the Belt. It's good practice, but it ain't the real thing."

"It's work," Al said.

"Lord is it not work!" Jack sighed, rolling his eyes. Then, patting his belly, "And it's three square banquets a day. But where does it lead, is what I'd like to know. Comes Labor Day, you got nothing to look forward to but Decoration. Look at us. Do you realize there's a whole army of us with pine needles in our hair, full of food and health, thrown into the city streets every autumn, out of work. Let's face it..."

"You'll come back," the unsleeping girl said. She was pretty in a way that, for Howie, hadn't much meaning. Her shoes lay in her lap and her bare brown toes were tipped with crimson. "How could we live without you?"

"Thanks, honey," the man called Jack said. "I appreciate the false sentiment."

"Not false," Honey said with fervor. "I mean it." The sleeping girl, her face buried in the green plush, switched her rump.

Howie stared, straining to understand. It was unbearable that he should not know what they were talking about. It was unbearable that the sleeping girl should not awaken or, at least, turn her face toward him so that he could fall in love with her. It was unbearable to be out of it, not to know the combination. Try, Howie, try. He leaned forward and, touching the plump man's sleeve, politely said, "Could I trouble you for a light?"

"Sure," Jack said and, not looking at Howie, drew a shiny monogrammed lighter from a pocket and flipped it ablaze. Now, holding the light, waiting, his eyes swiveled to meet Howie's. For a long second, the two young men stared vacantly at each other across the flame.

Hell," Jack said, extinguishing the flame, "what do you want a light for?"

"That's funny," Howie said, blushing, patting his mouth. "I could've sworn I had a cigarette here."

The man called Jack looked doubtful for a

moment and then began to laugh.

"First you bum the cigarette," he said, holding his own pack out to Howie, "then the light."

Howie grinned, his heart leaping with hope, and reached for a cigarette.

"I'll never learn," he said dolefully. "I was a breech baby."

They all stared at him.

"Ass backwards," he said, his courage ebbing. "I mean, that's how I seem to do everything."

Something in his tragic disappointment, his helplessness, his idiotic face, his awful joke, something, he would never know what, must have touched them, for suddenly they all began to laugh. And although they were laughing at him, still their laughter was kind and inclusive. He felt embraced. He knew by his joy how starved he was for this kind of acceptance. It was one of those moments, so rare in recent months, when there was no need to put his hands on his body to know that he was there.

"What's your name, buddy?" Al asked.

"Howie," he said. "Howard Turgenev Marks. My father was a reader."

The train racketed on. They talked, they sighed, they smoked cigarettes, they yawned. Occasionally, one of them glanced out of a window at the sliding countryside. Carefully, Howie watched them and, listening, caught the rhythm of their speech and the sense of their words. They were entertainers. Jack was something called a standup comic and social director. Al was his right hand and stooge. The girls were dancers and Honey, whose name was really Harriet, also sang. The name of the sleeping girl was Shirley. She slept on and on, her face buried.

Howie began to tell them about the episode in

the train station. A funny thing happened to me on my way to ... And now, as his confidence grew, as his pain diminished, the old man became truly, wildly funny.

"Stationmaster? What do you mean station*master*? Station*slave*!"

On Howie's tongue, the old man grew into a caricature, a grotesque. Word by word, Howie stripped him of his uniform, of his reality, of his dignity, until he stood naked and shivering the middle of the club car, surrounded by their laughter.

"Don't give me arguments, sonnyboy. What's so terrible you missed a train, a strong young fella like you? In the whole world there's only one train?" Then, subtly changing his voice, making it soft and sly: "Anyhow, you wouldn't have liked that train. Trust me. The next train is nicer ... cleaner ... speedier..."

He couldn't let go of the old man. He was inexhaustible. He was all the old men of Howie's childhood, indignant, quarrelsome, cajoling, shrewd, kindly, reasonable, utterly insane. Good-bye, old man, forgive me, Pop, no you weren't like this, yes you were.

Jack pushed a button on the wall. A small, sad, black man appeared and pretty soon they all had drinks. The drinks were on Jack.

"Moneywise, it was a pretty fair summer," Jack said after a lull. "But God knows how long it'll have to last."

Howie sipped his drink slowly, thinking about the five dollars in his pocket.

"Where you coming from, Howie?" Al asked. "You been working?"

"No," he said. "I've just been loafing. A little

place near Wingdale."

"Unity?"

"No, a small place. You probably never heard of it... Mother Krieger's Bide-A-Wee."

"You're joking! Sounds like a place for stray cats."

"Smelled like it, too," Howie said, looking out the window. "Say, isn't that Poughkeepsie?"

"A gorgeous town," Al said.

"Vassar's in Poughkeepsie," Howie said. "Did you go to Vassar, Harriet?"

"No, Bryn Mawr, dearie."

"I knew a girl who went to Vassar," Howie said, thinking of Violet who might never get out of the Institution. Poor Violet. He wondered if she had made that up, about going to Vassar. He had chosen her to dance with at the Saturday night socials, affairs so fraught with nervous decorum that Violet, who dressed like a gypsy, was a standout. Sometimes, between dances, she was asked to sing. She had a clear, sweet contralto voice, but the only song he'd ever heard her sing was "Sometimes I Feel Like a Motherless Child." She sang it so that there wasn't a dry eye in the house. Still, mothers weren't her problem, she said. Her problem was that she hadn't been able to find a suitable father figure in the world since Einstein had died.

"Einstein was your father figure? Try me," he suggested lasciviously, doing Groucho Marx's eyebrows. She was always too busy confiding in him to hear a word he said.

"Mummy was a lesbian and Daddy kept trying to commit suicide and failing. I slept in the middle."

After that, there wasn't much left to say, but she kept talking anyway. She talked about many things: the stage, sex, recipes.

"You are très sympathetic," she kept telling him, pressing herself against him so that he could feel the outline of her whole body. "But remember, you mustn't put the oregano in until the last minute or else it's completely wasted."

"I'll try not to," he would mumble, conscious of her body.

"And never, never anything but brown sugar!" She pressed a little deeper into him as if she were trying to engrave herself indelibly onto him. It was hard to follow her thought.

"I wouldn't dream of it," he mumbled. "I promise."

In a little while, a nurse would appear and peel Violet off him. The nurse would lead Violet away, leaving him sexually aroused and starved for a good plate of spaghetti.

Too bad he couldn't tell them about Violet. There was a wealth of humor there, and laughter was so important to them. Instead, he said, "I don't know how I got mixed up with a Vassar girl. I grew up so poor. I mean, really poor."

"Me too," Jack said with enthusiasm.

"Poor? I was eighteen before I found out that a tangerine wasn't a sexy dance."

"My cake for my seventh birthday," Jack said dreamily, "was a Mallomar with a candle."

"Hah! Exactly what I got," Howie said. "Our mothers must have grown up in the same shtetl. I had to blow out the candle quick so we could use it again next year. But I was allowed to eat the Mallomar."

"My idea of a wild time was riding the escalators in Penn Station. When the other kids were in the movies, that's where I was, living it up."

"To me, the height of luxury was to own an umbrella. Imagine! An umbrella! To think, it could rain but it didn't have to rain on you. I was always being rained on," he remembered mournfully. "Soggy all the time. Now, whenever I'm depressed, I can't help it, I buy myself an umbrella. I must have twenty-seven umbrellas.

"We didn't even have a bed," Howie went on. "Me and my brother Sidney. We slept on these two trunks pushed together with a mattress on top. I still have that mattress. Sentimental value." Dr Krieger had made much of the mattress. He'd kept coming back to it. For mattress, read mother, womb. Read roots. Read safety. Ah, those Freudian nuts! "The trunks were empty, but not the mattress... it contains all my worldly goods: stocks, bonds, mortgages, fiefs, chattels, forty-two dollars cash, liens, an Eversharp fountain pen guaranteed for life..."

"This is an amusing little fellow," Jack said.

"But wiry," Howie said, warming to the praise. "Sinewy." He flexed his muscles. "Don't ask me why we had two trunks," he went on. "We never went anywhere and, as far as I can remember, we never came from anywhere. Maybe they were left over from some previous tenants. My parents had the room on the airshaft and we kids had the outside room. Outside! All night long outside the window, the sign blinked on and off... atessen, atessen, atessen. To fall asleep, I counted atessens."

"Atessen? "

"That was all you could see from our window. You had to go to the toilet for the Delic."

At last, the sleeping girl stirred, turned, sat up. She stared blankly at Howie. She was beautiful and he was prepared to love her. She yawned and stretched her tanned arms and, rising unsteadily, crossed to where Howie sat.

"I've been listening to every word," she whispered, sitting beside him. "You're crazy".

He blushed. "Give me a break," he pleaded. "Don't tell."

"Like a loon," she said. Her upper lip was thin and bloodless, but the lower lip was full and ripe.

"I love you," he said, his voice trembling.

"Of course you do, you poor slob," she said sadly and yawned again. The interior of her mouth was as lovely as the outside. He couldn't take his eyes off her.

"What I want you to do," he heard Jack say from somewhere on the other side of the world, "is write all this material down."

Howie was overcome with shyness. He couldn't think of anything to say to her.

"Did... you have a nice summer, Harriet?" he said, at last.

"My name is Eleanor, " she said.

But Jack was standing between them, swaying with the train's motion, snapping his fingers in Howie's face, leaning down to talk to him.

"You're not paying attention, young man,." he said severely.

"Me?" he said, tearing his gaze from Eleanor's marvelous, sleepy face. "You talking to me?"

"Move," Jack said, shoving Howie over and sitting between him and Eleanor. "I want you to write this material down."

"Material?"

"I can use it. I'll pay you for it ... as soon as I get work."

"Material?" Howie said again. "You mean my

... life?"

"Whatever. That stuff you were telling us. It's not bad."

"You mean, write it down?" Howie asked.

Jack sighed. "Yeah, you know, like a writer? Here." He reached into his pockets and, after some groping, found a card and a pencil. On the blank side of the card he wrote his name and address and telephone number. He handed the card to Howie. Howie stared at it for a while, then turned it over and stared at the printed side. It read:

RAPPAPORT'S BAR-B-Q & TEX/MEX SHACK
24764 AVENUE B
NO CONNECTION WITH ANY OTHER
RESTAURANT OF THE SAME NAME.

He studied the card. It was an interesting card. "Good ribs?" he asked.

Not that side, the other side," Jack said, pulling the card from Howie's hand and turning it over. "That's where you can reach me. Tell me, am I getting through to you? You look sick."

"No, I'm all right," Howie said. "I understand."

"Maybe you better give me your address."

"I'll call you," Howie said. "Don't worry."

"You'll write it down?" Jack said carefully.

"Write it down. The material. Yes."

Outside, the city had sprung up on either side of the train. Soon he would have to leave this world and start life all over again. At his side, Jack talked on and on, like an insecure salesman.

"There's good money in comedy," Jack said. "And I like your approach. It's fresh. It's a little wild. You stick with me, kid, and as soon as I get work, we'll go places. Maybe sooner." He patted Howie's arm.

The train burrowed underground. Jack got up and he and Al began to gather their bags together. Honey put her shoes on. Howie looked at Eleanor, feeling desperate, as though in five minutes the world might end.

"Don't leave me," he said urgently, startling her. "Please." She stared at him. Her eyes narrowed. The lights in the train went off and came on again and still she stared at him. At last she spoke.

"All right," she said.

Walking up the ramp from the train into the station, he felt like a slug coming up out of the earth, out of the cold and dark wintry earth with its silences, through the crumbling crust, into a place full of spring, though it was autumn, a sky full of sunshine. He was carrying Eleanor's bags. They were unbelievably heavy, as though loaded with paraphernalia for some secret vice like weightlifting, but still he managed to keep his step light. Eleanor's miraculous hand was curled inside the crook of his arm. He had a girl ... maybe. He had a job ... sort of. He had five dollars. His name was Howard Turgenev Marks.

"What I'm going to do," Eleanor said, leading him firmly along, "is make you over."

"I can hardly wait," he said.

"Come, we'll go to my place."

He shed upon her a look flooded with love. "Yes," he said, grinning. "Sure. But first maybe we'd better just go and see if my mattress is still there."

TURN YOUR BACK AND WALK AWAY

It was necessary, in the dream, to keep the old lady on her feet. That was the struggle between them; if the old lady were to fall, then Jane must fall with her, and to fall would be to smother in the old lady's stranglehold. The smell of stale urine thickened the dream's air. Repelled, Jane breathed reluctantly and longed, while she fought it, for suffocation. She must not let go, yet the pull of the old lady's weight grew stronger as her own strength diminished. But she must not let go! From time to time the old lady gasped and once, in terror, screamed.

Jane awoke at last, exhausted, ejected into wakefulness spent and empty of everything save the knowledge that she had failed in something; the failure was crucial and would be forever too late to undo. The sense of her shame and guilt suffused her as she lay throbbing with misery in the dull half-light of daybreak. Next to her, Steve lay peacefully apart from her world, curled like a baby in the crook of his own arm, sweetly sleeping, sweetly, softly breathing, hair sweetly fallen disarranged across his untroubled brow. The myth of marriage, she thought with bitterness, and because she couldn't bear to hate him as she was, at this moment, hating him, because she hadn't the strength for it, she prodded him gently from his world into hers. He opened his eyes and stared blankly at her.

"What?" he said. "What's the matter?"

"Bad dream," she said, feeling foolish. "Talk to me."

He sighed. "What time is it?"

She strained toward the clock. "Five-thirty," she said.

"Oh, for God's sake, go back to sleep." Then, to soften his impatience, he kissed her on the nose. The inadequacy of his gesture appalled her. She turned from him, desolate and lonely, shaken by her resentment. She shut her eyes and, drifting dream fragments seeped back. The old lady's hands were claws, but yesterday they had lain crossed in her lap in dignified repose (or was it resignation?) and she had regarded them with love, remembering them in the knowingness of all their past labors, in all their confident doing, for they were her mother's hands, of course they were her mother's hands.

"...because I've got to get a full night's sleep. Just once," she heard him mumble into her back.

To touch, she thought, with yearning, drifting away from the voice in her back ... to reach out just once and touch. But the foul old smell was in her nostrils, the collective odor of unwashed age, the monstrous mechanism grinding out at its end the last slow clumsy turns of a lifetime's rote of daily acts. Function, malfunction, non-function: life, age, death.

"I can't leave her there," she murmured. "I can't leave her in that place."

He groaned. "Not again!"

"But don't you see..." Her voice trailed off on the realization that it didn't matter if he saw or not. They had been over it so many times and he was al-

ways, unshakably right. They were doing the right
thing. She was getting the best possible care. They
were paying for it, and it wasn't cheap. They
couldn't sacrifice their lives to what remained of hers.
It was the best, the only, possible way.

"You're always so reasonable," she mumbled.
"You're always so damned right!" But what, she
thought, has reason to do with the middle of the night,
with the dark, with dreams, with fear and guilt and
love?

"All right," he said, lurching to a sitting position, from which she guessed his anger, for his anger
required som degree of perpendicularity. "Let's not
be reasonable, if that's what you want. This is the
way it is: I don't want her here. I just simply do not
want her here! I owe her something because she's a
sick old woman and because she's your mother and
I'll pay it and go on paying it ... within reason!"

"Thanks," she said. "You have my undying
gratitude."

"Oh, Jane, please! What the hell do you want
from me?"

"Go back to sleep," she said, pulling the covers
over her head. Behind her closed eyelids, she had a
vision of all the words they had ever spoken to each
other collected, a huge sack of them, labeled:
"USELESS SOUNDS."

When she opened her eyes again the cold winter sun was full in the room. Steve was gone. The
whine of the vacuum cleaner sucking up the dust of
night told her that she had overslept again, and that
Judy, too, would be gone by now, fed, dressed, dis-
patched to school by Emma with easy efficiency
while she had lain impotently glued to sleep. Her re-
luctance to meet the new day came as no surprise to

her; it was visiting day again.

The single dismal elevator at The Home was little roomier than a coffin and its progress to the fourth floor was halting and unsure.

Pausing for a moment in the doorway, unobserved, Jane surveyed the room in which she had spent so many painful afternoons, trying to see objectively this cell to which she had sentenced her mother, probably for the rest of her life. It was, after all, not so terrible --- a large, bright room that must have been a parlor in this converted once fashionable brownstone. It now held comfortably six beds and night tables, and there were three long, narrow windows and a fireplace that had not been called upon to serve for years. The room's ceiling was lofty, and above the fireplace mantel there hung in a cheap varnished frame a painting by a former resident acquiescent to therapy. Its subject, done in insipid colors on a marked and numbered canvas, was one that, in this place, invariably startled her, for it dealt with heavily armed spacemen sturdily facing some interplanetary crisis.

Beneath the painting, Jane's mother sat motionless in her wheelchair, huddled between the frail twin pillars of her shoulders, staring inward into some corner of the past ... waiting, waiting ... and Jane was again reminded that her mother had all the hours of the week to live through, somehow, not just those five or six hours that Jane spent with her. Seven times twenty-four, she thought, how did they pass? She walked quickly into the room to her mother and, bending to kiss her, saw the old woman make the quick voyage from past to present, saw the face light as surely as if a match had been struck, and knew that what she brought to her mother in that instant was nothing less than the gift of life.

"Thank God! I thought you were never coming."

"Why?" she asked, sitting beside her mother in the visitor's chair. "What's wrong?"

"The meshugenah," the old lady said, shaking her head sadly and indicating old Mrs. Benson, who, unvisited, lay fully clothed and fast asleep on the next bed. "All night she kept me up. She walks the floor all night, back and forth. Only in the daytime she can't move, the nurse has to help her."

There were, at the time, four residents of Room 401, of whom Mrs. Benson was the senior.

"She reads ghost stories," Jane's mother said. She spoke haltingly, her voice weak, hobbled by a respiratory difficulty. "In the middle of the night ... she says she read it ... one of us is going to die tonight. 'It could be me,' she says, 'or it could be you.' A regular Dracula!"

The old lady began to laugh. Now, shared and in the light of day, Mrs. Benson could strike her as funny.

"But who needs it?" she gasped, and Jane, smiling uncertainly, saw that Mrs. Benson lay curled, or, more accurately, bent, in the fetal posture, an ancient, blue silk hat tilted crazily on her head.

"She's wearing her hat," Jane said.

"She has something about hats," her mother said. "She thinks she's going somewhere. She thinks she just dropped in." Again the laughter came, but this time the strain was too great and she began to choke.

"The inhaler," she gasped. "Over there." Jane reached for the bottle and, squeezing the atomizer, sent a spray into her mother's mouth, upturned and open like a feeding baby bird's. In a moment the old woman's breathing settled back to its normal rhythm.

"All right?" Jane asked. Her mother nodded, her mouth drawn down, chastened.

"Ahhh," she sighed, "we live too long. What's the good?"

"Don't talk like that, Mama."

"It's true. Nothing works right inside. And still we live."

For all of them here, because it hadn't come suddenly, or prematurely, or even on time, there was the leisure to watch death's slow approach.

"I want to go home," the old woman sighed. "I want to die in my own bed." And there it was again, like a litany chanted at regular intervals, to a God who is not at home. But it was she, Jane, who would have to answer.

"When you're better," Jane lied. "When you're a little stronger."

"I'll never get better here!" And now she spoke with bitterness, her faded eyes misting. "Nobody gets better here. Here is for ... rotting."

It was true. She had deteriorated here. Each day, because there was nothing to see, there was a little less vision; because there was nothing to hear, her hearing dulled; because there was no power left to her, her strength diminished. The losses were gradual, the retreat inevitable.

But each day she's a little older, Jane reminded herself, and it was Steve's voice she heard. "She's an old woman, Jane. It would have been the same at home."

"At home I'll get better," her mother was saying. "Stronger. I'll be able to eat the food. Here it's garbage, it's all I can do to look at it. You'll see,

Jane darling, once I'm better I won't need so much help."

She's pleading with me, Jane thought dismally, assaulted by memories of all the other days. Pride, she thought, remembering her mother's straight back, her serene brow, the humor and compassion in her level gaze. The pride has been tortured out of her. She eats pap that dribbles down her chin, and if her fingernails are dirty someone else must clean them and sometimes at night she wets her bed and the nurses talk to her as if she were a child. She's completely at the mercy of her body --and that's the shock of this place, the final horror, the indignity of being so dependent and so unprivate.

"Soon, Mama," she said. She took the old lady's hand and held it. Gently, she toyed with the gnarled, inbent fingers, straightening them (not thinking what she was doing) in a wistful denial of time. But released the fingers crabbed back into their present shape. This hand, she thought, these hands that have done so much in so many places. Quick hands, darting in and out of the folds of cloth, the needle glinting like the eye of a sun-caught bird in sudden flight. Hands supple and strong, floured, working the Friday-smelling dough. Hands sharp and powerful in the instant authority of a slap; gentle in the instant caress. All things she was, the Mother, looming, filling the house and all its corners, the source of so much, reward and punishment, nourishment and succor, yes and no, denial and love, fear and calm, thunder and peace and comfort. She put the hand gently back to rest in the lap where it had lain now so many months, useless, impotent, as surely dead as though it rested on her coffined breast.

"I'll give you a haircut, Mama," she said.

"I've brought the scissors." The old lady's eyes kindled. Here, at least, was a break in the routine, an unanticipated attention, an event.

"Good," she said, nodding. "It's shtroogily."

"It's what?" Jane laughed. Her mother's approach to the English language had always been oblique. She had come to it by way of Yiddish and Russian and, unintimidated, made it her own simply by bending it to her will. In need of a word, she instantly found one, whether it was there or not, fashioning it from the tatters of all her tongues and from the strength of some poetic intuition.

"It's..." She looked at Jane with suspicion. Was she making fun? "It ... could use it. Get a towel. In the night table."

Jane draped the towel across the hunched shoulders and, standing behind and over her mother, looked down at the narrow gray head, the yellowing scalp showing through the coarse hair. For a moment she was reluctant to touch it (when had they washed it last?) and then, remembering with anger that this was her mother, she stroked the hair into place and began to cut, thinking of the way it used to be, hanging almost to the knees, for it had been her mother's pride that her hair had never been cut in her life (it remained for the exigencies of invalidism to strip her of even that), and of the morning ritual (she, the daughter, had long associated it with daybreak, as though the two things. the ritual and the new day, were somehow interdependent) of binding and plaiting, of reducing the four or five feet of shining dark hair to a few inches of bun that lay coiled at the back of her head like a slipped crown. For the first time in many years she thought of the yellowed irovy box that had sat on her mother's vanity with its cache of thick hairpins, and her fingers felt again the neat, satisfying way the box's lid used to click into place. The box had a mate, something called a hair-catcher. As a little girl, she had got the idea that during the night, when everyone was asleep, the hair-catcher flew about gathering up the day's fallen hair. Remembering, now, she felt with a sharp and sudden ache what it had been like to be a little girl half in and half out of life. The feeling was so real and immediate that the focus of her relationship to Judy, her daughter, and to the old woman, her mother, slipped and blurred.

Snip, snip, snip. The gray hairs fell upon the towel. Parting the thinning hair with her fingers, she saw, for perhaps the first time, her mother's neck with its thin parallel bones and the hollow between, pathetic and shrunken and vulnerable, the rod that held the weight of the housing for all thought, all sorrow, all memory.

And now, unaccountably, the old woman began to tell jokes.

"Did I ever tell you the story about when the little boy asked his father why do they call noodles 'noodles,' and the father said, 'Such a stupid question! They're long like noodles, aren't they? And they're soft like noodles, aren't they? And they taste like noodles, don't they? So why shouldn't they be called noodles?'"

Snip, snip, snip.

"I don't know why," the old lady said softly. "Sometimes I sit here and they just come into my head, the old stories. Remember what Papa used to say when I'd tell him to close the window, it's cold outside? 'Nu,' he'd say, 'and if I close the window will it be warm outside?'"

Snip, snip, snip. "There," she said, brushing the loose hairs from her mother's neck, "that's better."

She held a mirror for the old lady to see, and the faded, failing eyes narrowed in critical self-scrutiny.

"A beauty," the old lady said, bobbing her head. "A regular beauty queen I see in the mirror."

Miss Martin, the floor nurse, strode briskly into the room, came to an abrupt halt, clapped her hands together.

"Why, you've had a haircut," she exclaimed, her quick perception a gift to her charge. "Why, Mrs. Karp, you look beautiful!"

"And why not?" the old lady said, twinkling. "In the morning I'm leaving for Hollywood on the Silver Streak Special. Mr. MGM personally signed me a contract."

"Don't bother," Miss Martin said at Jane's efforts to gather the fallen drifts of hair. "The porter will sweep it up."

"There's a draft on my shoulders, Miss Martin," the old lady said. "Could you get me my sweater, darling?"

And now Mrs. Benson stirred on her bed.

"Miss Martin?" she rasped, her eyes fluttering open beneath the crazy blue hat. "Have you got my new medicine? When do I get my new medicine?"

And across the room, old Mrs. Verdon, who was completely bedridden, who was perhaps nearest to death, called weakly, "Please, Miss Martin, could you move my pillow a little higher?"

All of them, Jane thought, with their terrible need for attention. They couldn't let Miss Martin pass without some sign from her that they were still there, filling some small void in space, in time. The request, its fulfillment, this was their final power. Bereft, now, of all need to make decisions, to order their lives, their advice unsought in the lives of their children, their husbands dead in spite of all their tender care, in spite of all the shoes taken to be resoled, the suits to be dry cleaned, the darned socks and the turned shirt collars, the meals planned and marketed for and prepared with pride, the children hushed on Sunday mornings; dead in spite of the years of seeing that the supply of toothpaste never ran out. Now, not even the butcher to be reckoned with, a cut of meat to be declined, an extra scrap of fat trimmed away before the weighing. The power of giving and the power of taking. The power of being. Nothing now. Nothing but Miss Martin.

It was nearly four o'clock. Visitors were not supposed to stay past four, when the elevator was needed to carry dinner trays to those residents unable to make their way to the dining room. Dinner at four had seemed so shocking in the beginning, such an unnecessary indignity, making the long nights so much longer.

"I have to go now, Mama," Jane said, longing all at once to be home. At this moment, Judy would be home from school, bursting through the door like a small cyclone, carrying the freshness of this March day in her hair and on her frosty apple cheeks.

"Mom," she would call, "Mom?" and then, remembering that it was Wednesday, go into the kitchen and, dropping her books on the kitchen table, tell Emma whatever it was that couldn't wait another moment to be told. The young are so impatient; it's their only wisdom, the knowledge that life cannot wait.

"Is it time already?" the old woman said dully, and sighed.

"I'll be back on Friday," Jane said, slipping into her coat. "What can I bring you? What do you need?"

"Nothing. Don't bring anything."

"Lemon drops?" Jane shook the candy tin that was always there on the night table. "It's almost empty."

"All right," her mother said, "bring lemon drops." But her voice, her eyes, clearly indicated that she had withdrawn already to that private place where she dwelt when Jane wasn't with her, the terrible, lonely place that was, perhaps, that absolute bottom whose avoidance we spend most of our lives pursuing. Forgive me, Mama, she thought, trying to harden her heart, forgive me for leaving you with only this, and the lemon drops, to look forward to in all of life, forgive me for leaving you at all and for being glad to leave, as I will one day leave you, by simply turning my back and walking away, in the cold, alien earth, in that strange, ugly place where Papa is buried. Forgive me, Mama, for not being God, for being only as human as you, as subject to all the conditions of life, for not being able to give you back your youth, your strength, your beauty, your life; oh, God, oh Mama, have pity on me, my hands are empty of everything but tears and lemon drops!

"I love you, Mama," she said, kissing the warm, dry cheek and, turning her back, she walked out of the room.

CHARITY

It was one of those last days of autumn, an unseasonably warm, bright day. She took her book out to the garden, partly for the sunshine and partly to escape the telephone which had been intruding at intervals as regular and as insistent as labor pains. It was the season of appeals, the time after the summer hiatus and before the Christmas money-sapping days, the fund-raising season. Every misfortune seemed to have its organization and every organization its clarion call.

Still, how say no to orphans, to the indigent aged, to disabled veterans? Yes, she said. Yes to heart, to cancer, to arthritis, to muscular distrophy. Yes to Alzheimers, nephritis, nephrosis, nepotism and impotism. Yes indeedy to the Community Chest, the Hospital Fund, the Red Cross, the White Feather, the Four Horsemen. Yes and yes again to Catholics and Jews, Blacks, Asians, Native Americans, scouts of both genders, and the Salvation Army.

She pulled a chaise into a position beneath the partly leaf-stripped oaks where the sun, for perhaps quarter of an hour, would shine directly onto her face. Cautiously, she arranged herself on the chaise ... tentatively ... prepared to bolt on the instant.

She closed her eyes. In the empty house the

telephone rang, and rang again. The high school band, rehearsing not far away, sent the thumping and rolling of drums into the aluminum frame of the chaise, the vibrato penetrating her body..

She opened her eyes to see a dog --- a large white dog finely spotted black as with a rash --- lope confidently through the open gate into the garden. Ignoring her, the dog sniffed the base of the furthest oak and, liking what he sniffed, raised a leg to salute it.

Privacy, she thought. They were her oaks, yet to any dog who strayed here they were comfort stations.

"Go away," she said, and at the sound of her voice the dog's tail shot up and violently beat the air.

"I don't want to be friends," she grumbled. "Go somewhere and find a boy." But the dog, en-. couraged, licked her hand in an effusion of joy.

"You don't understand," she said. "We're nothing to each other." She opened her book and forced herself to read, to ignore the intrusion.

"Measured and even, despite slight variations of amplitude and rhythm perceptible to the eye but scarcely exceeding six inches and two or three seconds, the sea rose and fell..."

The dog stretched out on his belly at the foot of the chaise and, resting his head between his paws, gazed lovingly up at her from soft brown eyes.

"Go home," she said. "One thing we don't need is a dog." She closed the book and, sighing, got up and walked toward the gate.

"You really do have to leave," she told the dog. "I can't stand you looking at me that way." The dog's gaze shifted self-consciously, but otherwise he didn't stir.

She held the gate invitingly ajar, smiling encouragement. Embarrassed, the dog closed his eyes, feigning sleep. She sighed again and, leaning against the fence, looked out at the orderly street. It was an attractive street, the houses set well back on their wide, neatly separated plots. They were older houses and although there were no two alike, one being Georgian, the next Tudor, a third partly Norman, still they were all somehow similar, solid and settled, rubbed by the years to a dull finish, and surrounded by towering oaks and beeches. At this moment there was no one about. The children were in school, the men were in their offices at the other end of the railway lines that scraped the countryside clean of them each weekday, the garbage had been collected and the mail distributed hours ago. Where were all the women? Poking about in supermarkets, palpating vegetables? Of course... they were on the telephone, calling each other for contributions.

Turning the corner into her street, appeared the figure of a shambling young man carrying a battered suitcase. His clothes were dusty and too dark for the season; he wore a flapping overcoat under which he must have been much too warm. The blur of white, which at this distance was all she could see of his face, was too pale for this suburb where tans were just beginning to fade. The approaching figure was entirely alien to the landscape so that her heart began to beat just a little faster in what might have been the beginning, the merest warning of fear. But of course it couldn't be fear and, as the young man drew abreast of her front lawn, she didn't hesitate to call out to him.

"Hello!" she cried. "Have you lost a dog?"

He looked around and behind him. If the dog

was his, he hadn't yet missed him. "I guess so," he said. "Is he here?"

He took a few steps toward her. His face, set atop a long, soiled neck, was pasty white, as though he had only lately emerged from prison or a childhood spent in a closet. He essayed a smile full of broken teeth, but his eyes were out of it, flat and dead. With a conscious physical effort, she prevented herself from recoiling at his advance.

"If there was a dog with you," she said, "this must be it."

She stepped aside to let him through the gate, the flimsy suitcase banging against his knee at every step.

"Here, Pimples," he called. "Come, boy."

The dog looked up without moving. His tail switched tentatively, then fluttered still. His eyes closed again.

"Pimples!" she exclaimed. "What an awful name." The young man turned his wan face toward her and stared at her out of shallow gray eyes. She might as well have spoken in a foreign tongue. Then, all at once, comprehension spread across his face like a summer dawn. He smiled again, but this time the smile surfaced from within.

"Yeah," he said. "My kid brother named him. What a dopey kid. Arthur."

The thought of Arthur transformed the ugly dead mask, lighting it with something that was close to charm. "You have any kids, mi—madam?"

"Yes."

He set the battered suitcase down at his feet and, standing very straight, almost at attention, focussed his sterile gaze on a point about four inches to the right of her nose. He gulped and began what was obviously a set speech.

"Would you by any chance be needing," he said mechanically, "a very fine set of the Encyclopaedia Britannica? Practically new?"

"No, I don't think..."

The young man took a deep, anxious breath. His eyes had gone blank again.

"This encyclopedia," he said without expression, "will place a world of information at your family's fingertips. It is a treasure-house of knowledge to have in your home." His voice dropped several tones, becoming more personal "It was Arthur's, this set. I have no doubt that it was in large part responsible for the excellent marks Arthur always got in school." He paused to think this over and then added, "Of course, Arthur was very smart anyhow ... but it certainly could not have hurt him, having this world of information at his fingertips."

"No, I suppose not," she said uncomfortably.

He slid his gaze a little to the left, daring a brief look at her face. Then, apparently finding nothing helpful there, he looked down at his shoes. They were as worn and as dusty as the rest of him. Patiently, he waited.

"Do you... live around here?" she asked at last, not knowing what was expected of her, wishing he would go away, back to wherever he did live.

"Oh, no," he said, looking up and around him, as though only at this moment noticing where he was. "What town is this, would you say?" he asked politely, not really interested.

"White Plains."

"White Plains," he said, dreamily, his confidence inexplicably growing. "A nice name. They must have named it during the winter. My home is in

Schenectady, which is an ugly name, don't you think?"

She smiled, fumbling in the pocket of her slacks for her cigarettes. She had the odd notion, from the expression on the young man's face, that he thought he'd made a friend.

"Of course, I've been away for a long time. Ever since Arthur died."

"Oh," she said, extracting a cigarette and putting it between her lips. "I'm sorry."

He shifted his weight from one foot to the other, staring hungrily at the cigarette. Clumsily, she held out the pack to him, but he made no move.

"Go on," she said, pushing the pack closer. "Take one."

He reached out a flaccid white hand, his fingernails overlong and filthy. With grotesque daintiness, thumb and index finger closed on a cigarette and drew it from the pack. "Thank you," he said, placing the cigarette in the exact center of his mouth. She lighted hers and handed the matchbook to him. He took the cigarette out of his mouth and put both it and the matches into the pocket of his coat.

"Well," she said, taking a step backward, "I've got to be ...."

"Oh, no!" he said. "Don't go." Then, embarrassed by his own vehemence, he added, "I mean, I wish you'd give this encyclopedia a little more thought. Let me show it to you." He dropped to his knees and slapped the catch on the suitcase with the flat of his hand. The case sprang open revealing a knot of dirty rags and half a dozen scuffed volumes.

"It's not a complete set," he mumbled, anticipating her. "But I'm prepared to make you a very attractive price."

She shook her head, feeling suddenly terribly imposed upon. "I'm sorry," she said firmly. "I can't possibly use them."

He stared at her, his mouth open, hope draining from his face.

"It's not just anyone I'd sell Arthur's books to," he said carefully, his voice a whine, and she had the notion that he was trying to be crafty, abetted by a dim memory of some sales manual's exhortation. It occurred to her that the world was full of such half-mad incompetents and the thought frightened her. How did they survive? How did they manage from one day to the next?

"$2.50 a volume," he announced, trying to sound final and authoritative.

She smiled. "I'm flattered," she forced herself to say, "that you would offer to let me buy Arthur's books, but you see we really have no use for them. We already have an encyclopedia."

His mouth, which had hung open during her speech as though it were through this cavity that all communication must enter, now shut tight. His lips narrowed. He was tasting her words and finding them bitter. She watched on his face the struggle to accept her refusal and to find an emotion proper to that acceptance. She saw him waver between anger and despair. Then inspiration must have struck, for his eyes narrowed. He began to close the suitcase.

"You... Jewish ?" he asked, uttering the word as though it tasted of vomit. Her heart began to beat in her ears.

"Ah!" He snapped the catch shut triumphantly. "I thought so!"

And now it was her anger and her struggle to master it. Don't be a fool, she told herself.

The young man stood up and, looking at her with absolute hatred, did a strange, unexpected thing. Without removing his eyes from hers, he took the cigarette and matches she had given him from his pocket. Again putting the cigarette in the exact center of his mouth, he lit it and began to smoke it with deep, hungry, sensuous puffs. It was a performance at once so insolent and so oddly lascivious that she felt as though she were being assaulted. Now her heart was beating wildly. She thought about scream- ing, then tore her eyes away from the ugly white face of her executioner, understanding in that moment why the doomed are offered blindfolds.

She had no way of knowing how long she and the intruder were locked in this wordless encounter when, at length, apparently satisfied, he bent to pick up his suitcase and turned to go.

"Come on, Pimples," he called, turning his back to her and walking toward the gate. "Let's go, boy." Automatically, the dog rose and took a few steps after his master's retreating back. Then he stood stock still and, pointing his nose in the air, sniffed.

"Come on!" the young man urged, turning to see if the dog was following. "We haven't got all day."

But the dog, as though at an inner command, wheeled and loped back to his place at the foot of the chaise where, after circling two or three times, he sank down and, with an air of finality, shut his eyes.

"Pimples!" the man commanded. The dog trembled but didn't move. "What's the matter with you, boy? You crazy or something?" His voice rose and broke with exasperation. "Well, I'm going."

As purposefully as his peculiar gait allowed, he

strode down the street in the direction he had been heading. She, standing there in her garden, shaken, beseeched the dog to go. But the dog was adamant. She tried grasping it by its scruff and tugging it to its feet, but it eluded her, rolling onto its back and regarding her with the faintest rebuke in its gentle eyes. In spite of herself, she began to laugh. "Go, Pimples," she said, choking on the name. "For the love of God, please go!" But at the sound of her voice, the dog's tail thrashed the ground in utter delight.

The young man had reached the corner before he faltered. The dog was not coming. At last he turned and came shambling back. He stared over the fence, watching her futile efforts with flat despair.

"He don't want to come," he said without expression.

"Maybe if we bribe him," she said. "I'll see what I can find in the kitchen." She took a step but the young man's voice stopped her.

"He's not hungry," he said with outraged pride. "He just don't want to come."

And, indeed, while they conjectured, the dog had dug himself in deeper and was again shut away in feigned sleep.

"Of course he wants to come," she said desperately, seeing that the young man's eyes were blurring. "You know how loyal dogs are!"

The young man considered. "No," he said after a while, his shoulders sagging. "I guess I better be going."

"What about Pimples?" she cried. "You can't just go off and leave him here."

The young man paused and looked back at her. She saw, with horror, that he was crying. "He don't want to come with me. He wants to stay here." He wiped the end of his long thin nose with the back of his hand. "I don't care," he said. "You can keep him."

And now she saw that he was really going. At the edge of her walk he stumbled on nothing, on a blade of grass, and caught himself and went on. He was a member of the legion of the helpless who stumble always on nothing, who miss the point of everything, who suck the blood and will not leave one alone, who are hideous and demanding and dangerous and pathetic and with whom there can be no communication; yet it was unbearable that he should leave this way, so completely failed.

"Wait!" she called, without knowing what she was going to do next. Wearily, he stopped and again turned to face her with his blank, damp mask.

"Let me ... let me see those books again," she said. "Maybe there are one or two I can use after all."

He looked at her with fleeting suspicion, then came and opened the suitcase. She bent and made a show of examining the books, studying the faded lettering on their spines.

"I'm sorry," he said, slyly, "you'll have to take them all. I can't break up the lot."

She sighed, feeling like an actor in someone else's nightmare. "I'll give you $10.00 for the lot," she said.

"$12.00."

"$10.00," she said. " Take it or leave it."

He took it. She could see that he was deeply satisfied with himself, as though he had put something over on her. His step, as he went off down the street, was almost jaunty.

She sighed again, thankful that it was over. For the moment it was quiet, but it was nearly three o'clock. Soon the buses at the high school would flex their muscles, mesh gears, thunder and roar. The older children, the shouting, whooping, non-screaming children, would begin drifting home. It would be time to resume the round of maternal functions: to listen to the day's tragedies and triumphs, to urge the reluctant childish flesh to do its homework, to practice its violin, to hang up its jacket and swallow its glass of milk.

Then, a little later, the trains would start coming like spiders spinning neat webs across the countryside, disgorging for another night the workworn men. Alex would be among them. He would come in, put down the newspaper, kiss her, and in a little while, when he'd taken off his tie and washed, he would wait to hear about her day. "What's new?" he'd say, sipping his drink. "Anything happen today?"

"Well," she would begin, "we seem to have got this dog." And then she would stand, undecided, wondering how in the world she could possibly tell him about her afternoon in a way that would give it some kind of meaning.

THE END OF THE WEDDING

The plane was late. The time posted for its arrival was still half an hour off.

"Plenty of time for a drink," Jim said. He took her arm and she fell easily into step with him, their gaits matching still, though in the year past they had rarely had occasion to walk together. It would take more than a year to undo the habits of almost twenty. Some of them would probably never come undone.

They walked the length of the broad, antiseptic terrazzo corridor, past the souvenir shops, the tobacco stalls, the paperback books plastered against the walls like pop art murals, listening to the carefully antiseptic voice of a woman announcing arrivals and departures, and at last into the darkened antiseptic gloom of the bar. The walks they had taken together in recent months had been to the offices of accountants and lawyers but the last had been away from Garth's funeral. Though they had lost touch with Garth in recent years, his death had shaken them. He had been a friend during an early time in their marriage when they had been relatively happy, pleased with the apartment they had been so lucky to get in the huge complex of prison-like buildings where, if you leaned out the bedroom window, you could see a patch of the river. But their apartment had seemed huge and clean and bright, it was unquestionably efficient, they were young, and it was their own. And the light in the bedroom was good enough to paint by when she had the time. They had made a lot of friends, all in apartments exactly like theirs, so that when they visited, as they constantly did, there was no need to say that the bathroom was the second door on the left.

Garth was one of these new friends, drawn to them at first because he shared their opinion that Nick was the world's most remarkable four-year-old. Nick had not been remarkable, really, merely charming, happy, and beautiful. Garth had appropriated him for Sunday outings with his own boy, Willy, who was mentally retarded and sickly. Nick was one of the few children who could be counted on not to be cruel to Willy. At the time, she didn't believe that a four-year-old could be anything so civilized as kind, and she had attributed Nick's decency to his being too busy to notice that Willy was different. But later, in the years of his growing up, Nick had been kind, had instinctively respected the weak, sided with the underdog, found something to admire in the least popular child. He was so sure of himself, so devoid of any axe to grind, that he had never had any need of cruelty. He had inherited all of Jim's niceness without, she hoped, his irresponsibility.

Jim ordered drinks, knowing what she wanted without asking, and while they waited she told him about her triumph in the new apartment. She had put up a shelf all by herself.

"In the hall," she said. "Remember that slab or marble we picked up in Woodstock in that junk shop?" For years it had lain in the basement of their house in White Plains.

"You finally found a use for it?" he asked,

grinning.

"I bought a couple of ornate brass brackets. And a drill." Jim had taken all the tools. She had never used one in her life.

"Did you use a level?"

"No, but it came out fine. I measured up from the baseboard."

"That thing weighed a ton. What did you use?"

"Plugs. The man at the hardware store..."

"It'll never hold. Better not put anything on it. You should have used mollies."

"What are mollies?"

The drinks came while he was telling her. She watched him smile at the waitress, thank her, then turn and lift his glass in a small salute. She marveled that the separation, after all the years of their marriage, hadn't in any way scarred him. He was as easy with her as if it were any ordinary night when, meeting him in town for dinner, they would go home together to the same tube of toothpaste, the shared bathroom glass, the big bed (she had kept that). He looked the same, too, handsome, his slightly crooked teeth giving his smile a kind of lopsided trustworthiness; a little grayer, perhaps, but no more so than if it had been the work of time alone, unaided by adversity. Though the decision to end the marriage had finally been hers, his acceptance of it had seemed much easier than her own. His adjustment to his new life had appeared effortless. He had taken an apartment that he couldn't really afford, with an extra bedroom (for Nick, he said, whenever he wanted to stay there), and furnished it with taste and an air of permanence. He had bought rugs and paintings and his kitchen sparkled with gadgets such as she, a good cook, after all the years full of hours spent in kitchens, had never dreamed of. He had denied himself nothing and, though she was annoyed by his extravagance because his contribution to Nick's support was negligible and dilatory, and because the burden of Nick's college expenses was entirely hers, she knew she couldn't accuse him of selfishness. If you caught him on payday with a hard luck story, he'd empty his pockets for you; the next day you'd be too late.

"You look great," he said, as though he'd read her thoughts and turned them back on her. "How do you like the apartment?"

"It would be fine, much easier than the house, except for Arthur." Arthur was Nick's dog, acquired when they'd moved to the house in White Plains when Nick was eight. The dog was eleven years old and no longer too reliable in his habits. "I have to walk him six times a day. And he doesn't understand elevators. He stands at walls, now, and waits for them to slide open."

Jim laughed. "Maybe you ought to get rid of him."

"How do you get rid of a dog that's been in the family eleven years?" As soon as she'd said it, she was sorry. In a way it was true, though; it was easier to get rid of a husband than a dog. But Jim, apparently, hadn't made the connection.

"How are things with you?" she asked. "How's business?" It was a stupid question; she knew exactly how he would answer it. She was merely passing time.

"Pretty good," he said, giving the words an inflection that implied much more than the words themselves. She looked up from her drink and saw the glazed look in his eyes (how well she knew it!), a blind drawn against the truth, that told her he was launching a lie. "There are a few big deals cooking. If just one of them breaks..."

How many big deals she had lived through, the daily details like installments in a cliffhanger, the suspense mounting, the intricacies of all the strands being drawn tighter, tighter, almost into the pattern of triumph until at last the whole fabric tore and disintegrated and the big deal that they lived on, sometimes for months, was dead. It was Jim's genius that as one big deal died, another was just being born. They were never left without the imminent prospect of not merely success (he'd have had that easily enough if he had just stuck to his job and kept out of debt), but of some stunning coup. In the beginning, it hadn't occurred to her to doubt him. There was always a nugget of verifiable truth, but Jim could take a nugget and fantasize it into a mother lode. Also, she had never known anyone who told lies. Lies seemed infinitely more difficult than the truth, and the function of words had always seemed so clear to her, and such a sacred triumph in man's evolution.

If she were still married to him, she would be questioning him minutely, waiting for the inevitable inconsistencies, pointing them out, watching him defend them, alter them, hearing the words dissolve and run, all reason and logic turned into a thick, soupy mess, ungraspable, meaningless. And she would be silenced at last by frustration and despair, disconnecting herself from the sound of his voice. Hopeless. Thank God she didn't have to do that any more, had disconnected herself, finally.

It was Garth who first told her. Sometimes, while Jim talked, she would be aware that Garth was looking not at Jim but at her, watching her face as though he were waiting for something. It had mystified and confused her. And then, one day, impatient with her obtuseness, he told her.

"He lies."

"Who? Jim?"

"Almost all the time."

"What do you mean?"

"It's no good. He's a pathological liar. You can't do anything about it."

Though frightened, she had grown angry.

"You could trap him easily if you really wanted to. But you never do. You're chicken."

The moment he said it, she knew it was true. But of course she could do something about it. She only had to be patient, to find out why he did it, to make him see. Because Jim was real, and he was there. She had only to reach out her hand and touch him to know that he was real and reachable.

After that day, things were never the same again. She doubted everything, questioned endlessly, lost her temper. He admitted nothing, defended everything, remained imperturbable. Once, after a particularly harrowing battle, all her own, he said, "I saw an analyst yesterday. I'm going to be seeing him twice a week."

"Why?" She felt the spring of hope. Now was the time for him to say that, yes, he needed help, he did this thing and it was beyond his control.

"Because you aren't happy. Because things have changed between us and it must be my fault."

Only that she was unhappy. Only that there was an unpleasantness. Still, it was better than nothing. In the weeks that followed, he told her in some detail about his twice-weekly sessions with Dr. Campbell, about the man himself, his office the waiting room, so that in time she was almost as familiar with that part of Jim's life as if she were Dr. Campbell's patient. He told her things he was discovering about himself, too, in his sessions: forgotten episodes from his childhood in which he'd suffered defeats in some way at the hands of his mother, his older brothers, a teacher. He told her dreams that he had brought to Dr. Campbell and what, together, they had done with them. Although his insight was not yet profound, she was exhilarated that he was making a beginning.

In the playground one Saturday, watching Nick and Willy on the swings, Garth came and sat beside her.

"Still chicken?" he asked. She had to curb an unexpected surge of hatred, to remember that Garth was a friend.

"Jim's seeing a psychiatrist," she said. "A Dr. Campbell."

"Oh? Terrific. Have you talked to him?"

"His psychiatrist? No."

"You should," he said. "I'm surprised he hasn't asked to see you. It's not unusual."

"Isn't it?"

"You ought to see him, to find out if there's anything you can do, any way you can help."

"All right, I will."

He stopped to light a cigarette, his eyes on Willy who was standing motionless near the swings, waiting for courage. She knew that Garth was debating whether to help Willy or to wait for him to make his own move, and that the decision, either way, was painful.

"I think you'll find that Jim will be perfectly agreeable," he said, after a while. "But I doubt if you'll ever see Dr. Campbell."

"Why? What are you saying?"

"When the time comes, I think Dr. Campbell will get sick. He may even die."

"What are you saying?"

"I wonder if there really is a Dr. Campbell."

She had to wait a moment before she could speak. "Nonsense," she said. "This is true. He couldn't have invented this."

"How do you know?"

"I know. There are too many details. Unimportant, meaningless little things. Too much atmosphere. If he's invented this, he could write *War and Peace.*"

Garth laughed, but his voice, when he spoke, was gentle. "Well, it's easily verifiable," he said. "If you're not chicken."

She hated the phrase. She watched Nick's swing arcing higher and higher, curbing her fear and her impulse to call out to him.

"What are you trying to do, Garth?" she said. "Break up my marriage?"

"Yes."

"Why?"

"Because it can't work."

He was wrong. His sureness, the certainty in his voice, were part of his professional pose. He was older; he was wise; his circle of friends, idolizing him, literally sat at his feet waiting for the terror of his wisdom and the whip of his wit. But she knew he was fallible. He had failed in his own marriage. He made mistakes with Willy out of the bitterness of having at last, in his middle years, produced a child and that child deficient. What could he know about Jim? How could he know that Jim, despite the barrier of his lying, was still the man she'd married. The shape, the bulk, his skin, his touch, his humor and gentleness, his eagerness to like and to be liked, his generosity, his absolute lack of malice, his easy, loving way with Nick, the rightness of their own lovemaking --- what could Garth know of all this? How could he weigh the one thing against the sum of all the others?

"I think I ought to see Dr. Campbell," she said to Jim that night at dinner. "I'd like to talk to him."

"I think you should," Jim said, not missing a beat. "He said the other day that he'd like to meet you. I'll set up an appointment."

Her relief almost overwhelmed her. Later in the week, he gave her the date of the appointment, a month away. Two weeks later, he told her that Dr. Campbell had been hospitalized with a heart attack.

"His office said it wasn't too serious. They don't expect him to be out more than a few weeks."

She looked up Dr. Campbell in the phone book. She found him listed at the address Jim had mentioned. She got him on the phone. He had never heard of Jim.

Days went by while she waited, unable to face the scene she was going to have to create. She felt dull, withdrawn, as though she were living in a closet. She couldn't bear to have Jim touch her; she could hardly listen to his voice. She hid behind an endless succession of books whose pages she turned, the words barely reaching her. Her apathy swallowed Jim, swallowed Nick, swallowed her, until she knew that if she didn't fight her way out of it, she could spend the rest of her life there.

One Saturday when Nick was away with Garth and she and Jim were having lunch, she said, her heart beating like a drum, "I saw Dr. Campbell yesterday," and forced herself to watch his face, the startled eyes, the sudden pallor.

"Oh?"

"He says he thinks you're making progress. But he says that it takes time." She had read whatever she could find on the subject in the public library. "He says that pathological liars are very difficult to treat, often impossible."

"Pathological liars?" His voice was so low that she could scarcely hear it. She was pitiless.

"They waste so much time. It's hard for the analyst, too, to separate the truth from the lies."

"You saw him?"

"He was very nice. Just the way you described him, so that I felt as though I knew him."

He began to cry. She had never seen him cry. She watched him for a while, feeling cold and heartless.

"Why did you have to make it up? Why didn't you really do it?"

His shoulders heaved. It was a while before he could answer. "I meant to," he said. "I almost did."

She went to the window and looked out. Sunlight dappled the tops of young trees below, rooted in oases in the concrete. The voices of children drifted up from the playground. It was the beginning of a season and, though they had lived through a war, the world was at peace. The calm Saturday air was full of hope. A scrap of a forgotten poem surfaced from the stored past: "Nothing can need a lie," she remembered. "A fault that needs it most, grows two thereby." She fought an impulse to say the words aloud.

"Why do you do it?" she asked.

"I don't know. To make you happy." She reflected, realizing that it was true. All his lies were, in a way, gifts to her. And to himself.

"It doesn't make me happy."

He came and stood beside her at the window. She could see that he wanted to touch her and was afraid.

"Is it really so important?" he said. He was asking her to accept it, to live with him as he was. But to do that, she would have to give up her reason and enter his fairyland.

"Do you know when you're lying? Do you know the difference?"

"Yes."

"Then each time you do it you have to make a choice," she said. "You have to choose away from truth. Why can't you choose not to lie?" He looked at her without comprehension. Later, she would learn that it wasn't so simple. It was like asking an alcoholic why he didn't merely refuse to drink. It was like telling someone in the depths of a depression to pull himself together. It would be explained to her that within the world as Jim created it, within the flow of his fantasy, the way he chose to see the things that happened to him, or did not happen, was logical and consecutive, truer than truth. But standing at the window that Saturday, groping for comprehension, she was as far from reality in her way as he was in his.

Fifteen years ago that was, she thought, sipping her drink, half hearing his patter about the millions to be made on this fantastic coupon scheme that couldn't miss. He talked always in large numbers, the only kind that interested him.

"It's all been worked out by a brilliant economist. I could show you the figures. Of course, they've been projected..." Such innocents they'd been that day! Still, that day had marked a beginning.

"We'll have to lick it," she told him. "I'll help you all I can."

"The chances are virtually nil," Garth said later. "You'll waste your life."

"He's a human being, Garth. He's young. Why do you throw him away so easily?"

"The only way they change is by desperately wanting to. There's no conscience, none of what we call a sense of responsibility, no habit of doing a thing the hard way. They don't see things as they are, they see them through their rose-tinted optimism. They can't make reasoned judgments."

Nonetheless, they went together from psychiatrist to psychiatrist. The first three were too busy to take on a new patient. The fourth told them frankly that, since his time was limited, he preferred to treat patients with whom he felt he had at least an even chance of getting results. It was selfish, but he needed more than monetary rewards in his work.

At last they found a doctor who agreed to a trial period, on condition that she cooperate. Rather than waste time, he would use her to check on Jim. Jim must understand and agree to it and she must be prepared to devote herself on a full-time basis to making the marriage work, if she was sure that was what she wanted. If there weren't a child, he might advise her to forget it. But since there was, they ought to make the effort. She would have to question everything, let him get away with nothing. She must be his conscience, a kind of transplant, until his own was functioning. Yes, she said, yes, yes, yes.

Fifteen years! She had played her role for at least ten of those years. She had shoved her paints to the back of a closet and, when Jim went into his own business not long after Nick started school, she'd learned bookkeeping and gone with him to the office every day. She paid the bills, kept accounts, saw that Jim was on time for appointments, tried to hold down expenses. For a few years they did well. Then Jim decided he wanted to move to the suburbs. He wanted a house. He wanted a garden. It would be a better life for Nick. The schools. Most of their friends had already moved out of the city.

They bought a house, a car, Arthur. For months she was busy with the details of getting the house ready and moving into it. She went to the office less and less often.

"I'll hire someone," he said. "You don't have to come in more than a couple of days a month. Just to make out the checks and bring the books up to date."

"But..."

"I'm getting to be a big boy now," he said, grinning.

The business failed that year. Within a week, Jim had a job.

"Thank God I don't have to be bothered with all those headaches," he said, as though the failure of the business was the happiest stroke of luck. "Now I can concentrate on selling, which is really what I do best. It's a good outfit. I'll make more money than I ever could have made in that set-up."

It was harder to keep a check on him now. It was embarrassing to ask direct questions of the people he worked for and with. She had to devise new methods, to grow cunning. Still, there were periodic crises. He gave an extravagant surprise party for her birthday and months later she discovered that he'd neglected to pay the caterers. He made promises to Nick and forgot to keep them. When she visited him at the office, she found old unpaid bills in his desk drawer, bills for things she'd been told were gifts. He borrowed money from friends and didn't pay them back. He told her stories full of discrepancies, so that she had to question him closely, trying to pin down the truth and keep him to it. At night, after Nick was asleep, they had long, anguished talks that left her limp with exhaustion.

"It wasn't a Christmas present. You bought it."

"No, it was a gift."

"I saw the bills. It wasn't a gift. Just say that you lied. Just say it. Say it once!"

"I didn't lie. The bill was sent by mistake. When I called them about it, they apologized."

"Then why did they send another? And another?"

"A screw-up in their billing department. Some stupid clerk."

"Oh, God, why can't you just say it? The sky won't come crashing down on your head. Why did it have to be a gift? Why does your paper supplier have to love you so much that he gives you expensive gifts?"

"It's not love, it's business."

Years and years of it. And then one morning she awoke and looked down at him sleeping beside her. He was no longer young, but in sleep his face, unmarked by care, had a sweetness and a serenity that stabbed her. Who the hell is he? she thought, hating him.

She signed up for a painting class that day. She took out her box of oils. The paints had dried in their tubes. The brushes were stiff and useless. She threw it all away and went out to buy new supplies. She bought extravagantly, thinking of all the money she'd saved in the ten years of not painting, and of all the lost time. She worked hard, trying to recover those lost years. After a few months, she rented a studio in town and went there every day. At night, she came home tired and happy, to cook dinner. Guilty, she cooked elaborate meals and tried to listen to Jim, to tune him in as though he were real. But her heart wasn't in it. She had discovered a new brush stroke that day, or a new way of using blue, or she had found something she could do that she hadn't known was in her, a way of handling light, and she was impatient for tomorrow. She was beginning to learn what it was all about. She was beginning to feel that she might even be good at it. She felt that she had just been born.

In the first months after Jim moved out, she was preoccupied with a thousand details. She had Nick to get off to college, the house to sell, an apartment to find, the dozens of accumulated things to confront and dispose of. And the hell of lawyers. It was more than she could manage alone; she had to dig for layers of hidden strength. Still, there were a hundred times a day when, hurtling from chore to chore, she would notice Jim's absence and feel her own aloneness. There was so much of him and of their being together, things that now, by his no longer being there, emerged from the shadowed background to scream their presence. Everything they owned together had its memory; all of it had been shared. Day by day, little by little, she learned the true meaning of easy familiar words like "separation" and "broken home." It was like death, only worse, for she had decided it. Over and over, she had to fight remorse and guilt and remind herself why she had decided.

But in sleep she was defenseless. She dreamed of Jim constantly, dreamed that she had murdered him, that he was a child lost in a desert, that he was an infant she had aborted. She would start out of sleep, her stomach knotted in guilt, asking herself, "What have I done?", knowing that, for better or worse, marriage was a sacred thing. And then she would tell herself that what she was going through was the normal wrench. You didn't get off scot-free. Time was what she needed, and there would be plenty of that.

Nick, too, so careful not to take sides, had finally added to her remorse. "I know the way Dad is," he'd written in one of his first letters from college. "But I don't think he can help it. Do you think maybe you let him down?" Though she had always believed that those who are aware must assume responsibility for those who are not, she raged against the accusation in Nick's letter, bitterly angry not at Nick but at Jim. What right have the weak to their tyranny over others? And, since they were so indomitable, weren't they really the powerful ones, the ones who prevailed? In her answer to Nick she wrote, "Sometimes it's not easy to judge who has been let down. Maybe the failure is always shared."

Still, there were days when she knew that if Jim had come to her with the right combination of words, and if she had somehow been able to believe them, she would have been prepared to mend the marriage. Knowing at the same time that if he had been capable of that, there would never have been the need to leave him.

It was her lawyer who returned her to sanity.

Hearing him distill the essence of her situation into legal jargon, apprehending his boredom, for what she brought him had been part of his daily routine for years, was in its way so frightening that it restored her. There was no room here for emotion. Though he wasn't an unkind man, feeling was beside the point.

She looked at her watch. Ten minutes more. She thought of Nick, encapsulated in that cold, silvered womb, streaking through the night. She tried to imagine the space that separated them and found that she could grasp it only in terms of time: ten minutes. And, though only this small black circle of Formica on which their glasses rested separated her from Jim, the forever of the future yawned between them.

"Did Nick say where he plans to stay?" Jim asked. It was a ticklish question. They both had a room for him, but he had lived in neither of them. She had sold the house and moved into the apartment soon after Nick left for college in the fall and, though she had disposed of many things, she had taken with her those remnants of Nick's childhood that he hadn't yet decided he'd outgrown.

"I imagine he'll divide his time between us," she said.

"I mean tonight. From the airport. Will he be going home with me or with you?"

"I supposed he'd be coming with me," she said. She had legal custody, a formality at Nick's age, and her address was Nick's official one. "But he didn't say." She saw, now, that by giving him a choice of two homes, they had deprived him of any real one. It wasn't fair that Nick should be faced with the need to choose. At best, his homecoming wouldn't be a happy one, but she hadn't foreseen that diplomacy would be required of him.

"Then I guess we'll just have to let him decide," Jim said pleasantly.

His blandness disconcerted her. Was it poise, she wondered, or insensitivity? Even as she asked herself the question, she knew its answer. It was neither. As with so much else, he had mislaid the reality of their situation by simply altering it to suit his comfort. She was suddenly dying to know what he had done with her whole life, all the years of it she had spent with him. She wanted to hear him sum it up. She leaned across the table.

"What did you tell people?" she said. "'When they asked you why we split up. What did you tell your mother?"

He shrugged. "I didn't tell her much," he said. "I told her it just hadn't worked out."

She heard the maniacal laugh burst out of her, as though she hadn't committed it, an alien sound, almost a bark.

"Is that all?" she said. "After twenty years?"

"She'd always felt I married too young." She stared at him. He was perfectly serious.

"But that was so long ago...," she faltered, thinking what of the years between? Don't they count? But it was clear that scar tissue had formed. Had there ever been a wound?

"Was it really so easy for you, Jim? The end of our marriage?"

He looked at her speculatively. She saw his eyes narrow as though he were trying to gauge just what it was she wanted.

"It wasn't easy," he said. "The first days were hell."

"Yes?"

"Right after I moved into the apartment, I went

across the street to the A&P for groceries. I walked up and down the aisles in a daze, filling the shopping cart with everything in sight. I didn't know what I was doing." He paused to smile sheepishly. "When I got back to the apartment and started to unload the stuff, I realized I'd bought as though I were shopping for the whole family. And it was only me."

"Then what did you do?"

"I called up every unmarried man I could think of and arranged a poker game."

She nodded. Yes, that was all right. "And then?"

He sighed. "Well, in the next few days I took stock of myself. I realized that what had happened had been for the best. I know I had problems, that sometimes it must have been hard for you. It's true that I always loved you but, you know, after the separation I realized that you weren't the right kind of wife for me. You were too critical. You never believed in me or gave me the kind of encouragement I needed. It was never a very good marriage."

So there it was. He had wrapped it up neatly and given her back this little gift package. Twenty years. She tried to finish her drink and found that she was unable to swallow. Her heart banged in her ears. Half the years of her life! She had spent them believing she was married, that what she did and what Jim did mattered. But none of it had mattered. She had spent those years locked inside her own sensibilities, he inside his, and they had barely brushed against each other. Alongside the string of his small fantasies, her own single one loomed like a monument.

"It's nearly time," Jim said glancing at his watch. He paid the check, then left a tip that was, as always, larger than necessary. "Too much," she nearly said, even then, then laughed at herself.

When they reached the gate, the passengers were beginning to file through. They were mostly college students, young, rumpled by their long flight and more solemn than bankers. In a moment, Nick appeared. She recognized him at once, though later she wondered how. He'd grown a beard and a moustache, his hair was nearly down to his shoulders, and he wore boots. The desert sun had burned him brown and, towering above the others, he looked commanding and patriarchal, far from the crew-cut boy she'd sent away. For a moment she was frightened, thinking that Nick, the one real thing they had done in their marriage, was a stranger, too, locked in his own life. But when he caught sight of them waiting at the barrier, his face shattered with recognition and delight. He was Nick.

It was hard to embrace him, he was so slung with cameras, his arms loaded with trivia, as though at the final moment of leaving he'd swept through his room gathering up all the odds and ends he'd forgotten to pack. He stood awkwardly, trying to put things down, passing them from one hand to the other while first she and then Jim leaned across his confusion to kiss him.

"Well!" they all three said, and stood there smiling hard.

"You both look great," Nick said.

"You've grown," she said. "I thought you'd stopped. You look fierce."

"Scared you?"

"I'll take you to my barber first thing in the morning," Jim said.

"No you won't," Nick said, fingering his chin. "This stuff is here to stay."

They prattled on. The trip was OK. They'd been held up for a while in Dallas. Yes, they'd had dinner on the plane, such as it was. No, he wasn't really hungry. Boy, he was glad to be back in New York.

"Give me your baggage ticket," Jim said. "I'll go collect it."

When Jim had gone, she kissed Nick again and said, "It's good to have you back. I really missed you." They grinned at each other.

"What's that?" she asked pointing to the welter of junk at his feet.

"This?" He reached down and pulled two crude clay objects strung on chains from the pile and held them aloft. "They're a present for you. Indian bells. They hang them from the ceiling and the breeze rings them. There were three bells, but I broke one in Dallas."

"They're lovely," she lied.

"I could have killed myself when it broke. I thought it would be safer not to pack them, but they were a pain to lug around. I'm sorry."

"Indians made them?"

"Well, not exactly." He laughed. "A friend of mine in the art department makes them. He sells them to the Indians to sell as native crafts."

She smiled. How much dishonesty there was in the world; how difficult not to be corrupted by it. Nick swung one of the bells. It sounded soft and clear.

"Listen, Mom," he said, his voice serious. "I thought maybe tonight I ought to go home with Dad."

"Yes, sure," she said, flustered.

"You don't mind?"

"No," she said, wondering how he had decided,

seeing in his face that the decision had troubled him.

"And I'll see you tomorrow? I want to go through my junk. I guess there's a lot we can throw away."

"All right."

"I thought it might be better..."

Jim was back with the luggage. "Let's go," he said. She watched Nick and Jim argue over who would carry what. Firmly, Nick won, appropriating the heavier suitcase and as much else as he could manage. So, he had decided. To do that, he must have judged them and then chosen. Out of what? Pity? She knew, during the scuffle for the bags, in the way he smiled at Jim, in the way he had talked to her, that he had judged Jim the weaker, the needier, ... the underdog. They walked out of the airport toward the parking lot where they said good night and parted.

Carrying her Indian bells, she found, as she walked toward the car, that she was having a conversation with Garth. "Taking the long, the anthropological, the un-chicken view of it," she said, "this marriage accomplished what marriage was instituted for. We reproduced the species and raised our young to adulthood. We paid our debt to life. All the rest is window dressing." She smiled, adding a final word, the agnostic amen: "Maybe."

She said good night to Garth, too, and drove away.

SOUP

"Do you know what time it is?" I ask my father, testing. He looks at the bedside clock. "It's two-fifteen," he says. I'm puzzled. It is two-fifteen. Why would he know this and not his beloved ledger numbers, the figures he so methodically entered for every transaction in his life? He's lost all those numbers; half his brain is dead. Is time so important that both sides of the brain master it? How little I know.

"Do you know who I am?" I ask him.

"Of course," he says again, but with less certainty. "You're Ann. Ann Silver." My maiden name, his name, which I've not used for over thirty years. "You're my daaaaughter," he brays.

He's in the bedroom in the rented crib-sided bed, dying. The doctor says it may be a matter of hours. I got here only this morning; I came to watch him die. How many times in my life have I wished him dead?

"I am a lucky man," he says. "I am full of joy, overcome with joy, drunk with joy, consumed with joy." Where has he found all these words, some I can't recall his ever having used. Fascinated, I've been sitting here for hours, listening to him slip from abusive rage to this uncharacteristic effusion of lyricism. Clearly, he is listening to the sound of his voice, repeating and repeating, but altering the vocal nuances. "Where am I? Home? I am home in my darling home with the ceilings, much too much ceiling, wall-to-wall ceilings, who needs all these ceilings?"

Claudia, his nurse for the past two years, comes in with a handful of pills and a glass of water. One by one he swallows the pills, encouraged by Claudia's little clucks of approval, this good and obedient child. He gives her a false, childlike smile. "Do you like this face?" he asks, grimacing sweetly. "This is a good face. A very goooood face. I want soup. I want six, eight, a hundred plates of soup. I want to gouge myself on soup. Is gouge a good word? Do I have any money left? Get me some soup."

"Gorge," I say, as I run to the kitchen to warm up a can of chicken rice soup. When I get back, he has already forgotten about the soup. I put it on the bed tray and begin to spoon it into his mouth. His hand sweeps away my arm and the soup sprays out of his mouth. He is an enfeebled powerful dying old man.

"What is that, piss? Take it away. Take it AWAY."

"He won't eat anything," Claudia says. "He hasn't eaten in two days."

"Go to bed, Claudia," I say. "I'll call if I need you."

The night is almost over. We've all been trying to stay awake. No problem for me; I wouldn't miss his death for anything. I have so many of his lousy genes that this is probably a preview of my own coming attractions.

"I guess I'm dying," he says sadly. "I didn't

think I'd ever die."

Nobody did. Megalomaniacal son of a bitch. I don't think he ever gave a thought to anyone but himself, or cared what anyone else was feeling, or so much as noticed. For a while, I tried to be generous, telling myself he didn't have the vocabulary for it, but there's nothing wrong with his vocabulary. Drowning, he's been reviewing his life.

"She used to make soup," he mumbles. He's talking about his mother. "Boy, did she make soup, lukshen, farfel, borscht, schav, she was a soup machine, her middle name was soup, she was the mother souperior, ha, ha, get it? When I went into business that first year, working day and night and sleeping on the cutting room table, she would come to the Place with a big jar of hot soup, I should only live and succeed. The meanest mother in the world, but this was about money, this was important." His voice trails off; his breathing is labored.

"Soup was love," I say.

"Soup was money."

"Money was love," I say.

"Money was money," he says, his voice fading. He sleeps for a couple of minutes, then, without opening his eyes, begins to talk again. "They used to say in the obituaries, 'he left an estate of over a million dollars.' That was always my ambition, to die with over a million dollars."

No kidding, I do not say. Reminding him that he wasn't going to be able to take it with him always made him furious. He didn't care about that; the accumulation was all.

"I'm pretty sure I'll leave over a million," he mumbles.

"They won't put it in the paper," I say, cruelly.

"They don't do it any more. Unless it's really a lot."

"Yeah. A million dollars used to mean something."

He falls asleep and I doze off for a few minutes, until the rattling sound of his breathing wakes me. Death rattle, I think, and I see on his face a look of intense concentration, as if beyond the closed lids his eyes are trying to penetrate some murky dark. He is working hard to master something, or to remember, and then I see him come half up out of bed to reach for a breath and not get it, and I know that what he was striving for was to keep his life in his body, and that he has failed. I touch his shoulder and feel the bone. He was such a bull of a man.

But whatever he was, he's stopped. I look at the thin line of his mouth that will never speak another unkind word. He's finally, awesomely dead.

THE DOG

When she was a child, Jane thought, trying to keep her mind off the road ahead, her parents used to visit her at summer camp. It was a drag for them, but they had never had to come as far as this.

The Chevy station wagon careened around an impossible curve. They were all impossible curves. Whoever had engineered this road, damn him to hell, was a vicious killer. She'd been sitting in the back seat for hours, her eyes squeezed shut much of the time in absolute terror. She could understand that they'd had to follow the mountain's contours; it wasn't practical to move mountains, and perhaps tunneling through them would have aroused the slumbering monsters within. But you'd think anyone could manage a railing, some sort of barrier between the narrow road's edge and all that sheer nothing falling abruptly off beyond it. No problem for them to plant those white crosses, so frequent along the way, that marked the end for some failed motorist. The bodies, she supposed, were irrecoverable and you had to pay some homage. Bloody pious Mexicans. She was very down on them.

Like those two in the front seat taking turns with the driving, if you could call it that. Not until they had the speed up to 90 kilometers did they seem relaxed. Ramos and Agostino. What was she doing in this Godforsaken wilderness with a brace of Mexican lawyers with whose mangled bodies her own, at any moment, might be condemned to lie forever, trapped in the twisted junk of this rattleheap, their blood all mixed together. As if they hadn't already bled her enough.

Ramos had assured her that kilometers were shorter than miles, that translated into miles, et cetera, but she was in no mood to do any translating. Too fast was too fast in any language, and it was all she could do in the few less heart-stopping moments of the road's winding, to absorb the staggering hostility of these mountains. Scarred, ancient, formed of eons of volcanic brooding and temper, they were utterly unlike the gentle green Berkshires of her childhood summers or the blue Catskills she had for a few seasons viewed from across the river. For long stretches, often an hour at a time, there was no sign of life (what could live here?), not a single picturesque person squatting at the side of the road, only vehicles hurtling at them, inevitably, around every second or third bend, like the elephantine bus that now suddenly loomed. Knowing that the road wasn't nearly wide enough to accommodate them both, and that neither driver would permit either prudence or courtesy to dent his machismo, she shut her eyes, cursing. She heard the whoosh of the bus as they flew past it and, spared once again, thanked whoever was still in charge of the miracle department.

She opened her eyes to stare with loathing at the back of Ramos' neck and saw that even Agostino was shaken enough to be muttering what sounded like a rebuke. Although Agostino had driven for the first two hours, and just as fast, she had sensed from the hunch of his shoulders and the set of his head that his trust was not in fate but in his own competence. Ramos, however, was insouciant, one hand loose on the wheel, the other lying across the back of Agostino's seat. From time to time, recalling that she was there, he would half turn his head around to make some unnecessary remark in his charming rotten English. Ramos, Spanish blood, well-born, spoiled son of an Important Man, letting her know he was the sportsman, keeper of polo ponies, with his handsome weak corrupt face, his soft pouting mouth. She'd give odds that he beat not only his wife but his mistress.

He was groping towards one of his little conversations and she wished he wouldn't. Because her Spanish was even worse than their English, the language barrier was almost insuperable. Still, she had no trouble understanding that they both lied to her and that they were robbing her. She pretended to be asleep, wishing it were true, but Ramos persisted.

"Is your God to taking care of us, Agostino, so nothing to afraid," he chuckled. Agostino responded in Spanish. "You know what he say?" Ramos called to her. "He say he not how you say selfish. He know his God good to him but he fear for you and me."

"Tell him thanks," she mumbled. She liked Agostino better than Ramos, but not much. Slight and dark, Indian, he seemed gentler, and once or twice she thought he had looked at her with something resembling sympathy in his soft dark eyes, as though she just possibly was not a cash register but a real live person.

"Why are we in such a hurry, Senor Ramos?" she asked. "No es possibile andiamo ahora a la penitenceria, no?" She spoke haltingly, cursing with half her mind Senora Gonzalez for the two years of high school Spanish that had rendered her so inadequate to this occasion, while the other half combed among the detritus of Romance languages that had accumulated there. "No es il giorno por visitare."

"Not understanding," he said reasonably.

"Tomorrow is visiting day, no?"

"Toorsday."

"So what's the big hurry today?"

"Is no big hurry," he said agreeably, soothing her, his foot no less insistent on the accelerator. "Is much time."

She sighed. She had long since learned on Dr. Kantfogel's couch that anger was often her way of dealing with fear. She was very angry. Think of something else. Think about how your parents had to come to visit you at camp (since that's where you were, unlike some people's children, who were in Mexican prisons). Once a summer, on visiting day, when all the parents came. Fever of preparing for them, scrubbing the bunks, rehearsing the play, clean uniforms, practicing the songs. Getting faces ready, brave and joyous. Then, truly eager to see them on the great day, anxious if they were a little late, hurt when so many others arrived before them and you were still waiting, your face beginning to freeze in its sickly half-smile, heart leaping as one day it would for lovers when they at last began to appear. Watching the strain on them of the day as it wore so slowly on, how tedious for them to spend all those hours viewing their child in this Other Environment. But it wasn't, from the moment they arrived until they were gone, another environment; she reverted to what she was at home, lost entirely the glorious new identity she felt she had forged in this place where she had at last come into her own: popular, good athlete, bright, inventive, funny, important, appreciated. Loved, even. Her parents were doing their duty; they patronized her with a humor that wounded. Nice that she'd won a blue ribbon in the horse show, that two of her paintings hung in the social hall, that she was editing the camp paper, that her team was ahead. How nice, her mother said, fussing with her hair. Big deal, her father said, chomping on his cigar. Though her heart had turned with love at the first sight of them (a habit), it was as much a relief for her as for them when they were finally able to leave and she could go back to being her unique summer self.

"Is much close to friend with God, this Agostino," Ramos was saying. As Ramos' assistant, one of Agostino's duties was to submit to persecution. "Too pure for marry, but he much love all children of his brothers."

The effort to communicate in unmastered tongues reduced them to idiots, robbed of all complexity and subtlety. Was that why she was thinking of her childhood, or was it the equation with Nick? But Nick, at nineteen, was no longer a child, and prison, let alone a Mexican prison, was hardly summer camp.

It had been one long nightmare, but she hadn't gone to pieces. She had swung into action the moment she heard. First the phone call to the consulate. They would make inquiries and let her know. Not much later, their wire (collect). It was a narcotics charge; they couldn't intervene. Narcotics? She knew Nick had chewed peyote at an Indian ceremony in the desert and that more recently he had been smoking grass. It hadn't occurred to him not to tell her and they'd had the usual exchange. "How old were you when you started drinking? Alcohol is more damaging." "How do you know? Besides, marijuana is illegal." "So was booze during prohibition, but that didn't stop anyone." Etc., etc.

It was the early sixties, impossible to see the configurations of the times, as one would later, in retrospect. As in the early stages of all epidemics, it was this stricken individual, then that one. So that when Nick was instantly drawn to the hippie scene (she thought of it then as a small group of misfits, and it was) on his arrival at college in Arizona, she at once felt the guilt of the failed parent. It was because of the divorce. But he was nearly seventeen when she and Jim had separated, and even Kantfogel, her long-ago psychiatrist, to whom she had run for advice, had assured her that, while it wouldn't be easy for Nick, he was at an age when most of his interests lay outside the home and he would survive.

Still, she hadn't been totally unprepared for what happened to Nick. His letters had led in an almost undeviating line to this moment.

"I hope you'll understand what I'm trying to communicate to you, Mom, as it's terribly important to me. I'm leaving school. Nothing I study here seems to have any relevance to me or to my life."

"Who are you? What is your life?"

"I don't know who I am. I don't know what I want to do with my life. That's what I need to find out and I'm not going to find it out here. I've got to knock around a little in the world. There's nothing here for me. I'm not an intellectual like you and your friends. Maybe I'm just not very smart."

"You're too dumb to know how smart you are. You're a lot smarter than you think."

"Anyhow, that's not important to me. Who you are, what you know, what you've done, those things aren't important to me. Being is important, and being beautiful."

"Soul?" she wrote, trying to swallow her impatience, trying to understand. "Are you talking about soul, and what do you mean by it?"

If he knew, he wasn't telling. The implication was that she, out of her background, was incapable of comprehending, and maybe he was right. Did he mean character, qualities of which he had so many to admire: goodness, kindness, gentleness, honesty, loyalty, sweetness? But what about the sterner ones: responsibility, strength, self-discipline, determination, if not for personal achievement then for the purpose of leaving the world a little better for having been in it?

"At least finish the term. Think of the wasted time, effort, money." Proving that she had missed the point entirely. Not for them the need for money, for time (Nick, when he got on his motorcycle and headed south, threw away his wristwatch), for approval, not even for a revolution. If only there had been that.

There were twenty of them, he wrote (at least he wrote; at least he still wanted the lines kept open). They were going to a little town in Mexico, San Blas, that one of them had scouted and found ideal. On the Pacific, with whatever the sea had to offer. A freshwater river, plenty of fish. Bananas. Mangos. They were going to form a commune. He had swapped his VW for the motorcycle. Less gas. I'll write when I get there.

But they hadn't counted on the Mexicans. The beautiful, simple, romantic natives. Who didn't want them. Who hated them, these spoiled gringo brats with their long hair so you couldn't tell the sexes apart unless there was a beard and some of them weren't old enough for that. Who looked dirty out of choice. Who were godless and immoral. Who were too tall, too young, ridiculous. Who had the gall to play at the poverty that for so many centuries had been their reality. Who had no money to spend in their town, where they did not belong. Watch out, Nick, here comes the real world.

"One hour only more," Ramos said. They were coming down out of the mountains and, though the road still wound perilously, the abysses that skirted them were beginning to have floors.

Fifteen hundred miles he'd journeyed on a beat-up bike that kept breaking down before at last, utterly exhausted, reaching nirvana. He hadn't been there five minutes when he was arrested, packed into the back of a truck and hauled off to Tepic, to jail. His friends, who had preceded him, were already there.

In the hours after the wire came from the consulate, she made dozens of phone calls, casting about desperately for someone, something in her life that could be helpful, discovering once again that only in extremis do we take the full measure of our limitations. Then she thought of Clara Nevelson. Clara was a lawyer for the Legal Aid Society, most of her work with juveniles, and she had friends in Mexico City.

"Oh, God, Mexico," Clara said when she'd heard the story. "Those Mexican jails are the worst. The first thing is to see that Nick gets some food and money. I'll call Max right away and get back to you as soon as I can."

"What do you mean, get him food? Don't they feed them?"

"Are you kidding? If they did, nine tenths of Mexico would be in prison."

Half an hour later, Clara called. "Max says to get down there right away. Tomorrow. Be at his office by late afternoon. She gave Jane the address. "And bring a lot of money. Cash."

Jim had gone with her that first time, holding her hand during the takeoff, knowing how she felt about flying. It was odd being with Jim that way. In the three years since the divorce, she'd had lunch with him perhaps half a dozen times to discuss money, or a problem with the children. Their only other meetings had been in the offices of lawyers or, briefly, when he brought Jed home from a Sunday outing. During those four days in Mexico City, however, temporarily reunited by the one thing that still bound them, that perhaps would always bind them, they were together almost constantly. They had separate hotel rooms, of course, but even that had posed a minor problem. The hotel desk clerk had had great difficulty understanding that even though they were registered as Mr. and Mrs. Jamie Becker, they required two rooms and only after a struggle during which he offered and they refused a suite, did he hand them each their separate room keys.

They spent most of that first day in the office of Clara's friend, Max Kurzman, an influential businessman, discussing the legal intricacies with him and his attorney, Ramos, turning the money over to them and dispatching Ramos to Tepic, along with a note for Nick. After that, there was nothing to do but wait for Ramos to return with Nick. He was confident, Ramos, that he would be coming back in two or three days; he had only to bribe a few people, file some papers. Waiting, infected by Ramos's confidence, there was nothing for them to do but turn themselves into tourists and enjoy the city where neither of them had been before. They explored the old city, found some good restaurants, went to the folk ballet and the anthropological museum, walked in the park, browsed in shops. Odd, after all those years of intimacy, the politeness and boredom between them.

Then Ramos had returned without Nick, shaking his head. It was more serious than they had known. Also, the judge was pretending to be incorruptible. Nick had gotten off two friends who had traveled down with him by declaring that the marijuana found on them was his, and that he had brought it with him from the States. Three counts: possession, dealing, transporting it across the border. A foolish boy, Ramos said, and more than that, he had been uncooperative, angry that his parents were meddling in what was his own problem, one that he would deal with in his own way. It would take more time, Ramos said. More money. There was nothing to do but go home.

Each week after that, Nick's release was imminent and each week there was some failure. The weeks turned to months. More and more money was needed, and then her signature on many documents. She decided to make the trip again, this time alone, and to go from Mexico City with Ramos to Tepic where he had to file more documents and speak once again to the judge. She was almost surely not going to be able to bring Nick home with her, but it was a long time since she'd seen him and she missed him desperately. She needed not only to see him, but to touch him. She needed to diminish the nightmarish quality of those months.

Surrounded by a high iron fence, the jail squatted, a small square building of no distinction except that it was painted in festive orange and blue, belying its dreary purpose. A guard passed them through the gates after an exchange of questions and answers and a show of identity cards. At the door to the prison they were questioned again and admitted. Inside, her first impression was of complete informality, despite the desk behind which an officer sat, his uniform only slightly less rumpled than those of the guards. Others, Mexican men in varying dress and undress, barefoot, wandered freely about, one of them mopping a passageway with a filthy rag at the end of a stick. At her entrance, all eyes turned towards her, brightly inquisitive; she was a curiosity, a white woman in American clothing, a head taller than anyone else there. She was aware, too, of a medley of odors which she was too nervous to sort out.

The officer at the desk inclined his head to her and greeted Ramos and Agostino with recognition and pleasure. He had been well bribed on Nick's behalf in the preceding months; he looked forward to more of the same. Almost slavering with greed, he turned again to her, the source, the cornucopia, and she saw in his glittering black eyes that he would do everything in his power to prolong Nick's stay; they were holding him for ransom. Her heart thumped with an overpowering surge of rage. She looked at the polite mask of the man's face, at the polite masks of the faces of her lawyers, feeling as though she had walked into a trap set by her own hand. Because of her concern for Nick, needing to see him, wanting him to know that he was not deserted, she had made a serious error. She should never have come.

She was ushered into an adjoining chamber, the visiting room, indistinguishable in its dreariness from any ordinary small town train station waiting room except for the absence of that numbing sense of transience. A wooden bench ran along two of the walls, empty except for a Mexican slumped in a corner, his bare feet not quite reaching the floor, deeply asleep. She sat down to wait, facing the far end of the room that yawned like the mouth of a cave, a black hole through which she guessed Nick would enter.

And remembered his first entrance, his birth. It was as though he had at last come tunneling out of not only her womb but the dark cave of her fear. She had greeted the onset of labor with relief and excitement, even hilarity. She and Jim, when she had finally gotten him to wake up, had giggled over her idiotic impulse to weigh herself as soon as she realized that what she was feeling was labor pains, and again at the odd assortment she threw together to take to the hospital, the carton of cigarettes, the acrostics, the unread back issues of the *New Yorker*, her journal, pads, pencils, pens. "How about a cheese sandwich on rye?" Jim had said. "How about my Swiss army knife?" As though she were off to a distant place where she would be isolated, where she would have so much empty time on her hands.

Even at the hospital's admitting desk, when the pains were severe and almost unremitting, and she'd had to stand half doubled over answering the clerk's endless questions, she'd found it funny. "Your mother's maiden name?" the woman asked and she had trouble remembering. "I'm not applying for a bank loan," she said. "I only want to have this baby." It was three o'clock in the morning, her doctor hadn't arrived yet, she was ten days early and they didn't have a room for her, she would have to go straight to the labor room, where Jim could not accompany her. There, a nurse, bored and sleepy, gave her a hospital gown, showed her which bed to climb into (the others were all empty), secured its crib sides, and vanished, leaving her entirely alone to stare at the one sad blue bulb dangling naked from the ceiling, giving off its dim light. It was then, in the silence and her aloneness and the increasing pain, that the fear began. Why had she been left alone? There wasn't even a button to push; suppose there were complications and she died? She was usually good about pain, but this was different; her body no longer belonged to her; it had become a ravening monster, an enemy. She had no idea how long she waited, trying to keep the panic at bay, before she turned fear to anger and began to rage.

"This is my first baby," she howled into the dark. "I don't know how to have a baby. Where is my expensive doctor? This is a hospital. With all the pills in the world, there must be pills for this." On and on. "Why must I suffer this way, like a peasant in the fields, in a rice paddy, instead of someone in a modern metropolitan hospital supposedly staffed with professionals?" She had set up such a racket and then not been able to stop, even after that cold and hateful nurse had appeared and, seeing that she was indeed close, began to prepare her. Later, when it was over, the nurse had told Jim, "Once in a while we get one like her."

They held Nicky up for her to see, told her he was a fine healthy boy, and she took one look and went blissfully, euphorically to sleep. When she awoke again the sun was high and her left hand rested in a bowl of tepid clam chowder. It was lunch time and a tray lay across her chest. "Must be Friday," she thought, licking a finger, aware of her deliciously unburdened body and in the same moment dying to see her new baby.

Jesus   in an Indian headband, tall and lean, came striding across the room towards her, a smile at once false and pure on his face. At his heels was a large brown dog with the physique of a starved goat.

"Nick!" she cried, leaping off the bench. She threw her arms around him and began to cry.

"What's that for?" he said. "Cut it out."

"Have you always had all these bones?" she said, feeling them through his shirt. She held him at arm's length, then, the better to see him. Though he was smiling, there were tears in his eyes, too. "Damn it," she said. "What's a nice Jewish boy like you doing in a place like this? How much weight have you lost?"

"Who   knows?   Twenty   or   thirty   pounds, maybe. I'm in real good shape thanks to the Tepic spa and health club."

He did look fit, the contours of his face strong beneath the beard, and, surprisingly, his skin was tanned. She had always thought him beautiful; just looking at him was one of the real pleasures of her life through all the stages of his growing up. He had never had an awkward age. When he had last gone off, the soft traces of adolescence still clung to him. She saw now that they were gone.

"It's not such a bad place," he said. "They only lock us up in our cells at night. The rest of the time we're free to wander anywhere we like. On the premises, natch. We're out in the yard a lot playing ball."

"Let's sit," she said and, clutching his hand, she drew him to the bench. The dog, who had flopped on his belly at Nick's heels was instantly on his feet, right behind them, and when they sat down the dog resumed his sprawl, his nose an inch from the tip of Nick's boot, his eyes feverishly fixed on Nick's face.

"Where'd the dog come from?" she asked.

"That's right, you've never met Albert," he said. "He's the dog I got out of the pound in Arizona. I wrote you about him."

"How did you get him here?"

"I sent him down ahead of me with a few of the kids who were traveling in an old milk wagon they'd bought. When I got picked up and thrown into this joint, here he was, waiting for me. It was a real touching reunion."

"He seems very devoted."

She remembered the letter in which he'd mentioned the beautiful beast he'd been so lucky to find in the pound, and how good it felt to have a family again. It was one of the least appealing dogs she'd ever seen, somewhere between goat and boxer with hints of half a dozen other strains, and with the frantic, darting, neurotic look and absolute lack of humor of a creature who has needed all his wits simply to survive.

"I guess I haven't done too well by him," Nick said mournfully, sensing her appraisal. "Out of the pound and into the pen."

Or by yourself, she bit her tongue not to say. Plus a short lecture about how you can't assume responsibility for another creature until you can assume it for yourself. Anger, again. My son and his dog, oh idiot, oh stupid and wasteful, oh what did I forget to tell you, there was something always on the tip of my mind to teach you and what was it again?

"I brought some stuff," she said, nodding towards the three huge shopping bags Agostino had carried into the waiting room for her. She had shopped in Guadalajara. Rice and beans and canned hams and soups and crackers and cigarettes and toiletries. Everything she could think of that he might need, which was just about everything in the market. And a stack of paperbacks she had brought with her from home.

"Wow," he said, lifting the bags and putting them on the bench next to him. He peered inside, pulling items out at random. "Wow and double wow! What riches."

"Though I hope you won't be here long enough to use it all up."

"It won't last very long," he said. "There are eighteen of us."

"Eighteen?"

"Angus and Linda are in the hospital with hepatitis. I mean eighteen in our group. The Mexicans, as you can see, have families."

A straggle of women and children had begun to file through the waiting room to vanish into the black hole that led to the cells. The children were barefoot and cheerful, the women, most of whom seemed to be pregnant, were poorly dressed, their faces flat and expressionless, like rough wood carvings, their arms laden with pots, sacks, buckets, string bags, dead unplucked chickens dangling head down.

"They're allowed into the cells?"

"Yeah. Twice a week. It's a day's outing for the family. They cook, eat, fight, screw, a little home away from home." He scratched his head. "I wish I could take you down to see our setup but they wouldn't give me permission. It's real groovy."

"Groovy?"

"We've got three big adjoining cells. We

painted the walls, murals, designs, with luminescent paint. It glows all night. We've done a lot of other fixing up, too. I made a great mobile out of those handsome little Mexican matchboxes. I keep adding to it."

Summer camp flashed through her mind again. She looked at his face. It was serene, untroubled.

Once, when we were both cranky for having been stuck in for a whole week during one of your illnesses, it was hard to tell which of us was crankier, but I being the mother said, okay, let's play, and you said what, and I said The Whole World. You'd never heard of that game because I'd just made it up. I began to push all the living room furniture against the walls and told you to bring out every single toy you had in your room, and I believe you had every toy there was, thanks to Jim who thought he was the number one father in the history of mankind because he denied you nothing, not even what you hadn't yet begun to want. Out you came with armful after armful and on the living room floor, on that expanse of green carpet, we began to set up The Whole World: here the airplanes, there the dump truck and the garbage truck and the tow truck and the fire engines and the automobiles, the lead soldiers, the train set with its little wooden houses and its tunneled mountain, here a wall out of the big wooden blocks, there a bridge and a skyscraper out of the Meccano set, a library with your picture books, a farm with the rubber animals and the cardboard barn. When I thought we had it all out, you came running in with your fishbowl in your arms, the little glass bowl with its one surviving goldfish slurping around in it, and you said, your face shining with delight, "Here comes the ocean, Mommy, we need an ocean." Yes, we needed an ocean.

Oh, we had a good time that day! Between us, we really did make a world and we both liked it so much that we left it there, using up the whole living room, for nearly a week.

"The kids want to meet you," Nick said. "Is it okay with you?"

"Of course."

"They're getting dressed up for you. They've been preparing for days. It's a big event for them. For us."

"How come?"

"You're the only one who's come."

"What do you mean?"

"From home."

"None of their parents have come?"

"No. Nobody. A couple of them get a little money once in a while, but that's it."

"Nobody? Nobody's come?"

He began to talk of their life in the prison. The state gave them a small allowance, a few pesos a day with which to buy food, enough only to keep them from starving. They got one of the guards to shop for them once or twice a week, for a fee, of course, and then they took turns cooking, beans and rice mostly, or they could get their meals at the cantina, an informal operation sloppily run for profit by an inmate serving a life term. Their own group was a tightly knit commune (as they had originally planned, though not in exactly these circumstances), pooling whatever resources it had and sharing everything equally. Nick was their spokesman; his four years of Spanish were serving him well, and since he had made friends with many of the Mexican prisoners, he had become fluent. They had retained a local lawyer to represent them as a group. He had been furious when Ramos and Agostino (Laurel and Hardy, he called them) had first appeared, because he didn't want special treatment, apart from the group, and because he'd felt, still did, that it was his own problem and that he must handle it his way, with his friends, without her and Jim's interference.

"But how could we have known that in the beginning?" she said. "We knew nothing. Except that they were going to get you out that first weekend."

Nick snorted. "Nothing works like that here. Mañana, mañana. First it's the jail captain, then the local judge, then a higher judge somewhere in the province, then some authority in Guadalajara. No trial. You post bail money, but it isn't really bail, God knows what it is. The legal procedures are all mysteries and they keep changing every day. One day they say one thing, the next something entirely different. All you can do is wait."

As she had already learned.

"But I'm sure you slowed it up. They'd have been glad to get rid of us sooner once they saw that no one gave a damn. We're costing them money, except for your bounty. All they had to do was see us across the border and never let us back in."

"You're probably right," she said. "But I don't see what else we could have done."

Was she really apologizing to him, feeling defensive? What did it mean? He was accusing her. Again, she tasted the edge of her anger and tried to swallow it, remembering how unnaturally she had bumbled about in the mother role in the beginning, in those terrible days when she was falling apart. And later? She remembered a moment: you had bought him his cub scout uniform with all the trimmings and

then, when he stood there decked out in it, his face so
naked with joy and beatitude that your heart turned
over, even while you hated it, and couldn't stop yourself idiotically thinking that this glowing eight-year
old with his eyes shining with utter delight and self-
love was an incipient storm trooper, so that you had
to say some nasty sarcastic thing he couldn't possibly
understand: clothes make the man, or: give a man a
horse he can ride, rotten mother, den mother. You
had to follow up, remember, think of projects for your
son and the four other *jugend* in the pack. We're going to sleep outside tonight, bring sleeping bags,
flashlights, and permission. And then you led them
across the back yard and over the brook that bounded
your property and was also the dividing line between
townships, and you said, "We're crossing into another
country," and behind the brook there was a small
woods, a watershed, where you'd found a little clearing and you made them all go to sleep in it, telling
them that in the morning we would cook bacon and
eggs on the terrace, and then you left them there, in
full view of the house, and went back to your bedroom and read *Mrs. Dalloway* and went peacefully to
sleep. It was a huge success.

Now, against the last of the tide of Mexican
visitors, the Americans began to appear, the group,
the children. Nick got up and introduced them one by
one. They were timid, they smiled, they shook her
hand and said how glad they were to meet her, to see
an adult American, someone from home, Nick's
mother. She made them homesick. They were very
young. They sat on the floor in a semicircle at her
feet, a softness in their eyes, a hunger on their faces,
a vagueness in their speech. She felt tender towards
them, a little embarrassed, and didn't know quite

what to say. She wanted to tell them stories, to make them laugh. She wanted to say, now that's enough of this stupid game, get your things and we'll go home. Instead, she asked them questions, where they were from, how old they were, how they passed the time here, was it very bad.

It wasn't very bad.

A boy named Eddie told her how much they all loved Nicky. He was the greatest. He was their spokesman and their protector. Just yesterday one of them had had his underwear and socks stolen and Nick had found out who had done it and gotten it all back. From a tough Mexican murderer, a lifer, and the cat had a knife a foot long, but Nick wasn't afraid of him, he was afraid of Nick.

Alarmed, she looked at Nick. He smirked at her, embarrassed, his look saying: it was nothing. Yes, as usual, he was the tallest, the strongest, the handsomest, and now, with his black beard and long hair, the fiercest. She looked back at the children sitting at her feet and saw that their eyes were strange, a little too soft, almost glassy. She looked at Nick and saw that his eyes were the same.

"Are you stoned?" she asked Nick.

"A little."

"Are you all stoned?"

"We're stoned most of the time," Nick said, smiling.

"How?"

"Easiest thing in the world to get hold of here. Good stuff, and cheap. Everyone's got it."

"I don't understand."

"The stuff they grow around here is really the best," one of the boys said.

"But that's what you were jailed for."

Nick laughed. "The guards sell it to us, the prisoners' wives bring it in, everyone smokes. It's more available than the air in here."

And now her anger was a wild pounding. There was nowhere to focus it. She clamped her teeth together and closed her eyes. She was an unwilling player in this nightmare, in this squalid jail, in this town whose name she could have gone through life without ever having heard, because her son, this romantic hero, had taken a stance that had led him here, that had made it almost inevitable that he be the ridiculous victim in an idiotic and meaningless charade. He had assumed that stance out of a need to feel himself separate and his own man, and this particular stance, because it was easy and available and required little thought. Ten years hence, history would teach her that he was part of an epidemic, but there was no way now to see him as anything but her son, this boy whose new self-image was also a rebellion, a rebellion that carried its accusation, as all rebellions do, and the anger behind that accusation.

She took a deep breath and opened her eyes and looked at Nick with all the objectivity she could muster: the scuffed cowboy boots, the worn jeans, the wrinkled white shirt he had laundered for this occasion, the long, unclean black hair held back by the Indian band across his brow, the chigger bites on his strong young arms, the untroubled eyes. This son of Hopalong Cassidy, Davy Crockett, Gene Autry, hero-worshipper for whom Scarsdale daddies with their skewed values were insufficient, despite all their fond words, heartfelt kisses, expensive gifts, patient indulgence, unquestioning love. What better world had he found behind his hair and beard and stoned brain? She wished she knew, but he was indeed separate.

She leaned back, feeling the tension go out of her. Memory was sentimental, fraudulent, a device for blackmailing the present, just as hope, false hope, was a way of blackmailing the future.

There was nothing she could do. Perhaps some day they could be friends.

Two men in wrinkled white jackets appeared at the entrance to the waiting room with the captain, conversing among themselves, looking towards them. The captain came over and spoke to Nick.

"Public Health," Nick said. "They're going to inject us all against hepatitits."

Groaning, they all got up off the floor and filed into the captain's office, the dog too, right behind Nick. One by one they returned. Nick, when he reappeared, had streaks of fresh blood on his shirt.

"I never saw anything like that," he said, shaking his head. "They didn't even sterilize the needle between shots. Probably gave us all hepatitis."

Even as he said it, she knew it was true, knew with certainty that that would come next.

The orange sun was low in the sky, thrusting brilliant shafts through the barred windows behind her. She was bone tired and her head had begun to ache. She was glad to see that Ramos and Agostino had reappeared. It was time to go. But now there was some commotion, an urgent discussion between the lawyers, the captain, the health officers. Nick went to see what it was about and she watched his face, saw anger there first, then acceptance. He came back to her, looking sheepish.

"They say you'll have to take Albert."

"Who?"

"My dog. They say dogs aren't allowed in the jail."

"But he's been here four months."

"Go argue with them! It wouldn't have happened if they hadn't seen you here."

"What the hell am I going to do with him?"

"It's all right," Nick said, looking sadly at the dog. "He'll be better off with you till I get out. I haven't really been able to feed him properly."

Ramos came up to them and she looked questioningly at him. He shrugged.

"We manage," he said. "We work it some way out. Is no choice. They insisting."

"I'll get some rope," Nick said. "I have a piece of clothes line."

With the dog at his heels, he disappeared into the hole for a few minutes and when he returned he had one end of the rope tied around the dog's neck. He handed her the other end and leaned to stroke the dog's head.

"It's all right, Albert. Be a good boy. I'll see you soon."

He turned to her. "Goodbye, Mom. Thanks for coming. Really."

She held him for a long minute, fighting tears. "Take care of yourself."

"Don't worry about me. I'll be all right."

Between the prison door and the iron gates there was a stretch of flat dead ground, a kind of no man's land. She walked across it, feeling eyes on her back. The sky was still very bright, very blue. The dog loped ahead of her and, when the gates were opened, streaked out, pulling the rope from her hands, deliriously free. It wasn't until they'd finally managed to coax him into the station wagon and were on their way that he realized that he'd been separated from Nick and began to howl.

PAST SORROWS
AND COMING ATTRACTIONS

Brenda Fiebleman, dreaming on the stoop, saw her mother turn the corner into their street. It was a long way from the corner to their front steps, perhaps an eighth of a mile, but she knew it was her mother because she had twenty-twenty. Her mother took credit for her eyesight.

"You think it's easy to raise an intellectual Jewish girl with twenty-twenty?" Having learned from Dr. Brady's newspaper column, she saw to it that the light was always angled over her left shoulder. "The heart side. To save your beautiful studious eyes."

She watched her mother's slow, spunky progress. She was a squat woman with a functional build and, though her arms circled huge shopping bags stuffed with provender hard won from her sly enemies, the Avenue J merchants, she didn't appear to be weighed down. The bags were extensions of herself, as natural as plants sprouting from an urn. Still, Brenda knew that after walking eight blocks, her arms would be aching. She considered going to help her but sat on, immobilized by her nervous breakdown, now in its fourth month. Besides, what about the shopping cart, her present to her mother three or four birthdays back, a simple mechanism, lightweight aluminum, big balloon tires. Other women took readily, delightedly, to shopping carts. A boon. Not her mother. Too much trouble shlepping. Unnatural. She, the daughter of peddlers who had wheeled their wares in gutters.

She turned her attention from her mother's progress back to her contemplation of the dead summer, the early Flatbush autumn, the changed air, the sharp new light, the shadows so different this morning from yesterday's shadows. The leaves on the maple trees, the sun-brittled grass of the small front lawn, looked tired, limp with disenchantment, mirroring her. It was her twenty-fourth autumn. Her shoulders sagged, her hands dangled. Though the summer had been hot, it was months since she'd had her hair cut, and it hung limp and dispirited. Her fingernails were bitten and ragged, her sneakers filthy, her jeans frayed at the knees. For a moment she saw herself as her mother saw the neighbors seeing her: she was a disgrace.

It was only ten o'clock. All summer she had slept till noon but the changed air had driven her from bed. Now, faced with a lengthened day, she had only the shards of the night's dreams to play with. Her shadow self had wandered in sleep from terror to terror, from symbol to symbol. She would spend the endless hours ahead translating the night's rubble into the solid bricks of cliche she was learning from Dr. Shapiro. Dear Dr. Shapiro, recharger of failed batteries, restarter of stalled engines.

Her mother clumped up the walk, passing her wordlessly, leaving in her wake an agglomerate smell, microcosm of her morning's travail: the bakery, the appetizer, the delicatessen ---the baked, the smoked, the cured --- the bloodless perversions of field and sea and orchard. So her mother wasn't talking to her today! Bewildered, she reacted to Brenda moodily, one day with anger, the next with passionate concern, occasionally with disdain, never with fear. Nothing was ever more or less than she expected; life held no surprises. What could happen that could be worse than she'd already lived through: nursing her husband through two years of cancer to the grave, her mother and brother and most of her cousins dead in concentration camps, the years of struggle, Sharon, now twenty-one, with her seven-year-old mind. What could happen to her that could equal her dreams: herself tall and slender and bejeweled, her older daughter a professor, but rich and married and the mother of fat pink babies, and, finally, a brilliant surgeon who, with a simple operation, would correct Sharon's defect, then fall madly in love with her, his creation, like a prince with a sleeping beauty.

Without turning, Brenda listened to her mother's struggle with the front door, heard the slam of it behind her and, in the shattered silence, saw her safe in her lair, the white kitchen with its new wallpaper, a dull dazzle of cups and saucers and teaspoons repeating themselves with geometric whimsy above the tile and around the breakfast nook. She would spend the next half hour happily sorting, repackaging, filing her purchases, humming and thinking menus, close to the source of things important and necessary, --- dead husbands, retarded and nerve-broken daughters forgotten.

Brenda looked up and down the quiet street, thinking of the fled companions of her childhood: Lincoln, Stanley, Ace. From the age of six, she had, against great odds, played only with boys. A natural athlete, coordinated and strong and quick, she had had little use for most of the pursuits of the girls on the block: jacks and rope-jumping and dolls. Because she was as good as the boys at their games, they had grudgingly admitted her, nicknaming her Bink. Brenda was an impossible name.

Lincoln was now a pencil manufacturer in Mount Vernon; Stanley a high school math teacher in Merrick; Ace in his father's advertising agency; all three of them married, Lincoln already a father. Except for themselves and the Kauffmans, three doors down, there was no one left on the block from the old days. They were still there because the house, long since paid for, cost only taxes and heat, and because she, Brenda/Bink, after the years of Brooklyn College and working after school in cafeterias, libraries, photo darkrooms, had failed to begin. She had achieved her B.A. and her M.A. and, all confidence, had embarked on her Ph.D only to wake one morning knowing, without surprise, that she had died. Respectfully, she had stifled the alarm clock and closed her eyes. Time passed. Her mother came and went many times. Her sister Sharon stumbled in and spoke her name. A doctor was summoned. Her response to all callers was minimal. She heard, she understood, but she no longer cared enough even to open her eyes.

"There's nothing wrong with you," her mother shouted at her as though, instead of dead she was merely deaf. "Heart, lungs, stomach, reflexes, all shipshape."

Ukrainian borscht, thick with meat and bone and marrow (her mother never skimped), appeared at regular intervals at her bedside and it was this that finally roused her. On the fourth day, starved, she knew that she couldn't be all dead. Later, she learned from Dr. Shapiro that it was her ego that had nearly perished, her id that had responded to the soup. The doctor was convinced that the cause of her failure of ego went deep but that overwork had triggered the crisis. She'd been pushing herself too hard. She must take a rest from her studies and slowly, together, they would "set her house in order."

For weeks, she had languished like a vegetable, fingering dreams, except for two crazy weeks when, taking the doctor's injunction literally, she'd plunged into a frenzied campaign of home improvement, climbing onto the roof to repair a leak, replacing the cracked toilet seat with a gleaming new one, papering the kitchen with paper of her mother's choice, repainting Sharon's room. She had always been the family handy-person, by default of its other members. She ripped out faulty plumbing and, with the aid of a manual from the library and tools borrowed from a hardware store, replaced it with expert proficiency. She painted the outside wood trim, bound up frayed lamp cords, fixed the venetian blinds, and silenced the refrigerator. Then, when there was nothing more she could think of to do, she went to her mother and said, "I'm finished. I'll be leaving now." She meant it. She had set this woman's house in order and now she could leave it. But the woman at the sink said, "Go wash up, Brenda darling, it's time for supper."

Summer had come and gone. Thrice weekly she took the BMT to Manhattan, to Dr. Shapiro's dimly lit cave where, supine on creaking leather, she mumbled nonsense through her disarrayed hair, distracted by the doctor's collection of treasures. The doctor was a cultivated man, no Spartan single-minded scientist, but a man of parts, proud of the diversity of his interests, the latitude of his libido. His walls were covered with second-rate contemporary paintings, surfaces littered with pseudo-primitive wood carvings, a jungle of knickknacks, mementos, and conceits. Also, the doctor was a dandy dresser. He was a homburg man, but otherwise his clothes were too original, too lovingly inspired, to have been merely purchased. Brenda suspected that the doctor made them himself. And when Dr. Shapiro spoke of sex, as he often did, his eyes glowed with such pleasure, remembered and anticipated, that Brenda, sallow and apathetic, was devastated by her own indifference. What had they in common, these two? There were only differences between her and the worldly doctor before whom she was endeavoring to peel off the layers of her pale Flatbush soul. Language was the most immediate difference, not that Brenda was unfamiliar with the jargon; on occasion she'd used it herself. As abstraction it was convenient, but applied to herself, the words were transformed into rigid nonsense, or too-easy sense. She was a bundle of ambivalence and ambiguity. She was id, ego and superego besides being oral, anal and, with luck genital. What had become of the comforting complexity of life? Where were good and evil, where were human values, where were justice, compassion and mercy?

She had it all balled up. She wasn't there to discuss philosophy but to be psychoanalyzed. Why was she wasting the doctor's time and her money? A form of resistance, a way of avoiding the unpleasantness involved in stripping away the neurosis. It was a way of sealing off the unconscious where the trauma lay. Back to beginnings. Back to mother and father. Back, back, back!

But it wasn't back that worried Brenda. It was the future, not the past that haunted her. There was nothing unusual in her past, nothing she hadn't long since come to terms with. Just the usual odds and ends: a strong, outspoken mother, the death of a gentle father, a mentally crippled sister, her own escape into books and studies. So what if her toilet training had come too early or she had been ashamed of her sister or her mother often got on her nerves? These were only the ordinary currency of life, humdrum. The future was another matter. How could she tell Dr. Shapiro about the future without running the risk of being considered a nut?

Her first encounter with the future had come not long after her mother's borscht had raised her Lazarus-like from bed. She was sitting in the armchair in her room, looking out the window at the sunlight on the Spanish tile roof over the kitchen just beneath her, thinking of nothing in particular. Afterwards, she couldn't tell if she had fallen asleep or into some kind of trance. Roof and sunlight disappeared as though a dial had clicked from one television channel to another. She was lying in bed, drugged and exhausted, and at her bedside sat a strapping middle-aged, anxious man, a little thick around the neck.

"It's all right, Mom," the man said, clasping her hand. She tried to pull her hand away but she was too weak. Looking down, then, at her free hand, spotted and veined, she saw that she was an old woman and she understood that she was dying.

"You have the key to the vault?" she said with an effort. "Don't waste time crying. Go straight to the bank."

"Don't worry, Mom, I know what to do. And you aren't dying. The doctor says you'll be as good as new in a week."

She was annoyed that he should lie to her even

while she understood that the lie, if it failed to comfort her, comforted her son. Her irritation with him was diluted by a peculiar tenderness. She wished she could remember his name.

"Sell the house," she said. "Take whatever you can get for it."

"All right, Mom. Don't worry about it."

There was something else she meant to say but while she was trying to think what it was, her son launched into a speech, a testimonial. "Listen, Mom," he said, and there was no stopping him, "I want you to know. Whatever. I forgive. Might not always have understood. Inspiration to me. Love you."

It was the kiss of death and she woke on it to the present, to her twenty-four-year-old self in March of the year 1952. She was shaken, knowing that she had neither dreamed nor hallucinated, that the vision she'd just lived through had happened just as surely as yesterday had happened. It had happened in some future past, a past that needed only some five or six decades to be shaped. She would have a son, God knows how, who would look like that, talk like that. Did it mean that she would marry? Or, since she couldn't imagine that, would there be some sort of unimaginable upheaval in the near future to change the condition of women like herself? And, less surprising, she would die. Her last concern would be for material things, the house, whatever it was she had stashed away in the vault.

Good God!

Having come through two deaths, the neurotically inspired and the previsioned, she realized that she was condemned to a long and ordinary life. The earth would not be blasted away, at least not for a while, and she herself would not wither of inanition. She would breed and she would accumulate. How? And more important, why?

The front door opened and closed behind her. She knew by the sharp brisk steps that it was Sharon negotiating the length of the porch. Because walking was one of the things Sharon could do, she brought to it the full measure of her unspent purpose and efficiency; she walked like a drill sergeant. She sat beside Brenda on the step, leaving room between them for the huge brown paper bag in which she carried her knitting.

"Mama says you'll catch cold sitting on the stone," she said, emptying the contents of the bag onto her lap.

"I won't catch cold."

She watched Sharon position the knitting needles with her long thin hands. Attached to one of the needles was the fruit of two years of labor, neatly folded. She had begun with what was meant to be a scarf, but she had gone on and on, unable or unwilling to terminate it, so that yards and yards of the stuff, all of it bright red (she would have no other color) lay mountain high, folded in her lap. She worked slowly, taking great pains with the one simple stitch she'd mastered, and the work was tight and perfect, an eternity of diligence.

"What are you doing, Brenda?" Sharon always asked her that.

"Nothing? What's that you're making?"

"It's knitting."

She watched Sharon's laborious pursuit of another meaningless row of locked yarn and wondered at the circuitous tissue of her secret, damaged brain, this odd Penelope (faithful to what?) spinning forth the patient, patternless, useless fabric of her days. She wished she could risk the danger of pitying her, but she had rarely pitied her. She had been ashamed of her, sometimes even hated her, but she had protected her. She saw in Sharon's face her own eyes, nose, coloring. Sharon was neat, her hair was always combed, she dressed carefully, she bathed as often as she was allowed, sometimes twice a day. Brenda had rarely seen her cry. Papa had called her "God's child, an angel," and, dying, wept for her daily.

"Why could I never pity her?" she asked Dr. Shapiro.

"Guilt, Brenda?"

"Why guilt? Because I wasn't the one? I don't recall ever feeling particularly blessed."

After Sharon's eighth birthday, they had risked sending her to school. Brenda was ten, in fifth grade, and every morning her mother said, "Look in on Sharon. See what she's doing." On her way to gym or the auditorium, passing the kindergarten room, she would peer through the glass panel in the door and find Sharon instantly, so conspicuous among the five-year-olds. She was always at the rear of the room peacefully scribbling with her crayons, and even then she would only use the red ones, as though blind to other colors.

"She was okay," Brenda would report later to her mother. "She was drawing."

Her mother, exasperated, would snort, "Again with the drawing! They call that a school?"

The next year, because of her size, they advanced her to first grade and when Brenda looked in she was still in the last row, still too large, but with her hands folded on the desk, wonderfully quiet, her lips parted, her eyes serenely empty. There was never anything on her desk but her clasped hands.

"She was okay," Brenda would tell her mother. "She was listening."

But that year, because Sharon was at school for the full day, Brenda would have to meet her in the schoolyard and walk her home. Once, Brenda found her backed against the chain fence by Allan Bernstein, a sickly grin on her face. Allan Bernstein's hand was up her skirt.

"I was scared to death of Allan Bernstein. He was a bully," she told Dr. Shapiro. "But I screamed at him to quit it."

"Ah, she don't even know what I'm doing," Allan had said.

"That makes it worse, you shit," she'd screamed, and head lowered, she bulled into him, knocking him down.

"Did a boy ever put his hand up your skirt, Brenda?" Dr. Shapiro asked. Brenda sighed.

"I didn't wear skirts."

"What did you wear?"

"Jesus, what do you think I wore? Pants. Jeans. I was a tomboy."

"Yes."

" And I didn't like boys. Not that way. I liked girls." She blushed and hated herself for it. "I had crushes on girls."

"All girls do," Dr. Shapiro said. "It's normal. At that age."

"Maybe. But I think..." She was finding it difficult to breathe. "I'm pretty sure I still prefer them."

"Nonsense," Dr. Shapiro said. "There's nothing in your Rorschach, nothing in your dreams, nothing in your transference, to indicate that you're a lesbian, if that's what you're trying to tell me you think you are. Did you ever have your hand up a girl's skirt?"

"Of course not!"

She hadn't even heard the word 'lesbian' or known there was such a thing until she was fifteen and someone had thrust *The Well of Loneliness* at her, commanding her to read it. Valerie something, in her French class, an overdeveloped girl with short yellow hair and bangs who sat on Brenda's desk before class and talked about books, a little too intensely.

"I was fascinated and repelled by the book," she told Dr. Shapiro. "And that's how I felt about Valerie. I took great pains to avoid her after that."

"Too bad. You should have gotten it out of your system."

She looked at the doctor with disbelief. He was the one who was crazy. "I'm not talking about a cold or an upset stomach," she said.

But she wanted to believe Dr. Shapiro. It was always possible that he was right, that it wasn't just wishful thinking on his part. And she had begun to like boys when she was in high school, and to date them when she was a junior and senior. She was a good dancer and, after her early teens, she began to be good looking --- even, in a way, or so boys told her, beautiful. When they necked and, later, petted, it was a relief to discover how much she enjoyed it. Later, in college, she had twice fallen in love, first with Andy for two years, a surprisingly passionate sexual relationship, and later with Ben, who was cerebral and gentle and who had gone to graduate school in California and married someone else. She was surprised, when she learned this, not to have felt more pain.

Yet even while she was in love with Andy and

Ben, there had always been something else, some woman she felt strongly attracted to, unwelcome feelings she had tamped down as though they were shameful and disgusting. The doctor knew all this.

"So you never did anything with a girl?" he now asked her. She felt herself redden again.

"Well, yes," she said. "Muriel Kauffman. When we were about eleven, I kissed her. I put my tongue in her mouth. I don't know what made me do it, we were playing some kind of game. She lived on the block."

Muriel Kauffman had laughed, then run away. After that, they had stopped being friends. Some invisible line had been overstepped and she couldn't be sure if she or Muriel was the more embarrassed.

It was around that time that her father died. She tried to recall what she had felt for her father. Relief, mainly, when he had at last died. There had been so many months of knowing he was dying, of watching him shrivel and shrink and suffer. She'd wept when her mother told her, "Papa's incurable." Afterwards, she had scarcely been able to look at him without thinking of what his skin contained, the inexorable growth that was devouring him. Her father no longer belonged to them, his family; he belonged entirely to his cancer.

Still, she had loved him. Twice a year, she drove her mother to the cemetery, an outpost at some muddled point where Brooklyn became Queens. She would stand in an island of silence, though airplanes droned overhead and children played across the street in the yards of shabby houses, while her mother walked the aisles of the cemetery hunting for some filthy, ragged, bearded old man with food stains on his lapels, a death bum, who, for a couple of dollars, would chant the mandatory prayers over the grave. Brenda would stare at the simple headstone that bore only her father's name and the years of his life. That stone, and her own standing there with her mother, were almost all that marked the passage of Sam Fiebleman through the long history of the world.

"Hello, Muriel," Sharon called, returning Brenda to the present. As if evoked by Brenda's thoughts, Muriel Kauffman had turned the corner and was heading up the street toward her house, three doors beyond theirs. She would have to pass them and, though she was still too far to have heard Sharon's greeting, Sharon's face was lit with happiness. Brenda watched Muriel's leisurely, regal approach. Her mother had often said that Muriel "carries herself like a queen." It was true.

"Hello, Muriel," Sharon called again. Smiling, Muriel turned up the walk and stood at the bottom of the steps.

"Hello, Sharon," she said. "What are you making?"

"I'm knitting."

"What are you knitting?"

"This."

"Hello, Bink. Brenda." Her eyes did not quite meet Brenda's. For a dozen years, Muriel had neither spoken to Brenda nor looked her in the eye. Today it made Brenda angry.

"It was your idea in the first place," she said to Muriel.

"I know it was," Muriel said angrily, in a rush, knowing at once what Brenda meant. "But I didn't mean like that."

Brenda began to laugh and after a moment Muriel laughed, too.

"You look like a couple of kids, sitting on the stoop like that," Muriel said.

"We are a couple of kids," Brenda said. "What are you doing home this time of day? Did you lose your job?"

"It's Saturday."

"Is it!"

"I love your shoes, Muriel," Sharon said. Brenda looked at Muriel's shoes. They looked expensive. So did the rest of Muriel's outfit. She knew about clothes.

"Thanks, Sharon," Muriel said. "I hear you've been having a nervous breakdown, Brenda."

"Not exactly," Brenda said, furious. Her mother must have told Mrs. Kauffman all about it, probably because Muriel was a social worker. Maybe her mother had spoken directly to Muriel, soliciting advice. Brenda could imagine her mother's train of thought: Muriel works with people. She helps them. Maybe she can help my Brenda.

"Are you better now?" Muriel asked. Her face was all kindness. Brenda's anger receded.

"You want to go to the movies?" Brenda heard herself ask.

"What?"

"Tonight. If you haven't got a date?" Brenda loved movies; she hadn't been to one in months..

"I haven't got a date," Muriel said. "I'd love to go."

"I'll come by for you around seven-thirty."

When Muriel had gone, Brenda sat on, amazed at herself. She'd never thought of Muriel as a possible friend, not after all this time. Muriel was a fixture in her life, entirely peripheral to it, like the street lamp across the way, like the six-cup percolator that had sat on the back burner of the stove for as long as she could remember, like the Avenue J druggist who had never handed her a filled prescription without saying, "Use it in good health." Muriel, a social worker, chic, with her regal walk, was everything that she was not. It would be a deadly evening, boring, boring, boring.

But Brenda was used to boredom. There was little in her nervous breakdown that hadn't been boring. Maybe boredom had been its cause. It had certainly been the theme, the heart of her second prevision, which had visited her a month earlier.

She was on a camping trip with two women. The camp site, in a state park, was a rounded clearing in a wooded hillside that circled a crystal lake and, though it was hung with oaks and beech and pine trees, the smell of the sea, a mile to the west, was sharp in the air. In her years of lived life, Brenda had had little contact with nature,--- occasional excursions to Rockaway Beach for the day, and twice to Bear Mountain on the Day Line. There hadn't been money for summer camp, or for a rented cottage in the mountains, or even a room in one, though her mother would never have tolerated a shared kitchen. The closest Brenda had come to camping out was one summer when she and Lincoln spent a number of afternoons crouched under a bridge table draped with blankets, eating Fig Newtons by flashlight. Yet here she was in this remote woods fiddling with fishing gear in the shadow of a well-pitched tent.

One of her companions was small and misshapen, virtually a dwarf, and the other a tall thin Southern woman, the trip's organizer, familiar with the complicated workings of the paraphernalia they had assembled to house and feed them and illuminate the night. Neither woman ever stopped talking. The dwarf was a pedant, unable to accept the least part of this experience, new to her, too, until she had approximated its literary equivalent. Wordsworth had been credited with portions of the landscape, and Defoe and Hawthorne shared responsibility for several of their endeavors, some of which were also distinctly Thoreauvian. Brenda couldn't decide which of the women was the more tiresome. While the little woman sat smoking on the sidelines, offering comments, Brenda helped Marysue erect the tent, a complicated affair with outside aluminum poles of varying widths and heights, with stakes and zippers and ties and cords. Instead of the ten minutes touted by the catalogue, erecting the tent had taken them an hour and a half, while Marysue chattered unremittingly about her expertise, about earlier tents she had known and places where she had thrown them up and the women lovers who had accompanied her and who had since betrayed her despite the idyllic times they had shared in nature's bosom. Still, Brenda felt a thrill of triumph when the tent was at last standing and their gear stowed within. The site was solidly theirs. But she knew that this was merely the beginning. There were still food, drink, warmth, and sewage to be dealt with, nature to be outwitted, wood collected and kept dry, water fetched, food procured and prepared and prevented from spoiling, insects and raccoons kept at bay, and darkness penetrated. At the moment, however, she wanted to go off into silence, to absorb nature through her pores, and in solitude. She wanted to go fishing. Alone. But the dwarf, like the ancient mariner, had her pinned where she stood, with her incessant talk, her beady eyes, her words sent forth on clouds of smoke, inhaled through a long cigarette holder clamped between her teeth, an arrangement that in no way hindered speech.

"You're a traitor to academia," she was telling Brenda. "It's unconscionable. I can't believe that you're really going to do it."

"But I am," Brenda said, oiling her reel, trying not to listen. "I've contracted to do it, and in good faith."

"With sixty-seven percent of the American dollar· going into space, you don't need experts to tell you where the economy is headed. What goes up may never come down, not from space. It's money thrown into the black hole."

"Smell that air," Brenda said, inhaling.

"Naturally they grumble, why wouldn't they? What does interstellar communication mean to the average person? What do they care about swapping beeps with some pointy-headed counterpart in another galaxy when they can't even communicate with their kids."

"They care," Brenda mumbled, spinning the reel.

"You'll see to it that they do. You'll sell it to them, like an adman, a p.r. person, like it was laundry detergent or toothpaste. The commodification of space. With your talent! Aren't you ashamed?"

"I came here to get away from space," Brenda pleaded, backing off. "To get out into the air."

"What I want to know is, are you sincere? Do you really believe in the product?"

Brenda began to walk away, out of the clearing, toward the lake. There wouldn't be any fish in the lake. And if there were, she'd never catch one. And if she did, it would be full of poisons.

"I'm going fishing," she said.

"Jingles will come next, I can see it now," the dwarf's shrill voice pursued her with its nonsensical accusations. "The poet scientist! Don't you think it falsifies to versify?"

As she emerged from the clearing, Brenda came out of the vision, out of the future, completely baffled. The nameless little woman, so deadly dull with her clever little face and her chain-smoking, had spoiled it all in the way that uninspired academics so often demystify what is romantic, profound, beautiful. And what were they talking about, anyway? Who was she, that Brenda? "I came for the trees and the sky and the lake and the earth," she heard herself shout back over her shoulder into the future as it dwindled into the present, as her voice faded. "It isn't often I can come." And why had she come, with those two women who obviously meant nothing to her?

At the movie house that night, Muriel Kauffman smelled wonderful. "Ma Griffe," she said, when Brenda commented. "D'you like it? I'll get you some."

"I don't use perfume," Brenda said, "though I appreciate it on others."

It was a double feature, both films with Peter Sellers, and they laughed a lot. Between films, during the coming attractions, Brenda offered to go for popcorn.

"Don't go," Muriel said, laying a restraining hand on Brenda's arm. "This is the best part."

She sat still, watching the previews of forthcoming movies. The first was about interns and nurses, hospital scenes filled with blood and sex. The second dealt with a turgid marital triangle, good man strong in riding boots, knocking down his blind wife's punk nymphomaniacal sister. Muriel giggled throughout the brief film clips while Brenda stiffened, feeling premonitions. "She knows," Brenda thought. "Muriel Kauffman is telling me she knows." But how could she? Nobody knew, not even Dr. Shapiro.

"Isn't it great?" Muriel said. "They give you these bits they think are provocative and you can figure out the whole plot, and then you can choose. You can choose to stay away."

"Oh, God, you know," Brenda said. "But how?"

"Know what, Brenda?" Muriel asked, covering Brenda's hand with her own. In the flickering, reflected light, Brenda searched Muriel's pale face, surprised that she hoped to find confirmation there. But there were only Muriel's features, the questioning eyes, the strong bridge of her nose, the soft uncomprehending mouth. Brenda shook her head, embarrassed, and they turned back to the screen where the second film had begun to unfold.

Afterwards, because it was just down the block, they went to Sidney's Versailles Snack Palace, a glittering eatery featuring waffle-based banana splits. They sat on crimson naugahyde, their elbows on pink Formica, and saw themselves repeated at a dozen different angles and removes in cracked and bronzed mirrored walls and columns. In the brilliant garish light from a ceiling cluttered with fluorescent chandeliers, Muriel's unretouched nose developed a slight shine. Brenda relaxed, feeling strangely happy.

"Will it embarrass you if I have one of the house specialties?" Muriel asked, while the waitress stood poised, waiting for their order. "I'm around deprived kids so much that I've acquired their gluttony."

"Have two," Brenda said.

Muriel described in careful detail exactly what she wanted.

"One scoop or two?" the waitress asked.

"Two. Both chocolate. Hot fudge on one, strawberry on the other."

"Strawberries on chawklit?" the waitress said, making a face. "What about whipped cream and nuts?"

"Yes. The works."

"I'll take the same," Brenda said. "What the hell."

"Though the truth is," Muriel said when the waitress had departed, "I can't remember ever seeing a kid, given a choice, order anything he couldn't smear with ketchup." She scanned the room. "Only middle-aged women with long-departed waistlines," she said glumly. "Consoling themselves."

"We can cancel the order if it's going to depress you," Brenda said.

"You, of course, don't have to worry. You look as if you haven't eaten since you were twelve. Tell me about yourself, Brenda." Her eyes shone across at Brenda. Was Muriel flirting with her, or was that her way? But before she could answer her own question, or Muriel's, the waitress was there with their order. It was only with an effort that Brenda could bring herself to look at the vulgar confections she set before them.

"They look like Miami Beach hotels," she said. She had been to Miami Beach once, the guest of her father's rich brother.

"It's vanilla," Muriel said, looking beneath the strawberries, her mouth grim.

"How can you tell?"

"Waitress!"

There was going to be a scene. While the waitress sauntered back, Brenda prayed that she would be one of the gracious ones, a philosopher.

"It's vanilla," Muriel told her. "I ordered chocolate."

"The other one is chawklit," the waitress said.

"Both," Muriel said. "They were both supposed to be chocolate."

Brenda steeled herself as she had so often done in similar encounters where her mother played the lead. They were both women, Brenda's mother and Muriel, who knew their rights as American citizens.

"Vanella, you said."

"Never. I never in my whole life said vanilla. Chocolate. I said it twice. Clearly. Distinctly. Emphatically."

"That's right," Brenda said. "She said it twice."

The waitress looked at Brenda with contempt before turning back to her true adversary.

"With all that gook on it," she told Muriel, "you won't even taste the ice cream." Brenda squirmed. The air was charged.

"Take it back," Muriel said.

"Be reasonable," the waitress whined. "Whaddyew expect me to do with this?"

"I am being reasonable," Muriel said in the most reasonable of voices. "You have many flavors of ice cream here, don't you?"

"Fourteen."

"And I chose chocolate. I was given a choice, I chose, I am entitled to my choice."

Defeated, the waitress took Muriel's dish back to the counter and shoved it across to the fountain boy.

"I ordered chawklit," they heard her say. "You put vanella."

"What about yours?" Muriel asked. "You probably got vanilla, too. Send it back."

"I don't mind," Brenda said, smiling. "But bravo. I don't think I've ever sent anything back in a restaurant."

"Do you want me to do it for you?"

"Please, Muriel, let's stop talking about flavors."

"Then tell me what you meant in the movies." She leaned forward. "When you said that I knew ."

"It was nothing."

"It wasn't nothing. It was something. I could tell. Something important to you."

Brenda felt both tempted and trapped. "It was about the coming attractions," she mumbled. "About the future, about choosing to go into it or to stay away. I'd rather not talk about it now."

"It's different with life," Muriel said. "How can you choose when you don't know what's there?"

But she did know. Fortunately, the waitress was back with Muriel's corrected sundae.

"Chawklit," she snapped, setting it smartly down.

It was after midnight when Brenda got home. From the hall, she saw her mother in the kitchen, hunched over the kitchen table, her rimless spectacles steamy from the tea she was drinking. Except for the circle of light in which she sat, the house was dark and silent. Her aloneness unnerved Brenda. Her mother had always been the president, the commander-in-chief, a shtarka. She was one of the angry old women, though she was not yet old. Life would never defeat her because she had never promised herself anything, not absolutely. In time her body would betray her, hardened arteries, arthritis, a stroke, but she would go down fighting, cajoling doctors, berating nurses, clutching at life to the last gasp. What courage. What tenacity. But at this moment, Brenda was touched by her solitude. She went into the kitchen.

"Have a nice cup of tea, Brenda darling."

"I'll get it," she said. "Don't get up. Mama, don't get up." Firmly, she pushed her mother back into her chair and fetched a cup and saucer from the cupboard, then sat at the table opposite her mother.

"There's plenty," her mother said, filling Brenda's cup from the teapot. "I made a full pot. You want some cake?"

"No."

"There's some nice sponge. Or a small piece of crumb I could warm."

"No thanks, Ma, I just came from Sidney's."

"You had a good time? She's a nice girl, Muriel?" Earlier, she had jumped for joy when Brenda mentioned that she and Muriel were going to the movies.

"I always liked her," her mother said. "She's kind to Sharon. Even as a little girl, she was never mean to her like the others."

Brenda sipped her tea.

"And she's smart, too. She has a good head on her. Like you, Brenda."

"I'm not so smart."

"You always got good grades. The highest."

"Anyone can get good grades."

"Don't talk foolish." She sighed. "Tell me, Brenda, heart to heart. Do you think you're getting better? Is Dr. Shapiro doing you any good?"

"I don't know, Ma."

"Because the money isn't going to last forever."

"I know. I think I can stop with Dr. Shapiro pretty soon."

"So what will you do? Go back to school?"

"Maybe. I don't know."

"Because you're already a master. I don't want to interfere, it's your life, but what's the good of being a doctor if you can't hang out a shingle? How much education does a person need to teach a bunch of school kids?"

"I'm not going to teach. I don't know what I'll do."

Her mother sighed. "I'm not really worried about you, Brenda darling. I have faith. But I don't understand these breakdowns."

"These? It's only one, Ma."

"A gorgeous girl with education, perfect eyesight, practically no cavities, excellent health. Your entire future is ahead of you."

"Everyone's future is ahead of them," Brenda said, wincing.

"Don't talk foolish. With me, my whole future is already behind."

"You should get out more, Ma. You're not old. You could do something."

"What about Sharon?"

"It's not fair for you to spend your whole life taking care of her. You're entitled to a life. There are places where she'd be better off."

"How could she be better off than here in her own home with her own mother? And what would I do, tell me? Go dancing? Go to the racetrack like

Mrs. Persky and bet on horses?"

"You could go to Florida and visit Uncle Jacob. You could meet a nice man, a widower. You could get married again."

"Sometimes I think that," her mother said. "Poor Papa." She sighed again, then her mouth tightened. "Is that what you'll do when I'm gone? Put Sharon in one of those places?"

"I don't know, Ma. You're not going to die for a long time. You'll live forever, if necessary."

"God forbid! Promise me, Brenda."

"All right, I promise."

"So what will you do with her?"

Brenda shrugged. "I'll buy her a mink coat and teach her to play canasta," she said. "Then I'll go to Seventh Avenue and find her a husband."

"What are you talking nonsense? She has a child's mind."

"Lots of people have, Ma, and nobody notices. Sharon knows how to dress herself, she can count change, and she knows how to hail a taxi. All she needs is a rich husband."

Her mother took the empty teacups to the sink. She stood there deep in thought.

"Canasta's complicated," she said. Brenda went to the sink and kissed her on the cheek.

"Goodnight, Ma."

For the first time in months, she fell asleep almost instantly. She awoke some hours later while it was still dark and lay comfortable and at peace, realizing that she hadn't dreamed. Maybe it just goes away, she thought, the way it comes. Still, the absurd, impossible, boring future lay before her, an undigested mass, booked as the next week's movies, coiled and immutable in their cans, were booked by the Midwood Theater. Was time an illusion and the future, as her mother had said, past? As a child, she'd been given a toy movie projector that cranked by hand and had a weak, battery-powered light. It wasn't much of a toy but, crazed with science fiction, she had made it the instrument of a complicated game. She had chosen a distant star, dreamed it rich with all but human life, named it the planet Brendith, surrounded it with an atmosphere that gave substance to shadow. Then, in her imagination, the projector grew enormous, its tiny bulb became a sun. She pointed the toy at the star and cranked it, unreeling the film, and said, "Five hundred light years hence, Donald Duck will live on Brendith and do these things and I, Brenda Fiebleman, long dead, am god of the planet Brendith." The responsibility was overwhelming. In time, she promised herself, she would make her own films, better ones. Sharon, her parents, one or two of her teachers, the kids on the block, she would beam them all at Brendith. She would give them immortality.

But the game turned on her and, in terror, knowing God was a child like herself, the earth his toy and Brenda his fiction, she hurled the projector to the back of a closet. Gradually, reassured by the quiet confidence of her arithmetic teacher and by the sound of her mother faithfully chopping liver in the kitchen, her voice quavering over some half-remembered song from her Russian childhood, Brenda watched the stars recede and time again became tick-tock, tick-tock, yesterday, today, tomorrow.

She lay in the dark. Between the rooftops a street lamp shone, trembling like a star. She groaned and turned in her bed, the sheets twisting around her legs. "Let there be a third vision to give me the an-

◆ 283 ◆

swer," she prayed. Three is the symmetry of religion, of fairy tales, of magic. She would wait for the magic third. And if an answer came, how would she know it, if she didn't know the question? She fell asleep.

In the morning it was raining. A wind had risen, driving the rain against the windows. She felt shut in and restless. It was Sunday, a long day, yet no longer than all the days of her recent idle past. There would be no Dr. Shapiro to break the pattern of emptiness with their mutual consideration of the furniture of Brenda's psyche: her feelings, her lack of feelings. But yesterday the pattern had been broken. Muriel Kauffman had looked her in the eye, and they had gone together to the movies. Muriel had made a scene and Brenda had actually admired her for it, even liked her. They had become friends. And who knows? Muriel had touched her a lot, her hand, her arm, had seemed to be flirting with her, had wanted to know all about her.

Her restlessness grew. After breakfast, she took her coffee into the living room and read the paper. On the sofa beside her, her mother picked up sections of the paper as Brenda discarded them. The radio was on and she sat, half listening. A sermon. Ethical Culture. Finally, driven from the living room, she prowled through the house.

She went into Sharon's room. Sharon was sitting in a straight-backed chair, still in pajamas and bathrobe, her hands cupping her small breasts, her mouth quivering, her eyes closed. Brenda stood in the doorway, afraid.

"What's the matter, Sharon?" she asked.

"Oh, Brenda!" She had never heard such sorrow in Sharon's voice. She came all the way into the room.

"What, Sharon? What is it?"

"I love him so much." Tears trembled in Sharon's eyes, waiting to fall.

"Who, Sharon? Who do you love?"

"Ben Casey."

Brenda tried not to smile. Until he had ridden off into the sunset, Gene Autry had been Sharon's love. She had remained faithful as long as he was there to remind her, dozens of his pictures adorning the walls of her room. Now it was Ben Casey, dark and taciturn, whose photos were everywhere.

Brenda sat on the neatly made up bed. Three dolls, carefully dressed, their hair neatly combed, like Sharon's, sat propped against the pillow sham.

"Why Ben Casey?"

"He's so handsome. And he... he helps people."

Brenda felt her heart turn. Should she tell Sharon that Ben Casey wasn't real, that he was a shadow on the television screen, an actor speaking written lines, that Ben Casey wasn't even his real name? No, of course not. What do people love, after all? Ben Casey wasn't real, but Sharon's pain was. What did it matter what it chose as object, as long as it chose ... this child's mind trapped in its hungry woman's body?

"I'll teach you a card game, Sharon, okay?"

"Old Maid?" Sharon said eagerly, her face lighting. "I know how to play Old Maid."

"No, a new game. Canasta."

The third, and what was to prove the last, of Brenda's previsions came to her an hour later. She had lost Sharon's attention for the dozenth time and had finally released her from the card table. Alone, she gathered up the cards. On the radio, the Philharmonic played the Sibelius First Symphony. The bass thumped a warning while the strings strained toward a passionate crescendo. Then click! The radio went dead, the cards, table, room, vanished, and she was in a small kitchen. It was night. There was another woman, young but out of focus, blurred, so that afterwards Brenda couldn't identify her, standing at the sink. Brenda stood, conscious of her hands dangling at her sides, and of a trio of conflicting emotions battling for ascendancy.

"May I take out the garbage?" Brenda asked.

"No," the other woman said without turning.

Her heart beat in its cage. She was wild with fury. Of the three emotions struggling for dominance, it was anger that won, but even as it did, she knew it was transient. Still, she stood trembling with it, battered by it.

The scene clicked off; that was all there was. She had missed only a few bars of the Sibelius, but there were tears in her eyes, real tears, and her head ached. She pushed away from the card table and went to the window. The rain fell in a straight, steady downpour. The wind had died. She looked up at the leaden, monotonous sky, the sky that would darken into night and brighten again into tomorrow and all the tomorrows of her ridiculous, impossible future, the years gathered there waiting for her to live them. If she chose.

What kind of woman says, "May I take out the garbage?"

Who was that other woman and under what circumstances would she answer, "No." To such a question!

She was dying to know.

And what had she been feeling? Angry, yes.

Abject (how had she failed the woman at the sink?). But what was the third thing, so strong, so vital, the thing that made the other two possible? Was it love? She was dying to know that, too.

She was dying to know. She thought she was weeping, still, but then she heard bubbling and growing in her throat that dark twin of tears, laughter.

About the Author

Edith Konecky was born in New York City and has lived there most of her life. She is the mother of grown children and the author of the novels *Allegra Maud Goldman* published by Harper & Row, Dell, The Jewish Publication Society, and currently by The Feminist Press, and *A Place at the Table* originally published by Random House and recently reissued by Hamilton Stone Editions.

Printed in the United States
2082